CHAPTER 1

It had been the most terrifying, miserable day of Tim Ryan's whole miserable life.

He'd just done it to show Hailey. Because...because she said he was too scared. He was. Every time he tried anything it always went wrong. Horribly wrong. And he wasn't a thief. Well, he didn't want to be. It was one of the few things his dad had ever really got angry with him about. And then he'd only been a little five-year-old kid helping himself to a chocolate bar in a store.

But Hailey...she said...and he'd do anything to get her.

He'd been just short of the door of the store when a big hand had closed around his upper arm. He'd looked up into the face of the store security officer. "Come along with me, you," said the man, his hand like a steel band around Tim's arm. The security officer had looked at Hailey. "He with you, Miss?"

"Him?" Hailey had said. "As if I'd hang out with that little creep. He's a loser. I think he's stalking me."

The security officer looked at her with slightly narrowed

1

eyes, and Tim's mouth had been suddenly too dry to
say anything. "Off you go, then," he had said, and he'd
marched Tim along back through the store to the security
office. Every cringing step Tim had been aware of the
eyes of the other shoppers on him, on his school uniform. The office door had been slightly ajar, and they'd
pushed through it, into a plain windowless room, with
filing cabinets, two big CCTV screens showing the shoppers, and a desk, at which sat another security officer,
who was talking on the telephone.

"Hand it over," the big security man with designer
stubble who had dragged him there had said. "You might
as well know our policy is to prosecute."

"I haven't done anything!" Tim had protested, his voice
going shrill as it did sometimes, still, when he was scared
or upset. The weight of the DVD hidden in his inside
pocket felt like half a ton of lead. If only he could have
dropped it or something...

The store security guy, his big hand still tight around
Tim's upper arm, had looked down at him. "It'd be a lot
easier on you if you just come clean. And I must tell you
the store is covered by closed-circuit TV." He pointed at
the black-and-white screens, showing the shoppers. "Even
in here—the camera is in the corner. When the police
get here, you'll be searched and charged."

"And then things will be really rough for you, sonny,"
the guy at the desk, who had a long nose almost like
a beak, had said, while staring down that nose at him.
He'd sounded viciously pleased about that, as he'd put
down the phone. Actually he'd sounded just like Brute
Meldrum at school, when he told you he was going to
beat the stuffing out of you after class. Tim had half
expected the guy to get up and start hitting him. Instead
he'd said to his fellow officer, "The cops say they should
have someone here in about ten minutes."

CHANGELING'S ISLAND

BAEN BOOKS by DAVE FREER

Dragon's Ring series
Dog and Dragon
Dragon's Ring

A Mankind Witch

The Forlorn

WITH ERIC FLINT
Rats, Bats & Vats
The Rats, The Bats & the Ugly

Pyramid Scheme
Pyramid Power

Slow Train to Arcturus

The Sorceress of Karres

WITH ERIC FLINT & MERCEDES LACKEY

Heirs to Alexandria series
Burdens of the Dead
The Shadow of the Lion
This Rough Magic
Much Fall of Blood

The Wizard of Karres

CHANGELING'S ISLAND

DAVE FREER

CHANGELING'S ISLAND

A Baen Books Original

Baen Publishing Enterprises
P.O. Box 1403
Riverdale, NY 10471
www.baen.com

ISBN: 978-1-4767-8120-4

Cover art by Tom Kidd

First printing, April 2016

Distributed by Simon & Schuster
1230 Avenue of the Americas
New York, NY 10020

10 9 8 7 6 5 4 3 2 1

Pages by Joy Freeman (www.pagesbyjoy.com)
Printed in the United States of America

AUTHOR'S NOTE

This book is a work of fiction; the characters in it are fictional and bear no resemblance to actual individuals, living or dead. What is real is the nature of the island community, and while I have taken some liberties with the geography, Flinders Island is indeed a magical place. I owe a debt of gratitude to Peter Frost for planting the seeds of this story and Pip Frost for encouraging me and being a test reader. I'd also like to extend a special thanks to Marion (Maz) Matthews for her input and kindness in being a first reader. I owe a great deal to many of the locals for their stories and advice, but a special debt to two books, *Against Pride and Prejudice* by Ida West, and *Grease and Ochre* by Patsy Cameron, for windows into the lives of the Straitsmen, and the Aboriginal people living on the islands. Any errors are of course mine, and not theirs.

In the corner, a large filing cabinet had suddenly flung itself open with a loud clang, and vomited a fountain of paper onto the floor.

"Blast it!" big stubble-face had said, as he'd looked crossly at the mess. "What made that happen? It's going to take me an hour to sort out those files."

"Must have been something jammed in it when you closed it," long-nose had said with a sigh, as he'd started to get up. "Hello. Whoa, Nellie! You're a quick little thief, boy," he'd exclaimed, pointing to the DVD now lying on the desk.

"Won't help you," designer-stubble had said, derisively. "Your prints are on it, and..." He stopped and sniffed. "Have you been smoking in here again, Johnny Belsen?" he'd snapped at his fellow security man.

"No. I told you, I've quit," the other store security officer had answered.

Tim—at a different angle to both of them—had seen it first. Numb with terror, he'd watched it crawl like some live thing out of the gridded duct behind them. It was, he realized, smoke. Heavy, oily smoke, and it was cascading out of the duct and down the wall. Tim swallowed. "Uh..." he'd pointed at it with a wavering hand.

"Good try, brat," the stubble-faced one had said, his eyes narrow, his gaze locked on Tim, not following the pointing hand for an instant.

But his long-nosed companion had looked. "Marx! Smoke!" he'd yelled, pointing too.

Abruptly, the wall-duct had spat a gout of crimson flames.

Its plastic cover had suddenly melted and dribbled in burning tears, spitting and bubbling black smoke, as they oozed down the wall. A piece of the burning plastic had exploded, sending a sticky trail of flaming goo across the desk, onto the scatter of papers there. The pointy-nosed one had slapped at it and screamed, clutched his hand. Then a siren began to yowl. On the black-and-white CCTV screen, people had looked up from their shopping in alarm.

"Fire! Fire! Everybody out of the building!" someone, out in the store, had shouted.

Then, finally, the store-security man had let go of Tim's arm, and Tim had done what seemed obvious right then, just stupid later. He'd run and snatched a fire extinguisher from the bracket in the corner. Pulled the pin, like he'd been shown in the fire-safety lecture at school. He'd let loose a blast from it at the burning duct.

It had hissed, gushed steam and a shower of crackling sparks...and the partition wall had collapsed, showing burning struts, and the store beyond, full of yelling running people. More flames blossomed instantly, and Tim had winced as the savage heat of it hit his face.

The grimacing long-nosed security officer, still clutching his burned hand, had staggered to his companion and pushed his arm down with an elbow. "Electrical fire, kid. Wrong extinguisher! Come on! We gotta get out."

Tim had just stood there, frozen, in the middle of the room.

The big guy had rushed for the door...and then turned and grabbed Tim's arm in the same viselike grip. "Come on, kid!"

His long-nosed friend had fumbled at the lock, and they'd spilled together out into the store, full of smoke and sirens. "Run!" the security officer had yelled in his ear. And, half-dragged, Tim stumbled along with them, out to the pavement, still carrying the little fire extinguisher.

It had not ended there, either. They had not let him go until the two police officers had arrived. That part on the pavement was now all a big, confusing, terrifying blur in his memory. Tim could still remember the police woman's words, though. He'd never forget them, or the shame and the relief. "Did you see him take the DVD?" she'd asked the security officer.

"Not actually," the store security man had admitted. "I picked the behavior, asked him to come with me to the control room. Marx and I were there, but the kid's a quick one. He took advantage of the filing cabinet flying open to dump it on the desk as we looked away, I reckon. Clever, but not clever enough. His prints will be all over it, as I said to him, and the CCTV record..."

The other police officer had looked at the store security man. At the firemen working. "You might be lucky. It's a pretty hot fire. Did he start it?"

The store security guy had shaken his head. "I'd like to say yes, but Marx and I are professionals. We had him on CCTV, told him so, and we were both with him. He didn't try and run away or anything when the fire alarms went off. He actually tried to use the extinguisher, which I hadn't thought of. No, he didn't start it. It was just his lucky day. But you can still prosecute on a witness statement."

The female officer pulled a face. Shook her head in turn. "We could. If you had seen him take the DVD, or found it in his possession. As it is...St. Dominic's kid." It was said with obvious dislike. "His parents will hire a lawyer that'll probably get the spoiled brat off. We'll just take him back home."

The scene, when he'd arrived at the flat with the two police officers, just as his mother got in, just having received a call from the school...was something Tim would rather forget forever.

She'd been silent. That wasn't like her. He hadn't said anything either.

They stood silent for what seemed like forever, until in desperation he'd said he was sorry.

And then the yelling started...but not at him.

Instead she was shouting it down the phone line to his father in Oman. And she normally wouldn't even speak to the man. Kept communication to snarky e-mails about money. Tim knew. He'd looked. Her password was so lame.

Accidents happen. Just more of them happen around me than anyone else in the world, Tim thought.

"I just can't cope anymore!" His mother had stormed.

Tim Ryan was used to that. She said it at least twice a day. Usually about him.

Huh. He couldn't cope with himself either, and he had no escape. He was stuck in his life; she could duck out of it. She didn't always have to be the one who didn't fit in, who didn't belong anywhere. But that was situation normal, making like it was her who had a problem that she couldn't cope with, not him.

"He's a changeling, Tom! He's not normal!" his mother yelled, as if Tim wasn't even in Melbourne, let alone the same room.

Like I can help the weird stuff that happens around me, Tim thought bitterly, looking out at the dirty sky beyond the high-rises of Williamstown. This poltergeist rubbish they accuse me of causing is all bull. I wish I could do it. I really do. Only he really didn't. All he wanted right then was for it all to go away.

Tim couldn't hear his dad's answer. But he was ready to bet his mother didn't even know what a changeling was. He kind of wished that he was one. It had to beat "loser." Maybe Faerie glamour let you look taller, cooler, like you had an iPhone. Maybe it let you get away with shoplifting without getting busted, he thought. He was sort of dead-man-walking resigned to the consequences by now. It could only get worse, but at least he wouldn't be at St. Dominic's anymore. At least he wouldn't be the new kid in the secondhand blazer, who didn't know any cool people or do any cool stuff. The kid whose friends from middle school were all in ordinary state schools. The kid everyone, even the losers, kicked.

"That won't work," said his mother, angrily. "The school has asked me to remove him. I don't know what to do, Tom!"

That must be the first time she's ever admitted that, thought Tim, sourly. He wasn't too good at it himself, but this time the truth was he didn't know either. He wished he was dead. Only that would please some people, he muttered to himself. Not Mum—it would upset her, he supposed. And she'd stop getting money from Dad then too, and that would upset her more. But Hailey—she'd said that he was a creep and a loser, and stalking her. She'd looked at him like she wanted him to drop dead. Well, he didn't feel like making her day. Not after she'd lied and left him to take all the heat. Put on that sweet, pretty, innocent little-girl look and fluttered her eyelashes at the store security guy and walked out, scot-free. His heart still ached anyway. She was...gorgeous. And, yeah, she was wild in a scary but still fascinating way.

"I can't," said his mother. "I can't afford it, Tom. The flights cost a fortune."

For a moment, just a heart-lifting moment, at the end of that day of shame and despair, Tim thought his dad was going to have him in Oman.

Yeah. Likely.

Not, his mind said.

But his heart was still beating faster when his mother said: "All right. But only if you pay for the flights. And only if you call the old bat to arrange it. She always gives me hell because you never call. Like it's my fault."

When she got to the part about "if you call the old bat and arrange it," Tim knew that his dad had slithered out again. Dad's a champion slither-outer, thought Tim, glumly. And everyone always says that I look just like him.

Tim knew then that he was off to the end of the earth. Being sent into exile. Transported. Being got rid of. Being dumped on his grandmother. Being sent to the worst and most boring place in the world.

Well. Flinders Island, anyway.

Then she put down the phone and there was more yelling.

Áed sat, as was his right, at his sleeping master's feet. Those few who could see him, and his kind, tended to take him for twisted bits of shadow and angle, which looked oddly like a sharp-faced little manikin, a tiny little man with black shards of eyes. There was no flesh or blood or true bone about him, but Áed was stirred by the boy's anger and fear, and numbed by his resignation. He didn't understand his master. Of course, as one of the lesser spirits of air and darkness, he didn't have to understand. His kind of Fae were bound to the bloodline, and only had to obey. Áed was loyal to this one, even if the child carried only a little of the old blood of the Faerie kings of the Aos Sí, and neither commanded his sprite, nor gave the traditional rewards and honours to Áed. The sprite knew the old ways and understandings were lost among modern men. That was the way of it, but he regretted their passing.

This day he'd served his master well. He'd woken the need-fire in an air-conditioning unit. Fortunately it was mostly plastic, aluminum and copper wire, with little cold iron. Even the iron bones in these buildings caused Áed discomfort. It had been hard to do. Raising fire was an achievement deserving of reward, uisge beatha or at least a bowl of old mellow mead . . .

It wouldn't be forthcoming, Áed knew.

Still, he was loyal.

✦   ✦   ✦

When he woke, Tim wasn't too sure how he'd gotten to his bedroom. He hadn't changed or anything, or even gotten into the bed that he'd fallen asleep on. He was still wearing the same school clothes with the smell of smoke from the burned-out store clinging to them.

He tried not to wake up. Tried to bury himself safe in sleep. It couldn't have been real. It must have been a really bad dream. Please? He closed his eyes again, determined to ignore the school uniform and the smell of smoke.

And then his mother was yelling at him lying there. That, at least, was normal.

"Get up! I don't know what is wrong with you, Tim! Have you been smoking that filthy weed again? I've begged you to stay away from that stuff. But would you listen to me? No!"

Tim sat, blinking, on the edge of the bed. "I told you, I only ever did that once. But you never believe me, do you?" he muttered, sullenly. It was true. He'd been scared to try it, but Hailey told him not to be a nob. And that the tagging that he'd done on the train had been so cool. He'd wanted to be cool, not a nob, so he'd taken the joint from her. And then he'd been really, really sick. Couldn't breathe, and saw weird things, which wasn't what happened to other people, from what he'd heard. Hailey had panicked, and had run away and left him. Some passerby had found him and called the ambos. The doctor at emergency said that he had an allergic reaction. The doctor hadn't been very sympathetic, but it was nothing, absolutely nothing, to the fit his mother had thrown—nearly as bad as last night. She didn't believe him, and she was at him all the time about it. It had been after the fight about the bill for breakages at Harvey Norman. She hadn't believed him then, either. Well, no one did. There had been a few other things when it had been him, he had to admit. But he didn't ever want to touch cannabis again.

His mother shook her head, her face set in that surly-cross expression, like a bad-tempered tradesman's dog, that she got when she was setting out to be really nasty. Her Irish accent came back strongly whenever she did that. "Not anymore, I don't. You're just like your father. And you've brought this on yourself. Pack your things, Tim. You're only allowed fifteen kilos of luggage, and Tom has booked you on the plane at midday. I've had to take another day off work for this. And you can clean up this pigsty before you go!"

He could hear the sound of rush-hour cars in the street, and see that the sun shining through the window was sparkling on the dust motes dancing in the air. If it was that bright and noisy he should be on his way to school, to another miserable but predictable day.

So. It wasn't all some kind of nightmare. He was leaving Melbourne. Leaving the life he knew, leaving everything and everyone. He hoped at least that that was true. He'd be leaving his friends, if he had any. At St. Dominic's there was only Hailey, and then, he had to admit, only if she didn't have an audience and if she wanted something. His heart still hurt thinking about her. She was drop-dead gorgeous, in spite of it all. He didn't even want to think farther back in his life. He'd been sort of happy here, once. Had a few guys he played about with at junior school, but then they'd moved, and he'd gone to St. Dominic's. Before his father left, before his unlucky thirteenth birthday, when the weird accidents had started happening around him.

He turned to his room, determined not to think about it all. It was like deciding not to think about pink elephants. So what did you pack when you could only take fifteen kilos of your life with you? Well. Not barbells. Not that he had any. He'd kind of wanted some, so he could get stronger and bigger... only, they were expensive and... Books?

Some of them. *Sabriel. Lord of the Rings.* The Harry Potters could stay. Did his laptop count? It was old and heavy, a hand-me-down. The battery only did twenty minutes. He was still sitting there, trying to reach decisions, when his mother bustled back in carrying a suitcase. "Haven't you done anything yet? Don't just sit there, Tim!"

And on his desk, just behind her and across the room from him, a pile of books tilted, tipped, and the first fell, bang! to the floor.

They both stared as the next book tipped over the edge and fell to land on the next. And then the next . . .

"I suppose you think you're incredibly funny with these tricks! Grow up!" shouted his mother, and stormed out of the room.

Tim sat and stared at the books. They didn't move again. So he got up, and went to the kitchen and had a bowl of cornflakes. He didn't really know what else to do, and he was past caring, and into the hopelessly resigned phase of coping. Books overbalanced, especially in tottery piles, when people stomped into the room. And actually, he didn't really give a toss what he packed. Well. He had to take a couple of books and his "I love Ireland" T-shirt. It was way too small by now. But like the stamp in his passport, it proved he'd been there. Looking back, he could see the trip had been his father's attempt to patch his failing marriage, taking Mum for that trip back "home" to Ireland that she'd always claimed she wanted. But at the time Tim had just enjoyed it. And there'd been something about that green and ancient place that had made him think it was sort of home-ish too. It wasn't, of course. This was.

He slouched back to his room. Looked at the case his mother had dropped. Groaned. It had a Spiderman II logo on it. He'd thought that was really flash . . . when he was nine. It had been cheap, getting rid of old stock, but then he hadn't cared. If anyone saw him with it now they'd crack up. He put it on the bed. Began putting things into it, more or less at random, after the books. He looked at the "I love Ireland" T-shirt. It was faded, the collar frayed, and it was way, way too small. He wasn't big for his age, but that shirt was, like, not going to ever fit again. He blinked. He wasn't going to let it get to him. He firmly put it back in the cupboard, walked out into the hall and dug in the top drawer of the cabinet. He fished out his passport. This was dumb, and he knew it. He'd never be able to afford the ticket, ever. But he still took the passport and put it into the zipper pouch of the case. And then picked up the T-shirt again anyway. He could always leave out something else. His deodorant was nearly empty. It had to weigh less like that, right?

Things went in. Came out. Went in again. It was... something to do.

"Tim! Are you finished? We've got to go. You'll be late," shouted his mother.

Like I should care, he thought, glumly. But he closed the case, slid out the handle—he had to sort of wrestle with it and it wouldn't go all the way back in either, and squeaky-rattled his way to the door, trundling the case behind him. He walked out, not looking back.

Áed waited. His kind had a poor sense of time, or time as it was in these earthly realms, anyway. He was not so much patient, as unaware of not doing anything. When his master left the building he did too, perched on the bag as it trundled on its erratic wheels, and he slipped into the boot of the metal chariot with it. Creatures of air and darkness do not have much in the way of weight, and so—as usual—his presence was not noticed. Only those humans with a trace of Aos Sí

blood who were gifted with the sight could see Áed or his brothers. And, mostly, they refused to believe what they saw. That was good too... which Áed could not say of the oil-smelly iron chariot he and his master were trapped inside, but that too could be endured, because it had to be.

Essenden Airport was almost exactly the opposite of what Tim thought defined "airport." It wasn't big. There were no queues, or moving walkways or announcements you could hear only half of. And the place wasn't full of strangers. Well, they were all strangers to Tim, but they all seemed to know each other. It made sitting there in silence worse. At least nothing weird happened, except to the scale when they tried to weigh his bag. The airline official just shrugged, and picked it up and said with an easy smile, "Bit heavy. But the plane's not full and he doesn't weigh much." That wasn't quite how he remembered boarding at Tullamarine International when they'd flown to Ireland. But he'd been younger then and excited and eager.

At last someone came along and said, "Well, we're all here. You can board now for Flinders." Tim stood up. His mother kissed him, half missing, on the jaw and not the cheek. "Try to pull yourself right, Tim."

There was an awkward pause as people filed past them through the open glass doors and onto the runway. Tim swallowed the lump in his throat. He wanted to hold onto her and beg her not to send him away, but all he did was nod. Anyway, he couldn't find his voice to say anything right then.

His mother patted him on the shoulder, awkwardly, and turned him toward the door.

So he walked, not looking back, out into the sunlight and to the waiting Metroliner. A very little plane, Tim realized. It had propellers! And the man who had said they could go ... was the pilot.

Áed loved flying in human flying-machines. They moved so much faster than creatures of air and darkness could fly on their own! He liked to sit on a wing and feel the rush of the wind blowing through him.

Besides, the air was cleaner up and away from the human habitations.

CHAPTER 2

He must have been running on autopilot, getting onto that plane, Tim realized later. He hadn't walked out the door when he had a chance at home. He hadn't gone to the gents' at the airport and not come back. He'd walked across the runway, and hadn't run off among the other planes. Just walked like a sheep, following all the other sheep.

The plane was tiny inside. Just two rows of seats, A and C. He had to duck his head to walk down the corridor between them.

There was someone in the seat he'd been allocated.

The girl gave him a nervous smile. She had braces on her teeth, and freckles, so many freckles that her skin was just about one big freckle. It might have been a bit more obvious than usual, because her face was very white between them. "I'm supposed to be sitting there." She pointed to the seat in front of her. "But, do you mind, I...I'd rather sit over the wing. Do...do you mind sitting one forward instead? I asked them to give me a seat

15

over the wing, but I guess, like, they thought everyone wants one with a view. But I hate sitting next to such a long way down."

She was speaking too fast. And she was plainly even more afraid than he was. That was kind of a shock to Tim. He wondered what sort of trouble she was in. "No worries. I don't mind." She'd stood up to talk to him. She was taller than he was. Skinny. But those were designer label jeans she was wearing. That brought back to Tim the misery of being an outcast in among posh kids, and made him feel awkward. She didn't seem to see it that way, though, as she leaned over his seat to talk to him. He looked about, trying to figure out where the overhead lockers were.

"I hate flying. But I had to go for my teeth. And Auntie Helen is paying, so it has to be Melbourne." She saw him looking about for a place to store the elderly laptop. "You have to put it at your feet. I'm sorry...some of my stuff is in there. Can you fit your bag in? My aunt bought half of Melbourne for me. She didn't think much of my clothes. I don't know anything about clothes. But I couldn't really tell her I don't care. I mean, she wants me to wear white trousers. Bunce, he's my dog, he'd just cover them in mud, like, instantly. He's a cross Irish wolfhound-Great Dane."

Molly knew she was babbling. At any other time, she would have been embarrassed. She didn't really know how to talk to people she didn't know, let alone strange guys. But right now she was too scared to care. She really was scared of flying. And she was scared of flying in small planes even more. So what made her parents go and live on an island? At the moment, talking was better than thinking. "Mom and Dad and I moved to the island a few years ago. And you can only really get on and off by flying. Well, it's that or a boat, and the ferry only runs once a week, and it doesn't take passengers unless you've got a car, and I've only got my P-plates. And I hate flying, but I had to. And we had a bumpy trip over. Do you fly often? I suppose you know all this, and you come from Flinders?"

He shook his head. "I've never been there. Well, not since I can remember. But I've flown overseas. To Ireland."

"Wow. I've never been overseas."

That got the first sign of a real smile from him. He'd looked like a bit of scary storm a few moments before, when she'd seen him looking at the seat number. He had very black hair, and his dark eyes had been all crinkled up. She'd seen that look before. She did a lot of babysitting, not that he was exactly a baby. When he smiled, and it wasn't much of a smile, you could see his eyes were blue, actually. "It's kinda different from this."

"Everything is different about Flinders. My dad says it's like going back fifty years. We've got a B&B over there. We only moved a couple of years ago, and I'm still getting used to it. Are you going on holiday?"

Tim was saved from having to answer by the captain giving them a talk about the life jackets, now sharing the space under his seat with his laptop. If he had to jump into the sea he'd better make sure to take the right thing. Not the life jacket! He could swim pretty well. Dad had liked taking him to the pool, back before he'd left. It was probably so he could look at the girls in bikinis, or that was what his mother said, but Tim got to go swimming.

Then it was seat belts and taxiing out onto the runway, taking off and flying above the city and out to sea. At any other time and place he would have been loving it.

Now...his thoughts were interrupted by a little whimpery noise behind him. He looked back, twisting himself around in the seat to kneel on it. She was staring blindly at the book in front of her. Tim knew she wasn't reading it, because she had it upside down. He could read it: George R.R. Martin...she read good books. He managed not to say anything stupid like "is something wrong?" Instead he said, "Do you want to talk to me? Keep your mind off it."

She nodded. Didn't say anything.

Tim had zero skilz at talking to girls at the best of times, but she needed his help. He groped around for something intelligent to say. The best he could manage was "So, what's your name?" It was noisy in the plane. She was leaning forward to hear. They were all of ten centimeters apart.

"Molly. Molly Symons. And yours?"

"Tim Ryan."

There was a moment of awkward silence. Grasping at straws, Tim said, "So...you said you had a dog called Bonce?"

It was an inspired, or at least a lucky choice. She smiled. "My Bunce. 'Cause he's, like, halfway between a bounce and dunce, my dad said. I love him to bits. He's got a moustache."

"A moustache? Way cool! You mean like Adolf Hitler? Or one of those long ones with curly ends?" The image was enough to make Tim smile, and to make the girl start giggling, in little snorts of the sort of laughing you do when it's laugh or panic, but that was better than straight panic. "And a beard?" asked Tim, following up while he was winning. "Like one of those goatees, maybe? Or a *Lord of the Rings* type plaited dwarf one? Maybe with a bone in it?"

That got still more laughter. "Poor Bunce. He'd be,

like, trying to eat his own chin, and when he couldn't eat it, he'd try and bury it."

The talk flowed easily from there, with the Irish wolf-hound–Great Dane cross getting more ridiculous costumes and hairdos, and curlers, and gel and bows on his tail. They drifted on to other things—books, the smell of dead wallaby, the school. Panic had been beaten, and so had some of Tim's own misery. It was still there, of course, but it had been pushed away to be resentful and nag in the background.

Outside the human flying machine, where the air was cold and delightfully sharp, Áed danced on the wing, enjoying himself. Far below, the sea, hungry and rest-less, moved and surged about isolated islands, drowned mountains of a long-ago that Áed could dimly sense, like an echo that one could see, with the old magics still walking there, deep and strong. There were traces too, far more recent traces, mere hundreds of years old, of Fae-work and the creatures from hidden realms, in the shipwrecks and the buildings on the islands.

Áed saw there was at least one of the Fae, an old, strong one, swimming far below him. It was almost as if she were chasing the flying-machine he perched on.

The little spirit of air and darkness did not see as humans saw. If they could have seen her from such a height at all, they would have seen a gray seal arching through the waves. To Áed, her true form was obvi-ous, and her long wavy auburn hair washed across her naked breasts as she half-turned in the swell, looking up at the airplane.

What did the seal-woman seek here, so far from the cold coasts of Ireland or Scotland?

✧   ✧   ✧

The plane banked steeply, giving the passengers a glorious view into the clear sea. Through the azure water, Tim could see patches of white sand in between the reefs and the weed-banks.

Molly went pale again, lost her smile. "You'd better belt up. We're coming in to land."

Hastily, Tim did, and looked out at the curve of the coastline—a strip of dark trees just inside the white sand. He noticed she'd stuck her hand up the narrow gap onto the window-side armrest. She must be lying forward on her knees. Her knuckles were whiter than the beach sand they were approaching. He tentatively reached across with his other hand, trying for the reassuring squeeze...only she grabbed his hand and held on, as, with a very slight bump, they touched down. It gave him an odd sort of inner satisfaction, being something of a comfort. She pulled her hand back as the plane slowed, propellers roaring. It swung round and taxied over to a tiny building in front of a car park...and stopped.

Tim blinked as the seat belts began their clacking. A sign on the building read "Flinders Island Airport." And he'd thought Essenden small?

The girl was standing up already. She wasn't pale anymore. Actually, she was blushing furiously through the freckle cover. "Sorry," she whispered, awkwardly.

"Um. Like, no problem. Just thought you were worried. I...I won't tell anyone," he said, because he knew he would almost rather have died than admit he'd been scared enough to clutch a stranger's hand. The hand of someone he didn't know, and younger than he was too.

By the look he got, he also got that right. "Thanks," she said, as she bent down and grubbed for her bags. "You're a nice guy." That was plainly embarrassing too, and, with haste, she grabbed her kit and joined the outflow.

Tim waited. He suddenly realized he had no idea what

his grandmother looked like. He wasn't sure how to deal with meeting her. But he was still riding on a little high. "Nice guy." Not "nice kid."

He was the last out of the plane, looking around at the scenery from the top step assessing his new prison-to-be.

It had a mountain. A mountain that seemed to be looking back at him, over the buildings and the trees, its distant bare-rock top lipped with cloud. It was really weird: part of his mind said, "I know that mountain, I've seen it so often." But he hadn't, he knew that. He was still looking at it as he clutched his laptop case and stepped down to the ground.

There must have been a static charge or something on the plane, because he got a weird sort of shock when his foot touched the tarmac. It was nearly strong enough to make his knees buckle, and he tripped and fell forward, only just stopping himself from face-planting onto the runway with one hand, and that gave him a shock too. He stood up hastily.

Everyone else was obviously over the static, walking cheerfully to the door of the curved-roofed airport building. Maybe it was something that always happened when you flew in little planes, and they were all used to it?

Whatever. He squared his shoulders and walked after the rest of the passengers. He could sort of remember what his grandmother sounded like, and maybe this island wasn't going to be that bad. It was strange. He'd never been here, but it felt sort of . . . familiar. Like putting on a pair of his old shoes.

He stepped through the door, into a crowd of people meeting, hugging, talking and laughing. It was a crowd, but not a big crowd. There had only been about fifteen people on the plane, and it seemed that all of them, except him, had at least two people who had come to meet them.

But there was no one there waiting patiently, stepping forward to meet him. There were several old women, but they were all meeting someone else. No one was paying him a blind bit of attention. Molly—the only person whose name he even knew—was heading out of the door, towing behind her a tall man with a retreating hairline and a ponytail, who was carrying all her parcels. She was in some kind of hurry. And then he heard a loud, deep bark-storm from outside, followed by little yelps of what was obviously delight. Tim grinned, despite no one being there to meet him. He hoped he'd get outside the terminus in time to see the dog with a moustache. He looked around for a carousel. It wouldn't take long to unload those few bags, surely?

Only there was no carousel. Not anything that could be one. Everyone was starting to drift out of the door... so Tim, not wanting to be left there standing alone, followed them out into the October sunshine. Everyone was heading for a lean-to roof next to the building, where a solitary, sturdy black-wheeled trolley was being pushed into place, piled with the luggage. Tim could see his Spiderman II bag near the top. He cringed inside a bit as people helped themselves to their suitcases and parcels and bags. Molly's father hauled a battered pink one off the pile, and she lifted out another bag from on top of his. She gave him a rather wary half-smile. "See you," she said, and set off for an elderly SUV—which had some mud, a few dents, and a huge, hairy brown dog panting out of the window. He did have a moustache—and about a mile of pink tongue too.

Tim's bag was the last one left on the trolley, so he took it. Everyone was heading for cars, and he really didn't know what to do now. He didn't want to go back into the airport building and look spare. There was an aluminum bench outside the door. He'd sit there. She couldn't miss him surely? There was no way to walk in without walking past him. He still had a few minutes of battery life in the laptop.

So he sat. Cars and utes—passenger vehicles with a cargo tray in the rear—left. Silence came down over the little airport. A kookaburra laughed at him sitting there, but no one else did, because there was no one else to see him. He couldn't even see any other buildings from here, just stark forested hills spiked with rock, and the mountain looking at him over the trees. He took out the laptop, started on Starcraft II. But the battery died before he did. So he just sat. Sat and felt hungry.

There was a vending machine inside, and a Lions' mints honesty box on the counter. But he realized that he literally didn't have any money at all. He'd spent almost the last of it with Hailey on buying the two of them milkshakes before his venture into being a shoplifter. The store security guy had taken Tim's wallet out of his pocket...and hadn't given it back. So it had probably burned with the store.

Time did not pass quickly or easily, or without everything coming back to plague his mind, while he was just sitting.

It was too easy to play "if only I had..."

Áed saw the place they had come to as it was, not as mere geography. It was a place of power. A place of sorrows and a place of gladness. A place of refuge. A place that had once been very much part of the magic of this ancient land. Forgotten magic now, but still as strong as ever it was. The creature of air and darkness was a little afraid of it. Of the big green and gray mountain to the south, of the spirit voices in the rocks themselves, singing songs in their own tongue.

But he was strengthened by it too. This was his master's place, and therefore Áed had a place here too. They were owned by this land, a part of its slow dance, just as it was a part of them.

It accepted them. But Áed could see that his young master did not accept it. Not yet. He might never. Humans were like that, sometimes. His master's ancestor had had the key to Faerie in his hand, and had still turned his back on a life of endless plenty and feasting, dancing, riding and womanizing with Finvarra's host, for the hardships and privations of this distant land.

Áed sat at his master's feet and kicked his heels, drinking in the strangeness, the beauty and the power of the place he found himself in. Time meant little to him.

CHAPTER 3

Molly sank back into the slightly saggy seat of the Nissan and drank in the comforting familiarity of it all as they trundled along. Dad was never going to be a speed-freak, and, as usual, after a trip into Whitemark, the boot was so full that Bunce had to share the backseat with her case and the bags. Bunce didn't mind as long as he could put his hairy head over the back of her seat and drool onto her shoulder, in between sticking his big nose out of the window.

"So, how was Melbourne?" her father asked as they drove past the old, burned-out gum trunk where some joker had hung a "the black stump" sign.

"Busy. Full of traffic. Full of people. Full of shops and shopping," answered Molly, looking at the empty landscape.

"Just like this!" he said, cheerfully waving at a handful of hairy highland cows in a paddock. "And look, there is another car on our road." He greeted the driver with a wave, as everyone did here.

"Well, it is kind of nice to have shops, but Auntie Helen dragged me through a lot of them."

"She would. So how was the flight, Molly?" He knew how much she hated being in the air. He was fishing.

Molly found herself blushing. Dad was a pain. He read her far too well, and noticed little things. He'd noticed the boy when she'd said 'bye to him. And he was as nosy as a bloodhound. It would be easier just to tell him. "Not as bad as sometimes. I talked to someone quite a lot of the way. A boy in the seat in front of me."

"We'll just have to see that there's always a boy on the flight for you to pick up then."

"Oh, pul-leeze, Daddy. He's far too young. He was just a nice kid."

"Practice makes perfect. Is he coming over on holiday or something?"

"He didn't say. And I didn't ask him what his parents did or where he was from, or what he wanted to do with his life, either," she said tartly. "So you can stop asking."

Her father grinned. "Name? Mobile number?"

"He said his name was Tim Ryan, and if I ever got anyone's mobile's number I'd never tell you, Dad. Anyway, I'm not likely to ever see him again. Now stop it. You're worse than Mom."

"Couldn't be!" he said as they drove over the ridge and looked out over Marshall Bay. He always took that downhill slowly to enjoy the view for longer. They talked of other things. Of bookings for the B&B and of the problems he was having with white cabbage moths. Being entirely organic in their gardening meant they got caterpillars in their salad.

Soon after they'd turned into the West End road, he jerked his thumb at a tired, saggy farm gate. "I think the name of the old duck who lives down there is Ryan."

✧   ✧   ✧

Tim looked at his watch again. It was three minutes since he'd last looked at it. And that was four minutes from the time before. He was starving, a little afraid, and not at all sure what to do next.

He took out his mobile. It was a hand-me-down of his mother's. Not the latest and poshest ear-ornament. He'd been too embarrassed to use it at school. He wasn't too keen on phoning his mother now either. He really didn't want to talk to her at the moment. He'd just had the bright idea of sending her a text, when he looked at the screen and found out that wouldn't be happening either. No signal. But he was right next to the airport! This place sucked!

He got up. Paced around. He didn't even know where his grandmother lived; otherwise, he'd have walked. It was an island. It couldn't be that far. He could go inside again and ask someone for help, just like some lost kid. But he wasn't going to . . . not just yet, anyway. That determination lasted all of ten minutes. He was feeling mixed up and angry and scared again. He walked to the door and opened it, still out of sight of the desk.

"Dammit!" yelled someone. "My computer just crashed. Have we had a power failure?"

Tim froze in the doorway.

"The lights are still on," answered a female voice.

A few seconds' pause.

"Who the hell unplugged the computers?"

Tim oozed his way back out of the doorway. He knew that somehow it would be his fault. Besides, there was a car driving in. They parked, took out suitcases . . . well, they weren't fetching him. But that explained it all. His grandmother must think he was on a later flight. No need for him to go and ask for help. It was only twenty past four. Not near sundown yet. No need to panic. He'd get a book out.

More cars arrived, with people getting out without luggage . . . none of whom looked remotely grandmother-ish. Several of them waved as if they knew him, and a couple even said "hi" and "g'day," but no one stopped to talk to him. A plane came in from the south. Not from Melbourne. More people with bags and cases arrived in a hurry. The passengers came out and collected their bags . . . and left.

Tim steeled himself. He was starving. And the sun was definitely getting lower. He had to go and ask for help. He'd just stood up when a shiny new green Jeep Cherokee came in, a little too fast on the corners, and screeched to a halt next to him. The window slid down and a cloud of air-conditioned smoke and loud music came out, along with the words "You Tim Ryan? The ol' woman asked me to pick you up."

Tim nodded, relief making him feel weak, and not ready to care if this was the devil in person fetching him.

"Put your bag on the backseat, and let's go," said the man. He was old. Like, about forty, and half-bald with a gold earring, and a bigger moustache than Molly's dog.

Tim did as he was told, got in, and, before he even had a seat belt on, found himself pushed back in the seat by acceleration.

"Sorry I'm late," said the driver in an offhand manner. "Island time," he said, beerily.

"Um," said Tim, "That's okay," which was just as true as the "sorry" had been. Nearly three hours of worrying did seem like kind of a lot, but what could he do about it? The air in the SUV was making Tim's chest tight. He wondered if he dared open the window a little. He decided he had to. The driver didn't even notice, and then it was better. They were out in the country—even the airport seemed to have no town around it, and Tim looked at trees and emptiness and the occasional house, most of them looking just as empty as the countryside.

"So the old woman tells me you comin' to the school here?"

"Um. Yes."

"It's useless. She should have kept you at St. Dominic's in Melbourne. My kid Hailey's there."

If Tim had been able to find a black hole to dive into right then, he would have. So this was Hailey's father. It didn't look like escaping his past was going to work out that well. He didn't know what to say. He certainly wasn't going to say "I was caught shoplifting while I was with her, which is why I've been sent here." While he was trying to think of what to say, they looped up the hill, crested it, and began heading down towards a vast perfect curve of bay fringed with distant islands, the glassy sea sparkling and shading from azure to deep blue under the westering sun. It looked like the cover of a fantasy novel, too perfect to be real. "It's supposed to be a good school," said Tim, warily.

"Yeah. I made a lot of valuable connections while I was there. Old school ties count for a lot." The driver didn't seem to notice the view and just kept driving, past a few houses and onto the gravel road. Tim's alarm grew. This was just...bush. They lost sight of the sea. There was nobody. No houses. It wasn't even farmed. At least most of it wasn't. They passed a windmill, some planted rows of cropland, a few sheep, and raced onward...more bush. The only signs of life were crows on the roadkill. There were plenty of crows. Plenty of food for them too.

They swung off the main gravel road and onto a smaller one...and skidded to a halt at a rusty gate tied with a piece of old rope. The dust caught up and swirled around them. "It's just down there," said the driver. "I'm late, so I won't take you in."

So Tim found himself with his bag and laptop, standing in the dust as the SUV turned and roared off. He took a deep breath, opened the gate, and set off down the rutted track winding between the she-oaks, walking into the setting sun.

They'd come to a place of old sadness and ghosts. A haunted place. A strong place too, in its own right. Áed could feel that Aos Sí blood had been spilled here long ago. And others of his own kind had left their marks, rather like dogs marking the edges of their territory. But the signs were old.

He was glad to be out of the cold-iron chariot. He hadn't liked it, and he hadn't liked the other human in it either. Ghosts or not, this place was open to the sky and the wind. It had a freedom about it.

Besides, the ghosts here were not inimical. Just present, and watching.

The rattling wheels on his Spiderman II bag were no use at all on the sandy track. And fifteen kilos had seemed like very little to fit your life into, but it got heavy, trudging towards... well, towards what? He had no idea.

The silence was frightening in itself. Partly because it wasn't silence. Just quiet, with none of the ever-present background noise of the city. It made small noises seem louder and... well, more worrying. There were snakes out here. And he felt as if he were being watched. But there couldn't be anyone out here...

The bushes rustled. Something was moving. Tim stood dead still, ready to run, his tiredness forgotten.

The terror stepped out onto the track and spread its tail. Tim was so startled he fell over his case. He lay there, hands in the dirt, feeling stronger, laughing with relief and just the sheer craziness of it all. A peacock? Here? In the middle of the bush?

The peacock didn't like its tail being laughed at and stalked off. Tim got up and started walking again. It must be a pet, surely. He must be close to the house now? Three small wallaby came out of a patch of paperbark trees. They didn't give him quite the fright that the peacock had, and they were plainly wary of him too. He stood watching. He could see their nostrils whiffle as they tasted the air, turning their heads. They seemed to take it in turns to graze, with him being watched, as he watched them, with the sun slowly sinking into the trees.

He had to get on. He didn't want to be here in the dark. *You can't be afraid of a wallaby*, he snarked at himself. But he was. Would they kick him? He took a step towards them and they bounded off, and he trudged on. He was a lot less close to his grandmother's house than he'd imagined when he saw the peacock. Maybe he should have taken that first faint track? This one didn't look like it had been driven down lately either. What...what if he was lost? What if he had to spend the night out here? It was long, long walk back to the last house he'd seen from the speeding car.

The sight of a light was a very welcome one. He walked a little faster, down the curve and toward the house. There was only one light on, the house itself a dark bulk against the garden. As if it were some kind of beast waiting to leap.

Someone stood up from next to a garden bed as he approached. A small, slight woman who somehow managed to look about two meters taller than he was. The first thing Tim noticed about his grandmother's face was her eyes. They were fierce, staring. And then she turned her head sideways, like she didn't want to see him. But he could see that she was still staring, just not directly at him.

"You took yer own sweet time, boy," she said, gruffly. He recognized the voice from the telephone. She never said much. Just "Happy Birthday" or "Merry Christmas." Never sent him anything either.

"No one picked me up until just before five!"

"That bloody Dicky Burke. He's no good," said his grandmother dismissively. "Well. I see you've got one of them trailing you around. You tell him he's not to make any trouble around here, or I'll give him what for. Put your bag on the verandah and come give me a hand."

Tim didn't know quite what to make of that statement. Hailey's surname was Burke, so that, he assumed, was "Dicky Burke," but was she talking about the bag trailing him around? Was she mad or something? Was he stuck out here in the middle of nowhere with a crazy old woman who wouldn't even look at him? He soon found out that, whatever else she did, she meant to make him work. Principally at pushing a heavy wheelbarrow. First it was weeds to the compost heap. Then it was hauling wood for the kitchen from the woodpile. She fed the chickens, and then told him to bring over two more loads of wood, as she went inside.

Áed knew she could see him. That was enough to worry him, without adding this place to it. Sadness and the murder hung about the building. Not the whole building, just the old part, built with salted timbers drawn from the sea.

Mary Ryan did not need to see anything much in her kitchen. It hadn't changed a great deal in the last fifty years, and she could put her hand to anything she needed in the pitch dark. With the way her sight was, these days, it was just as well. And right now her eyes were also full of tears. She couldn't see him well enough. But he sounded...and moved so like her Tom had, when he was young, before...before he'd gotten angry inside, before he'd left the island. Before he'd pushed away all that his people came from, pretending he was something he wasn't. Before he'd gotten involved with that Irish woman. It hurt. Heaven knew it hurt still. Having the boy here...was like a sore tooth that had been a mere niggle until one had a cup of coffee.

And yet...she'd desperately wanted him to hug her.

This youngster wasn't her Tom. That boy had grown up and rejected everything she'd fought for, worked for. This boy was like him...but not like him. And this boy had one of the shivery little people with him. Funny, she couldn't see the boy's face except out of the side of her vision, but she could see the little people just fine. They looked like the air over a hot road, but you could sometimes make out their faces.

She sighed and turned back to the wood-burning range. She pushed the pot onto the heat. It was bad enough that she couldn't really drive anymore, which made life difficult on the farm, but the boy would be expensive too. It was an expense that would have to be met.

After all, all of this was for him, eventually.

She'd promised her John, faithfully, when he'd gone off to war, that she'd look after the land. That there would always be a Ryan on it. Sometimes...sometimes she'd had the second sight. The inner eye that saw the future, and places far away. That always saw fragments...of truth. She'd seen her John die, her big, solid, beloved man, the only man who'd had the courage to come and dance with the black girls, and damn what anyone said. She'd seen him bleeding in the mud, three thousand miles away. She had known he was dead, long, long before they came to tell her. They'd said she was a hard woman. But she'd done her weeping by the time they brought the news. She was cried out by then.

She stirred the pot fiercely. She'd been strong then, and strong when Tom had wanted her to sell the farm. She'd be strong now.

When Tom had called to ask if she'd have the boy, she'd had a moment of the second sight again. Her eyesight was failing, but that inner eye still saw clearly. That inner eye showed her a vision, briefly, of a taller, broader boy than the one who had just crept into her yard. A boy with a straight back, in a red jacket, out on a boat with a stormy sky, and Roydon Island disappearing into the rain behind him, riding the wild waves, as if they were children's tame ponies, and him with a broad smile on his face.

It was a smile that took her back fifty years to a man she'd loved, and still did.

After the seeing, after that vision, she couldn't have said no, although she wasn't sure how she was going to manage.

The boy came into the kitchen from the yard. Didn't even take his shoes off by the sounds of it. He had a lot to learn. But he was her grandson. "Welcome home, boy," she said evenly, trying to hide the emotions he'd boiled up in her. "Now go wash yer hands. The bathroom's up there, to yer left. Yer tea will be ready in a few minutes. And next time leave your boots outside, see. We don't wear boots in the house."

Tim walked up the dark passage to the bathroom. The worn wooden floorboards creaked underfoot. The smell of food had reminded him just how long ago, and in what a different world, his last bowl of cornflakes had been. He was still tired, wary, and deeply unhappy inside. But it was kind of odd what someone saying "Welcome home" did to him inside.

It was almost as if, strange as the place was, it was home. Weird, he thought as he washed his hands. Home was Melbourne. It didn't have a wood fire in the kitchen and had hot water in the hand-basin. It wasn't a million miles out into the bush with a crazy old woman.

CHAPTER 4

Tim made his way back to the kitchen. It was a bit smoky in there, lit by a single bare bulb. Two places were laid on the scrubbed boards of the big, rickety table. A plate full of food—a generous plateful—stood steaming at one of them. His grandmother was dishing a second, much smaller plate of food from pots on the stove. Tim hovered, uncertain if he should sit and where. She turned from the stove. Gestured with an elbow at the plate at the table. "Yer making the place look untidy. Sit down and eat up. It's getting cold." As he moved to pull the chair out, she said. "Wait. Yer'd better give it a welcome."

She put her plate down at her place, went to an old rounded refrigerator in the corner, rummaged in it, and pulled out a bottle...of beer. Well, it was a beer bottle. She handed it to him. "Here. For your little friend."

Tim looked uncertainly at the stubby bottle. It had a cork shoved into it. Not a new cork, either. The bottle was about half full. Not quite knowing what he should do, he pulled the cork out.

"It's flat, but they don't mind," said his grandmother.

"Er. What is it?" he said, sniffing it from a distance.

"Beer. Not for you to drink, boy! Get a bowl from the dresser and put it in the corner where I won't kick it."

Tim did as he was told and came to the table. He was hungry, and it smelled good, even if she was crazy enough to have him pour stale beer in bowls.

"You're supposed to say 'Be welcome to the house and hearth,' when you put it down. My nan taught me that. They behave then," said his grandmother.

"Who behaves?" he asked warily.

"The little people," said his grandmother. "Go say it, boy. He's waiting."

She was crazy. But what could he do? It was dark out there, and he was hungry and tired. So he did it. "Be welcome to the house and hearth," he said awkwardly. Then he came and sat.

The food was good. More vegetables than he would have chosen to put on his plate, but the gravy was thick and herby and rich to disguise it, and the stewed meat was fall-apart tender. And there was lots of potato. Later he would say that was how he knew his gran's cooking, there was always lots of potato.

"You like it?"

He nodded. "It's great. What is it?"

"Roo-tail stew. They're a pest here. What you'll eat most of."

Tim thought of the little hoppers on the track. It wasn't exactly pizza or Chinese, which had been what they ate pretty often at home. But he supposed it was the nearest you'd get to delivery here.

When he got up from the table . . . he noticed the bowl in the corner was empty too.

But he was too exhausted to think much about it that night. He'd barely coped with being shown to a painfully neat bedroom and wooden frame bed with a patchwork quilt on it. He must have gotten his bag, brushed his teeth and collapsed to sleep in it, because he was in the bed the next morning, and his toothbrush was in the bathroom.

Áed took the welcome as both a comfort and a threat. A comfort: she knew the old ways and words, a pleasure in the tasting of the beer, as was his rightful reward. A threat: if she knew the words of welcome, it might be that she also knew the words of punishment or banishment. Áed did not sleep. Rest has a different meaning to the spirits of air and darkness, and he didn't need much. He was wary about leaving his charge, but he made several brief forays to explore.

There was another of his kind about. His kind weren't gregarious, and it was busy working on the farm.

Mary Ryan went to bed too, not even listening to the radio as she usually did in the evening. She had a lot on her mind. Mostly, money. She scowled to herself. There was probably money to be had from the Social Welfare at the Centerlink office. She wouldn't take the dole for herself; it went against everything she believed in. She was damned if she'd demean herself to ask, anyway. She had her pride, and if she lost that, she had nothing. For the boy, well, it was different. But... once they started sticking their beaks in, they'd find out about her eyes. They'd say she couldn't live here, let alone look after the boy.

She did the sums in her head again. Food, well, the basics, fruit, meat and vegetables anyway, were not going to be a problem. She couldn't see to shoot anymore, but her father, and his father before him, had snared wallaby.

The garden provided. But it was the rest: sugar, vinegar—or there'd be pretty few vegetables and no fruit in the winter. Tea, cooking oil, clothes, boots, soap, the extra electricity. She tended to sit at home in the dark most evenings, just to save that bit. You could listen to the radio perfectly well in the dark. The farm needed more work than she and her little helper could do these days, and the scrawny boy wasn't really up to it yet either. It needed work and money, and the stock just wasn't fetching what it used to on the sales. Dicky took her beasts in, and he said she was lucky to be getting what she got back for them.

Eventually she got up, opened the tin box, and took out the thin fold of money. It was so awkward having to turn the light on to see the value of the notes. There wasn't much there, as she'd known. But there was nothing else. The only other things in the ditty box were worthless to anyone but her, and too precious for her to ever part with. She couldn't see to read them anymore, either, but she knew all the words on those letters by heart anyway.

Her fallback money would just have to be enough, or she'd have to sell something. Heaven knew what.

Tim woke to the sound of a teaspoon being clattered around a cup, looked up from the pillow to see the spare figure of his grandmother pushing open the door. She put the cup down on the little bedside table. "Yer better get yourself to the kitchen pretty quick or I'll feed your breakfast to the chooks."

He didn't want to be awake. He really resented being woken, but there was no suggestion that she was not dead serious. Tim felt himself simmering with the feeling of being unfairly used . . . and she turned to the corner of the room. "And don't you even think of it, or there'll be no beer." And she walked out.

His stomach said it was hungry, and a hungry day had no appeal, even if he had no idea what the day held. Boredom here, he supposed.

There was a pot of porridge on the table. No cereal. Just a bowl, a spoon, a jug of milk, and an old sugar bowl.

"Go easy on the sugar. It doesn't grow on trees," said the old lady. "I cut yer lunch." She pointed at the plastic lunchbox on the corner of the dresser. She reached into the apron pocket of her pinafore. Pulled out an envelope. "Here. That's for the uniform. I spoke to them at Bowman's yesterday. Look after it."

"What?" he asked, feeling as if he were being spoken to in Japanese, for all that he understood. Uniform? Bowman's?

"Yer got to be waiting for the school bus at half past, at the corner. Eat up, or you'll be late. Have some more milk; it'll cool it down. We got lots of milk."

It tasted odd though. It had yellow stuff floating on the top of it...it wasn't actually sour or anything. Just not normal, like milk from the Coles around the block back home.

"Is this milk all right?" he asked.

His grandmother's hand wavered across the table. Tim noticed she didn't look directly at the table either, but side on. She picked up the jug, held it to her nose and sniffed. "Smells fine. Fresh out the cow this morning. You can learn how to milk her this evening."

As a reason to rush back to his grandmother's, that wasn't on the top of Tim's list. As a reason to go in a hurry, it wasn't bad. It was brisk and windy out, scudding clouds ripping across the tops of the old twisted pines. The place didn't look so frightening in daylight. It did look run down. The fences were rusty. The wire sagged, had been mended here and there.

He walked along to the main gravel road and looked about. He wasn't sure which way it was to the corner where he had to meet the bus. Probably back toward the airport. He'd had time now to start dreading it all. What did they know about him? About what he'd done?

A car came past in a flurry of dust...and stopped. It reversed, and a huge hairy head, with a windswept moustache, stuck itself out of the window and barked loudly.

"Tim? It's me, Molly. From the plane," the girl with the braces on her teeth said from the passenger seat.

"I would have recognized you even without Bunce and his moustache," said Tim, quite proud of that line. It made him smile. It made her flush red, which wasn't what he'd meant it to do.

"Can we give you a lift somewhere?" asked the driver. She was a middle-aged woman, who looked like an older, shorter-haired version of Molly, only with glasses, and a few creases between her eyes. "Only we have to rush for the school bus. We're running late."

"That's where I am supposed to be going."

Molly spilled out of the car. "I'll sit next to Bunce. He'll drool on you, otherwise. Hop in the front."

Tim did so. Clicked in his seat belt.

"Are you going to school here?" asked the driver, accelerating fast enough to push him back in the seat.

"Um. Yes." Tim was worried they might ask why. They had to wonder.

"The headmistress will be doing her happy dance," said the driver, focusing on the road, not looking at him.

"We need numbers," explained Molly. "There are too few kids in the senior grades. It's, like, just a handful of us."

Great, thought Tim. *And I wanted to be invisible in the crowd.*

"What on earth are you sniffing at, Buncy?" asked Molly.

Tim was grateful for the distraction provided by the

dog, head cocked on one side and great big black nose and moustache twitching as if he'd smelled a really bad fart.

"Don't bark! You'll send Mum off the road," said Molly, grabbing him.

"Fortunately, we're here," said Molly's mother, pulling off the road and onto the broad verge. "And we've beaten the bus. Let the big moo out, Molly. He can have a run around."

Molly leaned across and opened the door, but Bunce wasn't going anywhere. Just sat there, staring cross-eyed at something, and giving a little wary burr of a growl.

"Goodness! I hope he's not sickening. We really can't afford vet bills now!" said Molly's mother, only, it seemed to Tim, half jokingly.

"He was fine ten minutes ago!"

"I think he's defending you, Molly," said her mother, suddenly, chuckling. "Tim, hop out, and let's see what he does then. Oh, how funny!"

By the look on Molly's face, she did not find it so funny at all. But Tim got out. "Thank you for the lift," he said awkwardly. In the distance he could hear the bus, and, now that he was out, Bunce bounced out too, and ran around like a mad thing, barking and leaping over bushes. His mistress had to run after him and drag him back to the car, and then grab her bag while Tim got onto the bus, feeling slightly awkward.

The bus driver gave him a lopsided grin. "Ah. You'll be Tim Ryan. I was expecting you." Molly also got on, her face as red as her hair, and promptly got called to "come here, Molly" by the two younger children in uniform. She did. Tim had already sat down near the front. He'd been hoping to find out a bit more about what he was in for, but he never got a chance. The driver did chat with him, however. "So old Mary Ryan's your nan, is she?"

"Yes."

"So your parents are in Melbourne, then? I remember your father. Hasn't been back for a long time."

He felt like it was a police questioning or something. "Mom's back in Melbourne. My dad"—his voice shook briefly and he was ashamed of it—"is in Oman. In the Middle East."

"Ah," said the driver, nodding. "Explains it."

He said no more, and Tim wasn't too sure what it explained. They drove on over the hill and past the airport and some scattered houses, set in fields with sheep, and cows...and a flock of turkeys wandering around as if they owned the place. Onwards towards the mountain. And then they arrived at a cluster of red-roofed buildings.

"Well. Here you are," said the driver. "Better go and see the headmistress, son. She's expectin' you."

Inwardly Tim groaned. What had his grandmother said about him?

Áed had been amused by the dog. It hadn't known what to do with him, or quite what he was. He'd been tempted to tease it, just for the mayhem he could cause. He'd been a lot less pleased to see the selkie, when he'd explored and his master slept. The seal-woman was still in her natural place, the sea. She sat on a rock sticking out of the water, and combed her long wavy hair in the moonlight. She'd seen him too. She'd smiled. It was not a nice smile. Predatory... and pleased.

It was the same fae he'd glimpsed from the flying device. Áed knew there could only be one reason the selkie was here. She was following him, or perhaps his master. In the water the seal shape-changers were dangerous. On land, less so, but they were not confined to the water, the way the lords of the hollow

hills were confined to the land by the salt water. Like Áed's kind, the selkies could go anywhere, even if they did not enjoy it.

She'd beckoned to him. "Come here, little one."

Áed, sensibly, had fled as fast as he could from even the sight of the sea. He'd sought out the other creature of air and shadow, the one living around the farm, one whose scent he'd recognized. The one who came to the kitchen and the barns and sheds, but no further.

The hairy creature was at work in the barn, no longer moving the beasts, as he had been earlier. It was a small fenodree, as suited the agricultural nature of the place. Hardworking, and not very bright, and a little wary about Áed. "You make trouble, I hurt you," he said slowly, nervously fondling the wooden shaft of an old two-handed scythe.

In the hierarchy of those of the hollow hills, of the creatures of air and shadow, the fenodree was low, below Áed. But they were strong and determined. "I don't wish to fight," said Áed. "I just saw a selkie."

"She's back, then." The fenodree seemed unsurprised and relatively unworried. He'd stopped clutching the scythe and was back to untangling his long fur with his blunt fingers. "She won't come out of the sea."

That was a comfort. "Why not?"

"She's afraid of the others. The old ones."

Áed had sensed them, caught the shimmer of them. But they had kept their distance. "What does she want here?" he asked. If the fenodree could live with these others, so could he.

The fenodree shrugged. "The boy. The key."

"What key?" asked Áed. The word in the old tongue they spoke had many meanings.

The fenodree shrugged again. "I do not know. She has looked for it for a long time. She is from Finvarra."

That was enough to frighten Áed even more. Finvarra was a king of the Shee and a great power still, in the hollow hills.

Áed would have to guard his master carefully.

Alicia Symons drove home slowly, thinking about the youngster they'd picked up. She'd not, at first glance, been too impressed. Actually she felt sorry for him. He was small and looked defeated and rather lost walking along the road with a lunchbox.

And then he'd smiled and confused her daughter. And it seemed Molly's dog had caught that confusion. It was something for a mother to think about!

She drove down through the she-oaks toward the house on the promontory. Not, for once, looking at the view from their hill and losing herself in the rapture of it. From the minute they'd seen the view, she and Michael had loved the place. They'd known they couldn't really afford it, and had gone ahead and done it anyway, because they couldn't bear to lose their chance. They should have looked at the school issues first. It wasn't that the school wasn't trying. It was just dying for lack of children. She should have been delighted that there was another child. But...well. Perhaps she was being overprotective.

Her husband was out working on the turbine. It was all very well being self-sufficient, and saying there was lots of wind for power, except the wild wind here was forever breaking something.

"We picked up a boy on the road today," she said, looking up at him.

"Ah. Molly picked up one yesterday, on the plane," he said, coming down and wiping his hands on his jeans. "Remember, I told you last night. She's growing up."

"It's the same one. He was on his way to school."

He knew her well enough to need no further explanation. "I'll phone a few people. This is Flinders. Everyone knows everything in twenty-four hours."

A few minutes later he came back. "Seems his parents have got divorced. He's staying with his grandmother. She's apparently an old tartar. They're 'real islanders.' Old family."

She smiled at the "real islanders"—you had to be here for fifty years to get considered more than temporary flotsam by some of the islanders. "That...might explain the look. Poor kid."

"The look?"

"He looked like the whole world was on his shoulders. And Bunce growled at him."

"Good grief. Well, if he gives Molly any trouble I'll growl at him too."

CHAPTER 5

Tim had been . . . well, terrified, when he went to the headmistress's office. Almost inevitably, just as he went in, a whole pile of paper sprayed across the room, and the lightbulb exploded with a loud pop.

"Goodness! What an entrance." The woman shifted her glasses back on her nose, and smiled at him. She didn't blame him! That was different. "You must be Timothy Ryan. I'm so glad to see you. Give me a hand to pick these up, will you?"

It was said in such a calm, easygoing way, and she really did seem happy to have him here. She talked while they picked up papers. She spoke so quickly that it was hard to get a word in edgeways, but she was also very good at asking the right sort of questions. And she wasn't in the least troubled by his lack of uniform. "I'll get you a shirt from the lost property box for now. Come to me at break and I'll take you down to town."

She never mentioned knowing anything about why he'd come. Neither did anyone else. The day, like any first day,

49

rushed around him in a confused welter of newness. He was introduced to a lot of people. He couldn't remember any of them. He was ahead in some areas, far behind in others. As for the place, he felt as if everything was moving around him, just as soon as he got his bearings. He was whisked away to a small shop in the little town, and paid over his grandmother's money, and left with a carrier bag and what passed for a uniform here. St. Dominic's would have sneered, but then he'd hated those clothes anyway.

And no one said, right out to his face, "Why are you here?"

Somebody had to know. Someone had to tell. And then...yeah, well. Shoplifting wasn't that big a deal, was it? But he'd worked out pretty quickly that here it probably was a very big deal. The kids had left lunchboxes, some transparent with chocolates visible, sticking out of their bags. You couldn't have done that at his junior school back in Melbourne without someone nicking something. St. Dominic's had been, if anything, worse. Here...they didn't even lock their cars. Or have burglar bars or security guys at the shop. Someone told a story in class about some stupid visitor locking a guest cottage, and the owner having to break a window to get in because of it. Tim had asked if the owner had lost his key. He'd got one of those looks, a look that said "gee, you're dumb." "No one has keys. We don't lock things up here. Why would you?"

Tim knew why. And from that he could figure exactly how they'd feel about a thief. He'd been in a school where he'd been the kicking-boy before. He didn't want to be there again, even if these country hicks weren't his kind of people.

Tim's mother had often used the expression "waiting for the other shoe to drop" and never quite explained why one was waiting, or just what shoes had to do with it. When he was much younger, he'd asked why you didn't just run away when you heard the first shoe.

"Because you can't. And you don't know if it will."

Tim understood the feeling now. His stomach was in a bit of a knot all day, just waiting. And he couldn't run away. He was stuck out on an island with no way off that didn't cost a lot. And he had no money, nothing, not even a working phone. It was just like a prison, really. He might as well have been charged and been sent to jail, as to this place. It would take hours and hours to walk to this town from his grandmother's house, if you could call the town a "town." It was more like a pub, a little supermarket, and a post office, and a few houses. No mall. No movies, no . . . no nothing. Nothing for a guy to do. No place to hang out.

Just a granite mountain that seemed to be looking at him.

Áed liked the school-place. He liked laughter and noise, and he liked the opportunity the place gave him to serve. He liked to work with things like wood and paper, rather than metals, and there was plenty of that here.

There were little twists of hot air rising above the road, and Áed swirled with one. He was not strong enough to make it into a true whirlwind, to tear roofs and break walls, but he could spin it faster and direct it. His master was upset and worried about these humans. Best to distract them from him. Give them something else to think about. He headed the spinning vortex of air toward a group of children who were talking about his master.

✧   ✧   ✧

"Look!" yelled someone as Tim mooched along towards the bus, thinking. Trying to ignore everyone. Look like he wasn't there. They were talking about him, he was sure.

He looked up as a column of dust whirled towards the other kids. He was not in its way...

Not again! It would be his fault. It always ended up being his fault.

This time he got angry. He just had half a chance to start again, even in this dump! Instead of running away like the rest of the kids, Tim turned and faced down the willy-willy. "Stop it, now. I don't need any more of this here!" he screamed at it.

"Tim!" shouted someone. "Come away. You can't just yell at a whirlwind."

The air was full of grit, dust, sticks and leaves. The wind raged, lifting his hair.

"I won't give you any beer!" Tim had no idea why he said that. Just his crazy grandmother and her beer story last night had been playing with his mind all day.

"Tim!" Two of the others had reached him. Grabbing his arms... It was Molly and the big, rather slow-seeming Henry. "Come..."

"It's stopping." Henry said, as the dust tower turned abruptly and collapsed, bits of leaf and stick falling. Seconds later it was gone, and there was just a little dust in the warm spring air.

"That was lucky!" said Molly.

"It listened to him, see," said Henry, cheerfully. "Next time Dad wants to set cray pots and it's blowing, I'm going to tell him to offer the Beastly-Easterly wind a beer to make it go away, instead of drinking it himself." Quite a few of the kids laughed.

"Where did you get that idea from, Tim?" asked someone.

"Um. Something my nan said."

"My nan only ever says 'have you washed yer hands?'" said someone else.

"Come on," said Molly. "Killiecrankie bus has to go. That's us, Tim."

Tim found he'd accidentally broken a few of the rules that morning. The older ones were supposed to sit at the back, and there were a few extra littlies for the trip back who told him so. Not very politely, in the case of one little boy.

"Oh, shut up, Troy. He's new. He doesn't know yet," said Molly.

Several people asked how his first day had been. Tim didn't say anything about being trapped with zombies on the island of the living dead, but made polite "yeah, great" noises.

They all seemed to be happy with that, and he had survived all the way out to the lonely turnoff. Only it wasn't so lonely now. A new Subaru whisked two of the kids away—Troy and a younger one who had to be his sister—in a spurt of gravel and cloud of dust. The elderly Nissan SUV didn't have a dog with a moustache, but did have a smiling man with a retreating hairline and a ponytail leaning on it.

"Would you like a lift?" asked Molly's father. He couldn't be anyone else. He looked just like her when he held his head like that and had that half-smile on his face.

"Thank you, but I'd like to walk," said Tim, lying, but embarrassed. "It's not far, and, um, I need the exercise." It was better than facing any more curiosity.

"Well, we're going past," said Molly's father.

"No, really," said Tim digging deep in memories of things people said about the country. "It's...it's just nice to enjoy the fresh air. And, um, the sounds of nature."

His parroting of this load of bull seemed to go down

well with the guy though. "Exactly what I'd do on a day like today. Too nice to be stuck in a car. Come on, Molly...Unless you want to walk too?"

"It's about five kays along the road, Daddy. And I've got a ton of homework to do," said Molly, shaking her head at him. "See you tomorrow, Tim."

And with that, she got into the car, and they left, and Tim looked into the dust-trail at the walk ahead of him for a while. Well. He couldn't just stand here, so he started walking. It was a lot farther on foot than it was by car, and the "fresh air" was hot and the "sounds of nature" could have been made a lot better with an iPod. It was hot and still and the only sounds were the flies. The roadkill was buzzing with it.

He trudged on. A car came past. It was Hailey's father, but he didn't stop. Probably heard all about me, thought Tim, gloomily. He wondered what Hailey had said. "Loser," probably. It still hurt, thinking about her.

He was so deep in thought about this, so hot, and tired of walking, that he didn't actually notice the white Land Rover ute with the inflatable boat on a trailer behind it. The pickup truck's bonnet was up, and it was parked at the side of the road as he walked around the corner. It took the man working on it to swear before Tim suddenly became aware of it.

The guy under the bonnet must have heard something, because he turned. He was a lean, suntanned-to-old-leather-faced guy, with a neat little clipped beard, no moustache, and very blue eyes. "g'day," he said, like he hadn't been swearing ten seconds before.

"Hi. Can I help?" said Tim, knowing he couldn't. He didn't know much about cars, and didn't even have a working mobile. That still galled him. How could the place be so...basic?

The stranger looked Tim up and down, thoughtfully.

And nodded. "Maybe you can, sonny. My hands just don't fit down there. It's pretty hot though. I just burned myself."

"I could try, I suppose," said Tim, looking at the gap that the man was pointing down into.

"That pipe there has to go onto that flange on the other side. But be careful, it's hot."

Gingerly, because he could feel the heat, Tim reached down, trying not to touch anything, and got hold of the pipe. The problem was there was just no space. While trying to be careful not to touch anything, it was very hard to push sideways at near-full stretch. It was the sort of job someone with strong hands and arms could do in ten seconds...if the engine was cool.

"I just, ouch, can't push it on," admitted Tim after a minute or two.

Heat meant little to Áed as he clambered down his master's sleeve to avoid the nasty iron in the steel. That could and would burn him in a different way. He was quite strong, and, once the Master let go, it took all the time of the blinking of an eye to push the rubber pipe in place and slip the clip back on.

"Oh, well. Don't burn yourself trying. I'll walk up the road and see if I get mobile reception," said the man in a resigned tone. "I've got a load of fish and it won't do them any good sitting in this heat. Hello..." he said, looking down and then having a closer look. "You've done it, youngster! Well done. You even got the circlip on. Good lad!"

Tim looked down into the heat of the engine. The pipe was on, and a little brass clip around it. He'd swear he hadn't done that. "I didn't think I had gotten it on," he said, doubtfully.

"It looks pretty solidly on to me," said the man, looking at it, then grinning at Tim. He wiped his oily hand on his jeans and stuck out the hand. "Didn't introduce myself. I'm Jonno. Jon McKay. One of the local ab divers. You must be the new kid at the school. Ryan, I think."

"Uh. Yes, I'm Tim Ryan. How do you know who I am?" he blurted out.

The diver laughed. "This is Flinders, mate. Get used to it. You can't keep anything a secret here. My deckie's girlfriend works up at the school. The headmistress was celebrating having a new student. Now, can I give you a lift? It's a scorcher for walking, and old Mary Ryan's place is a good couple of kilometers still. I imagine that's where you're going."

"I'll be fine. Really," said Tim, wondering just how much of his past had already not been kept secret.

Obviously his voice betrayed him. "Don't be such a martyr," said McKay. "It won't take me five minutes, and you just saved me a long walk, and my fish from getting too hot. I owe you."

"It's not the way you're going."

"Even towing a boat, I can turn around," said McKay cheerfully. "Get in, will you? I'll go up to the corner and turn around. It'll be easier."

So Tim got into the truck with him. It was obviously a working ute, with the foot-well full of spare parts and jumper cables. More to make conversation than anything else, because he knew nothing about boats or fish, Tim asked, "So what kind of fish have you been catching?"

McKay chuckled again. "Muttonfish. Or that's what they call them here. I dive for abalone. Have you ever dived?"

"No. I've never actually been into the sea."

The diver looked at him, his mouth open, and then hastily back at the road as the tires bit the soft gravel on the road margin. "You're kidding me, right?"

"No. I guess... my dad didn't like the beach. He hated the sea, I remember him telling me when I asked him to take me."

"But you were in Melbourne. Didn't your mother like it either, then?"

"I think my mom only likes shopping malls and theaters and stuff. She used to take me to the pool quite often. I can swim pretty well, just not in the sea. I might have gone to the beach to play in the sand when I was, like, really little, I think. I suppose we were quite close to the sea really, but, well, we never went. But I used to go swimming quite a lot. I can swim well," he said defensively, feeling, somehow, that he'd moved down in McKay's estimation of him.

"I suppose you've never been on a boat either?" asked the man, a smile twitching his lips.

"No, I haven't," admitted Tim, feeling like he was saying he hadn't done his homework, and thinking just how unfair that was. Something about this man made Tim want to be liked by him, want to be respected.

"Hmm. I'll take you out sometime. We'll go and catch a few flathead. It's a part of your heritage. I reckon you'll see enough of the beach here. You can get down to Marshall Bay from Mary Ryan's place. There's a track through the scrub."

They'd arrived at the old gate. "I can walk from here. Really. It's not far."

"Hop out and open it. It'll be easier for me to turn around down at the house, if I remember it right. I came down with my uncle Giles when I was about your age to go netting off the beach."

So Tim did as he was told. Letting the ute and the boat go past before he closed the gate, Tim got a really good look at the boat on the trailer for the first time. It was obviously rugged and cool looking, metal underneath, with long, sleek blown-up pontoons on the sides.

They bumped down to the farmhouse. "Stock looks in fair shape," said McKay, sounding faintly surprised. "I don't suppose you know much about sheep or cattle either."

"No. I have to milk a cow this afternoon," said Tim.

That got a snort of laughter. "You're going to have some fun out here, youngster."

Tim hadn't quite thought of it as "fun."

They arrived at the house, and his grandmother was striding towards them, garden fork under one arm. McKay got out of the ute. "Mrs. Ryan. I'm Jon McKay. You probably don't remember me, but I used to come along with my Uncle Giles to net garfish about, oh, fifteen years back."

Something about the way the old woman walked changed. That might almost have been a smile on that severe face of hers. "You want to net some more fish?"

"No, I'm diving abalone these days. I just brought your boy home. I was stuck at the side of the road and he gave me a hand to fix the ute."

"Ah. Not in trouble, is he?"

"No. He was a real help," said McKay. "I said I'd take him to catch some flathead someday."

"I haven't had a good feed of flathead for a while," said Tim's grandmother. "If he'll go, he can."

"If we have some decent weather on the weekend, I'll take him. He's got some adventures ahead of him. I hear he's learning to milk a cow this afternoon. And he says he's never been to the beach or the sea."

His grandmother snorted. "That's the trouble with city people. They can't do much."

"Yes," said McKay cheerfully. "I came from Lonnie for holidays. Best time of my life was learning stuff from Uncle Giles. Anyway, I have to get these fish packed and down to the airport, and my deckie has taken off again. Would you like a few abalone for your tea, Mrs. Ryan?"

That was almost definitely a smile. "That'd be good. Yer want some spuds?" asked Tim's gran.

McKay nodded. "Please, if you can spare some. Mine aren't doing as well as yours. I've got a place up towards Boat Harbour. The soil is pretty sandy."

"This was too, but it's had fifty years of manure in it. Here, Tim, run and get a carrier bag from behind the door in the kitchen, and you can take the fork and dig up some potatoes."

Tim fetched the bag, was handed the fork—his grandmother and McKay having walked over to the vegetable garden, talking—and realized he had a problem. There were a lot of plants there. None of them had a sign on them that said "potatoes."

Áed could see the fenodree, lurking among the broad beans, scowling. The woman of the place might regard this as her domain, but the fenodree regarded it as his. If he took offense, well, he could do mischief. Or worse, he could just lope off. Áed realized the little one did a lot of the farm work, and enjoyed it. "He's still young. Like a new puppy. You will have to teach him."

The fenodree blinked. "You teach him. The potatoes are nearly ready, but he's about to stick the fork into the asparagus bed."

Áed leapt and pushed the shaft of the fork, wooden and easy to push, so it swung down away from the thick feathery leaves.

The master looked puzzled, and narrowly missed his own foot.

But at least the fenodree laughed.

✧   ✧   ✧

"Put it in the edge of the earthed up bit, that mound," said McKay. "And then stand on the fork and lean it back. I bet you have never dug spuds before."

Tim looked down at where he turned the earth up. It was quite loose and easy to lift. He could see the round shapes of potatoes in the dirt, and he reached down his hands to lift them out. The soil was slightly warm around them. It was kind of neat hauling them out. If only they came out as crisps, he could do this all day.

"The old ones like him," said Áed, for he and the fenodree could see what the master could not, in the lines of force and strength that ran through this land and crackled with its lightnings into the boy. Ochre patterns that ran all the way to the mountain, had run the length of the land for always and always, still ran down into the water where the sea had tried to eat them away, from times when the land had been much wider.

The fenodree nodded. "We'd better see to the teaching of him. He will be good for this place."

Feeling good about digging up potatoes had lasted a few minutes, until McKay took off and Tim found out that digging, and worse, was more or less what the afternoon held for him.

"Where'd yer think yer going?" his grandmother asked as Tim walked toward the house, and McKay and his boat bounced off up the road.

"To put my lunchbox and things away."

She'd nodded, still not looking at him, but at the space to the right of him. It really felt creepy. "Yes. Put yer old clothes on, and yer'll find a hat on the stand. We need to turn the compost."

"I thought I might relax. I, I've had a hard day. I might watch some TV, and, and, I've got to check Facebook." Somehow he hoped there might be a message from Hailey. Or something.

His grandmother gave a cackle of laughter. "Yer out of luck. No TV. And I don't know what this face book thing is, but yer can keep your face out of a book while we've got light. This garden is what feeds us, boy."

Tim swallowed. "You've got to have the Internet? I can't not go online."

"I'm not sure what line you're talking about, but you can't use the phone all the time. I can't afford it. Yer can write letters."

Tim felt as if his whole face was going to crumple up. He went in to his room, and plugged the laptop in to charge. He wasn't going to garden. No way.

Only... it didn't switch on. It kept starting up and shutting down.

He wanted to scream. And scream.

He could sit and look at the wall. But he wouldn't bet she would give him any food if he didn't go and work.

So he changed out of the school clothes, and went out, still angry. It would serve her right if poltergeist stuff happened to her!

Only it didn't.

CHAPTER 6

The week was one long drift of confusion, every waking hour. Tim was as careful as he could be at school not to draw any attention to himself. They were the living dead, but he was stuck here. And at least they had computers and a school library. He didn't want to do the stuff he had to on the farm. He resented it. Why should he? Only... it was so difficult not to. His grandmother worked at everything next to him. He'd gotten used to looking to see what she was doing, so he could learn how to do it, as most of it he had no idea just how to manage. And, well, she must have eyes in the back of her head. Or the little people she talked to must be telling on him, which was just as crazy.

About the only good thing he could say was walking eight kilometers a day, four there and four back, having to get up far too early, mostly because he wasn't going to be embarrassed by a lift again—he didn't want them seeing that he had to walk—and then digging, or sawing, or hauling poles around, well, he was so tired he nearly fell asleep into his food every night.

He was locked down into "survive" mode. He could handle it for a few weeks until his mum sorted things out.

Áed, now with the little fenodree helping, steered the master past disasters. He would have cut his foot half off, and been kicked by the cow, otherwise, as well as gotten lost. They'd had their hands full that week.

Áed realized he'd better brave finding out what the selkie was after. When the master was safe asleep, and the fenodree was out cutting hay for the beasts, Áed went down to the wide and wasteful ocean. It was, as the sea always was, hungry. It frightened him, but unlike the great ones in the hollow hills, for Áed the sea itself was not accursed and deadly. He could cross it by boat or plane, or even fly above it himself, quite cheerfully.

The selkie must have been watching, because she came. But the fenodree was right: when Áed backed off she would not follow him onto the dune. Well, he'd seen the powers of the land here. "What do you want?" he asked in his own tongue, as she crooned. He felt her drawing spell, but it had little effect on him. That, too, was good to know. This place must protect him too.

"I want the key, little one."

"What key?" Áed asked, warily, knowing a little, but fishing to find out as much as he could.

"The key to the door into the hollow hill, where King Finvarra feasts with his host," she answered.

"And what would that be doing here?" asked Áed, doing his best at innocence. Such a precious thing would not be given to mortals, but only those of the blood.

The selkie looked at him and put on the appearance of a teacher. Such things amused the seal-people. "It was given, as such always are, to the royal halfling child which was put out as a changeling to live among humans, so he can return to the hollow hills when he is grown. Only this child did not return. Neither did the key. It was taken away, beyond the reach of the king. He wants it back."

Áed knew that the blood of the Aos Sí kings ran in his master. That was why Áed himself had been drawn from the hollow hill, to the boy. The master had been a boy then, and not a man, as the people of the hollow hills and old country called being of age. Humans and indeed the Aos Sí were of age when they could father children, not before. It had only been when the master had begun to change from a boy to a man that he had become Áed's master.

The Aos Sí lords and kings got bored sometimes, and mixed with mortal men ... or rather, with the women, with inevitable results: children.

The hollow hills were not good for those children of mixed blood though. They seemed to need sunlight. Áed liked sunlight himself. The half-bloods were exchanged for human babes, and fostered in human homes. When they came of age ... they came home. The human children stayed among the Aos Sí, and did not return to the sunlight. They died in the hollow hills.

Humans lived such short lives, in exchange for souls.

Áed had never heard of a changeling who had not gone back. Sometimes they left children of their own behind, under the sun. The green land of Ireland was full of such traces of Aos Sí. Áed knew that others of his kind were sometimes drawn to such, until they were banished again.

The selkie spoke again. "King Finvarra wants his key. He wants it back with or without the one whose birthright it is. It has passed through too many generations unclaimed. It should never have left the old country. I have searched for a long time to find it again."

"Then why don't you collect it and be on your way?" asked Áed, knowing the answer was important, and suspecting that he knew the answer already, but wanting it confirmed.

The selkie smiled, a nasty smile, all teeth and no humor. "This place. The land. It binds, little one. It will bind you too. If I leave the ocean, it would bind me. I don't want to age and die, trapped here. So bring it to me. Bring me the key, and I will free you too. I do not wish to do you, or your master, ill. I just want the key. But if I don't get it, I will hurt him. Kill him, if need be."

She was lying. Only the master could send Áed away, and that would be in disgrace and back to the hollow hills, rather than freedom. "You will have to fetch it yourself. Or ask my master. It is his birthright."

The selkie had tried to splash him. That was pure spite, Áed knew. So were the names she called him as he left her sitting in the salt water.

For Tim the week came to a final low on Friday night. He was tired. Well, he had been tired every night, but he'd been coping pretty well, he thought. But then the phone rang.

His grandmother answered it. "Yes," she said. "Yer can talk to him."

Hearing his mother's voice on the phone tore Tim up inside. In the background he could hear the sound of traffic. The sounds of Melbourne. "When can I come home? Please?"

There was a long silence down the phone. A sigh. "I shouldn't have called. My friend Melanie said to let you have a month just to settle. Look, you're not coming back to Melbourne for now, Tim. I . . . I just called to let you know the police were here today. They're investigating a case of arson at that store. I had to tell them where you were. Someone may want to talk to you."

"I didn't do anything. I want to come home!"

"You can't. Look, it's for your own good, Tim. You're there to keep you away from... from that stuff."

"I told you I didn't. I didn't, I didn't! I need to come home. I hate it here!"

"Look, Tim, you'll just have to get used to it. Maybe next year..."

"A year! You can't. You can't!" he yelled his voice cracking.

"You brought it on yourself. Now try and..."

Tim slammed the phone down. He looked at the bare, empty dining room, with its single globe. At the darkness outside the curtainless windows. It still frightened him. He wanted to go off and... and just go. But where? How?

He walked to his bedroom, slammed the door, and threw himself on the bed and lay there.

He didn't even answer when Gran called him for supper.

He just lay there, wishing it would all go away. Wishing he could make all of them as miserable as he was.

Gran didn't call him again. And somehow he slept, a sleep full of troubled, angry dreams of burning stores, a weeping mother, and tall people on horses, with lances and pennants, riding across the night sky.

He woke once, enough to think the last part of the dream was weird, but then burrowed back into sleep; even if it was odd in his dreams, at least it was escape from here.

When the woman phoned, Mary Ryan had been half tempted to give her an earful. Now, after sitting in the kitchen, listening... she really wished she had.

She hadn't thought how unhappy the boy must be. He kept his feelings in, and she couldn't see his face well. He didn't say much at all. Well, she didn't either. But she'd heard those cries from the heart. It had not occurred to her that her grandson might not think of this place as "home."

She sighed. He'd also sounded just like her son, his father. Using words he'd used, later, when he'd suddenly decided he had to go out into the wide world, and that anything was better than Flinders Island.

She'd always taken on the knock-downs by getting up and fighting on, even that worst knock-down, when her husband John had been killed. She'd had to, for her boy. Well, she had to now, for this boy. She wouldn't take help for herself, but, well, that fellow seemed good with Tim. She went to the telephone, wondering just how she'd get the number. She could call Dickie Burke... The phone burred under her hand and she picked it up before it could ring. If it was that woman again...

But it wasn't. It was young McKay, the very person she'd been planning to call, to remind of what he'd said, and feeling very uncomfortable to do so. "Hello, Mrs. Ryan," he said. "I'm going to get a few flathead with a mate of mine tomorrow. Would your boy like to come along?" he'd asked.

That he'd remembered impressed her, warmed her. This McKay was like his Uncle Giles, a good man. He'd been one of the few who had never looked down on her, and had done... little things she hadn't appreciated much at the time, when John had died. He'd also always remembered what he'd said, and kept to it. "It'd be good for him," she said gruffly. "Tell you the truth, I was goin' to ask yer. He's a bit low. Missing home. He's in bed now, but... where are yer launching from?" That could be very awkward. Driving was not easy or safe, really.

"West End. We're coming right past. I'll pick him up if you like. Easier. I'll give you a buzz in the morning when I leave here, I should be there in twenty minutes. Probably about sevenish for the tide."

That was a relief! "I'll try to have him at the gate for yer. I don't drive much so I'd be grateful."

"Not to worry. I'll come down to the house, that way it won't matter if I'm a few minutes out. I'll have Malcolm with me—a friend of mine from away—to open the gates."

"'Preciate it. The boy needs to have a good time."

There was a brief silence. "He should be having one. I did when I was his age here. I lived for coming over to Uncle Giles. And if he likes catching fish, we'll see what we can do."

"He was a good man, yer Uncle. He'd be proud of yer."

"He'd give me a thick ear for the state my boat is in, but I'm going fishing tomorrow anyway. I'll call, unless the weather turns bad."

Gran shook him awake. Tim had heard her coming with the cup and teaspoon clatter, and simply burrowed himself deeper into the pillow. He was not going to get up. Not going to dig or weed or carry hay or muck out the milking shed. Not!

"Yer friend McKay will be here in less than half an hour. You need some tucker in you if you're going to be out at sea all day," she said. "Porridge will be ready in a few minutes. Better look sharp or he'll go without you."

Tim sat up. "What?"

"I said porridge will be ready in a few minutes. And Mr. McKay is on his way. He phoned about ten minutes ago. Not a lazy beggar like you. I said I'd wake yer to talk to him, and he says no, just tell him to have his lunch and hat ready to go fishing. Yer better take a coat too. The weather could come in." She turned and walked out. Tim could hear her opening the oven in the kitchen. Stirring something.

Tim took a deep breath, and without thinking about it, reached out and took the cup and drank most of it in a gulp. It was half cold. That really wasn't normal. He usually had to blow on it to not have his mouth scalded. Had...had it been sitting in the kitchen? Had his gran not planned to wake him or something?

That thought got him out of bed and scrambling into clothes. In the kitchen the porridge was ready, along with the smell of new-baked something. Spicy, yeasty and rich, it had been calling him from halfway down the passage. "I made yer some cinnamon buns to take to sea. There's hot tea in the flask," she said, pointing to a bag. "Yer take care of it, see. It was yer...grandfather's flask." She looked, for once, straight at him. "I'm trusting yer with a lot."

Gran sounded really a little odd when she said that. Like she was giving him a Blackberry and an Xbox together, and they were made of thin glass. And like she didn't want to, but still did it. "Thank you. I'll try my best."

"You do that, and I'll be well pleased, I reckon. Now you be polite to young McKay. And make yerself useful on the boat. Don't wait for him to tell yer what to do; ask and watch. Then he'll maybe take yer again."

Tim nodded. "I thought he said he'd take me...just to be polite."

"His Uncle Giles was a decent feller. Kept his word. Seems like this young feller is like him. I made extra porridge, as I reckon you'll be hungry after last night."

He was. Starving, actually. He had three platefuls, and was just finished when his grandmother cocked her head. "I reckon I hear yer ride coming." She didn't seem to see too well, but his gran could hear a mouse tiptoe across the barn from inside the house.

CHAPTER 7

Tim found himself cramming into the front of the ute with another plump man. "Mally, this is Tim," said McKay. "Tim is coming along to show you how to fish."

"Last time you tried to do that," said the other man, offering a sideways hand to Tim, and grinning like an overexcited kid. "And I remember the score was ten: three, even if you don't."

"This time," said McKay loftily, "it will be different."

"Ha ha. We'll see," said Mally, with a wink to Tim.

"Seriously, this is Tim's first fishing trip, and the first time he's been to sea," said McKay.

"I bet he still catches more than you do," said Mally. "You'll have to get the gate, Tim."

Tim didn't say much on the trip to West End, but McKay's friend Mally made up for it. He made them all laugh quite a lot. They turned off the main road next to a lovely old colonial house, and bounced down to the coast on a bush track. In front of them lay the rocks and the crystal-clear, turquoise sea, and across the water

71

stood an island that looked just like something out of *Treasure Island.* "Roydon. It's pretty," said McKay, turning the ute and reversing the boat toward the sheetrock at the end of the track.

"You live in paradise, mate," said Mally reverently.

It did look like a travel brochure for some tropical island holiday.

"Yeah. But wait until you try it in winter with the westerly pumping, rain coming down, and you have an abalone order to fill. Come on, we need to take off the ties and get the bungs in. The fish are waiting and the tide doesn't."

So they got out, and Tim tasted the breeze off the sparkling water. He learned what bungs were, and Mally took great pleasure in telling him how his friend had, when they were at Uni in Melbourne together, omitted to put them in once.

Tim had mostly forgotten about being miserable for now. The mention of Melbourne brought it back, but then McKay was expertly reversing the boat down the curving rock into the water, and, two minutes later, Tim was out on the sea for the first time in his life, catching the spray from the bow in his face and heading away from land, and then seeing his first ever wild dolphins swimming past.

"There goes the fishing," said McKay, as Mally tried to photograph them.

"Ah, but they're a beaut sight. And I'll swear I saw a seal too," said Mally.

"They're even worse for fish. We'll run to the eighteen-fathom line. Leave them behind, with any luck."

They did, and then McKay cut the outboard, and they were bobbing silently a long way out from the island. Tim looked around for fishing rods. He didn't see any. He was handed a big plastic spool with a thick green cord wound on it, with two hooks and a heavy weight on the end. McKay had a bait-board and was cutting strips off what looked like thick, semi-see-through plastic. "Here, Tim, weave a strip of squid onto your hooks like this," said McKay, "and then you let out the line until it hits the bottom."

Tim joined in doing as the others were, and let the line down. The boat was drifting and the line didn't go straight down, and he wondered how he'd ever know if the weight was on the bottom. He felt it bump, and then something began jerking the line. "Uh, what do I do . . .? Something's pulling my line."

"Wow! You're in! Just pull the line up, hand-over-hand, like this."

Tim hauled. He could feel the line thrum and wriggle, and he kept pulling. It was a lot of line, and a heavy weight to pull.

"Don't slow down!" yelled Mally.

"Keep it coming. Keep it coming!" shouted McKay, looking down into the blue water at the white and brown shapes. "It's a double hookup. Here, hold my line. Let me swing it over for you. If you bump the hull with the fish, they'll get off."

Moments later two enormous, ugly, mottled flat-headed fish, with eyes that looked to Tim like something out of a fantasy novel, were in the plastic bin, thrashing and flapping. McKay grabbed a cloth. "You got to watch it. They have big spines on their gill-covers. Ouch. Makes you bleed like a stuck pig, they've got some anticoagulant on them. You stick the knife through the head here, on this pattern that looks like a map of Tassie, to kill them, quick and clean."

"I think I have a fish on yours too," said Tim.

Áed could see the selkie, down in the depths. He wondered if the seal-woman would tip the boat or stir up the sea. Or drive off the fish. But she was playing a long game. She was making sure that if he would wish to fish, he could catch fish, and come to the sea to do it. She'd get him that way, eventually. He'd go fishing alone...and she would work her magic on him, get she wanted, or maybe hurt or kill him if she couldn't.

Áed would just have to see that it didn't happen.

The fishing was fast and furious for a time, and all of them bled and laughed, and cheered and hauled fish into the bin, tangled lines, baited hooks, and got teased by Mally, who was always the one to have his fish tangle in the lines or miss the box and go slithering around the bottom of the boat, putting feet and the inflatable pontoons at risk with the spines. Tim got spiked getting his fifth fish off the hook, and it hurt and bled a lot. But no one else seemed to care about their wounds, and he didn't want to make a fuss, so he went on fishing. He forgot about it when the next fish pulled like a train.

"I think we've just about bagged out," said McKay a little later, looking at the fish bin.

"Last cast," said Mally. "I'm still in the lead. Well, I would be if you hadn't brought your secret weapon along." He pointed at Tim. "And you told me he'd never been fishing before. Ha. He's an islander, born and bred, I bet."

"That's because we had to untangle the mess you made dropping your fish in our lines," said McKay. "Okay, last cast. Then we'll go over to the island and clean fish and have some grub."

"Hmm, division of labor!" said Mally cheerfully. "I'll eat and you clean the fish...Whoa...Tim, that thing is pulling the boat!"

"Shark. Get your line up, Mally, or it'll cross our lines and get off," yelled McKay, pulling his own in hastily. Tim was too busy fighting the fish to pay attention. The cord cut at his hands, and it fought much harder than the flathead had. He could see the gray and white shape surging through the clear water.

Áed could see the selkie coming up, pulling at the line, working her magics. Was this her plan? To get on the little boat, perhaps set them all to fighting? Or had she really been caught? Áed doubted it. She was too old and too cunning and too used to fishermen for that. He prepared himself to break the line, just as what the humans saw as a fish surfaced.

And then she let go.

Hearing the cries and watching the master and the other two humans on the boat, Áed realized that the selkie understood fishermen very well indeed.

It had been a bit of a letdown to not get the shark into the boat, but McKay had been adamant. "No more. We've got fish to clean, tide to make for getting the boat out easily. Besides, the sea is picking up. There'll be another time. And we've got more than enough fish. Leave some for next time."

So they'd gone across to a small cove on the nearest little island. Here there'd been a bit of tricky work getting them, and the fish bin, and their lunch off, and the boat safely moored so it wouldn't ground and wouldn't swing into the rocks. "Food!" said Mally. "I'm starving. And I've only got dried fruit and nuts. My wife thinks I'm a monkey."

"A fat monkey," said McKay. "It's all the exercise you do, sitting at that heavy desk every day."

"It's a dirty job, but someone has to do it," said Mally cheerfully. "But I've been smelling something fresh-baked since young Tim got into the ute. And it's not him. He must smell of something the fish like. I hear you blokes use squid essence for hand soap."

"It's all we can get in the bush," said McKay. "I brought a spare sandwich, because last time you only had fruit and nuts, and you ate most of mine."

"Nan made me some cinnamon buns," said Tim, opening the bag, hoping that he wouldn't be embarrassed by them, like he was about the homemade bread sandwiches at school. His grandmother either thought he was going to be stuck at sea for a week or that the others would share. There were eight of the buns, sticky with sugar and trailed with spice and popping raisins.

"You beauty!" said Mally, diving in, not waiting for an invitation. "You can keep your sandwich, Jonno. And you can come again, Tim, as long as you bring the baked goods."

"It's my boat," said McKay.

"Then you better have a bun. Just one, mind. Oh man, they're just a little warm still. They must have been baked this morning. You're one lucky kid. If she was my nan, I'd be fatter than a house."

"You're working on it already, Mally," said McKay, having a bun too.

Áed left them eating and moved watchfully to the rocky point where he'd spotted her in the water. Maybe the selkie could come ashore here, even if the main island was off-limits.

Her teeth were sharp and he could see each tooth had three points to it. Humans might see her as beautiful woman, but Áed saw past the glamour. "Still watching

and guarding, little fae?" she asked, from in among the kelp fronds.

"It is what I am," said Áed. "And I watch you."

"All I want is the key," she said, smiling. "I won't hurt him if I have that."

"It's his birthright. His to decide to use, give to you, or his to pass on to his firstborn child."

She said nothing. Just smiled again, all sharp teeth.

"Hey! That flask looks like one of the original Colemans! My uncle had one," said McKay. "But it looks brand new."

"Nan said it was my grandfather's."

"They don't make them like that anymore. That's quite something. You better look after it."

"Is it worth a lot of money?" asked Tim, grasping an idea. Not a nice idea, but...

McKay shook his head. "Probably not, unless, like me, you remember having picnics on the beach when you were a kid. But it's such a neat thing to have. A lot of memories attached to it, I'd guess."

Thinking of his grandmother's voice when she'd told him to take the flask made Tim feel a bit guilty to have even thought about selling it.

"I seem to recall my Uncle Giles saying your grandfather was killed in Vietnam," said McKay. "It looks like she kept it without using it since then. You should be proud, son. Look after it."

But she didn't even *like* him much! Tim was still thinking about this when they got up and gutted and filleted the fish on a low rock, putting the skins and heads and guts back into the sea to "feed the sharks so they can eat me when I'm working here," according to McKay.

Then they had to get back into the boat and head for

shore. The wind had picked up while they'd been on the little island, and so had the swell.

"I'll be lucky if I don't lose my lunch," said Mally uneasily.

And he was rather quiet and a bit of an odd color on the way back. It was quite a wet, bumpy ride until they got into the channel. Tim had briefly wondered if he would feel seasick. He'd heard about people throwing up, but actually he didn't even feel queasy. It was like a really cool roller coaster ride, and you could imagine you saw things in the waves too. Mermaids, sharks, ichthyosaurs...

He was rather sorry to have come to the end of it. The minute the water calmed and they were back to the shoreline, Mally recovered and made up for his silence with a great performance of leaping ashore: "Land, land! We're saved," he yelled, and kneeled, and artistically kissed the rock, and then slipped on some seaweed as he stood up, and slithered down the slip and into the water. "It's out to get me!" he said, shaking his fist at the sea, as he stood up from it, dripping.

"I can't blame it," said McKay, laughing with Tim. "I suppose now that you're all wet I'll have to reverse the ute and trailer down."

Mally shuddered. "Anything to avoid that. I can't do it."

"Watching you try is a great comedy number though," said his friend, cheerfully.

They hauled the boat up onto the trailer with the winch, unscrewed the bungs, and watched half the ocean run out from under the boat's floorboards. "A wet ride," commented McKay. "She handles it well, though." He patted the boat affectionately. "Okay, Mally. There's a towel behind the seat. I'll drop you off first, if your missus will be back by now. Or you can come up to my place. I've got a boat to scrub."

"She should be back. Personally, I think photographing the dawn is overrated. She's a prizewinning photographer," he explained to Tim. "Learn by my mistakes. Marry a prizewinning cook instead, like your nan."

"She's a prizewinning gardener too," said McKay. "You should see her spuds."

"Unlike the poor bloke we're staying with," said Mally. "He's one of those sea-changers and he's trying so hard. I reckon he's getting at least half a kilo of potatoes for every kilo of seed potato. Nice guy though."

They drove on, and then down a long hill back to the sea, to a beautiful decked house, and a slightly harassed-looking balding man with a ponytail, a muddy shirt, and an armful of tools. Tim recognized him as Molly's dad. "Hello. I've just got that tap fixed. How did the fishing go?"

"Fantastic!" said Mally. "And Tim here got a shark, but we lost it at the boat."

Molly looked out of the window on the stairs, on her way down, seeing the white ute and boat coming up to the house. It would probably be that Mr. Harrison back from fishing. At least he was a nice guest, not like some.

She was surprised to see Tim tumble out of the ute. He was smiling and looking a lot happier than he did at school, or on the bus, where he was like a little mouse. He and the other two were in animated conversation with her dad, which involved lots of gestures. Big gestures. She grinned, hiding her mouth with her hand out of habit, even if no one could see her. She hated people looking at her braces. Fishing stories. Like her dad, and the flathead that got away, when he went angling on the beach. It was always the big ones...

"Molly. Can you get us a bowl?" called her dad. "We've been given some fish. I'm a bit muddy for the kitchen."

So she brought one out to them. "Hi, Tim. Hello, Mr. Harrison. Did you have a good time?"

"Fantastic! This is my mate Jon McKay. I see you know our champion fisherman."

Tim looked slightly embarrassed, but pleased. He nodded. "Hi, Molly. I was lucky today."

"Lucky as all get out," said McKay. "He took to it like a duck to water."

"And he nearly caught a shark." Harrison held his arms at full stretch. "It was towing the boat."

"Nearly pulled us under," said McKay cheerfully. "And Mally was yelling 'Cut the line, cut the line' as we went skiing along. Good thing it came off, or we might have been in Perth by now. Tim was standing up in the bow like Captain Ahab, holding on, hauling it in, saying 'it's only a tiddler...' while Mally was begging and weeping."

"Ha," said Mally, gesturing widely. "That was you. I said we might make a new round-the-world record, and to hold tight. It was bigger than a blue whale. Maybe two blue whales."

"Aw, you blokes!" said Tim, grinning. "It wasn't that big."

"It was a good fish, though. Get up and pass us the Esky with fillets in it, Tim," said McKay.

Tim actually ran to do it. Molly had never seen him look so lively at school. He struggled with the icebox. He wasn't the biggest of boys, and it was obviously heavy. You wouldn't think so, though, by the way Mr. Harrison's friend McKay took it.

"How many did you get?" They were beautiful big fillets.

"Fifty-five."

"I thought you said we'd caught our bag-limit?" said Mr. Harrison.

"No point in taking all the fish in the sea," said McKay. "Leave some for next time. Besides, we'd still have been gutting, and the sea is a lot worse now. It gets up pretty fast around here. How many do you want, Mally?"

"Well, if I could freeze a few to take home, it'd be nice. Some for tea tonight. But we've got abs and that crayfish you gave me, and we're only here for two more nights..."

"So what did you need sixty fillets for, then?" asked McKay. "I want about twenty fillets, to stock the freezer and to give a few fresh ones to my neighbor. Tim's grandmother will want some for the freezer, but that's still plenty."

"My gran doesn't have a freezer," said Tim.

"Good grief. We couldn't live without ours," said Molly's dad.

Molly couldn't help noticing that Tim cringed a bit. He obviously wished he hadn't said anything. "Dad. You did promise me you'd take me up to my babysitting," she said, partly because it was true, and partly to change the subject.

"So I did. Is it that time already?" He looked at the tools in his hands. "Doesn't time fly when you're having fun?" He grimaced. "We'll take what fish you can spare, guys. And there is space to freeze a nice batch for you to take home, Mr. Harrison."

"So who are you babysitting for?" asked Tim as the fish fillets were divided up.

"More like child-minding really. Troy and Sammy Burke. They live just over the hill. In that big posh place with the all-glass front up the hill, a bit toward your gran's place. They've got a fantastic view."

She wondered what made him cringe about that too.

"You wouldn't like a job for a few hours?" asked McKay, as they drove up the track from Molly's parents' place. "Nothing interesting. Just scrubbing down the hull of a boat. But I'll pay you...oh, fifteen dollars an hour. I think that's the going rate for young'uns."

Tim nodded eagerly. "Yes, please." For a start, he didn't want to go back to the farm, where he'd be working anyway. For a second thing...he didn't have any money at all. Not that there was anything to spend it on. For a third thing, he'd rather liked Mr. Jon McKay and his friend Mally. Being out on the boat and fishing was some of the best fun he'd ever had, and he'd have done the boat scrubbing for nothing, just for a chance to go to sea with McKay again.

"I feel a bit guilty taking you away from your gran and the farm, but I really need to get this boat finished, and your gran's coped without you up to now. Amazing old bird, she is, running that place on her own. She must be glad to have you to help."

Tim hadn't seen any signs of her being glad. But then she'd lent him the flask. And she had said "welcome." But she was crazy, talking to invisible people. He said so. Maybe...

"Heh. I do that myself. You should always talk to the most intelligent person around, and a lot of the time it is just me."

During the afternoon Tim found out a fair bit about the abalone diver. The first thing he found out was that McKay had no plan to sit still and do nothing while Tim worked. After a while, Tim decided that McKay didn't really know how to sit still. He worked next to Tim, scrubbing and scraping the hull of the wooden boat. It was an old Cray boat that McKay planned to fit out with live tanks for prawns—a new idea that he wanted to try out. There was music from a CD player and they talked as they worked, about fish, about diving, about sharks, and about McKay's on-and-off girlfriend, and about his own trips to the island as a youngster.

And the man worked hard. Tim tried to work just as hard, but by the end of two hours he felt like his muscles were jelly. He was relieved when the abalone diver looked at his watch and said, "Right. I'd better get you back. You've done well, youngster." He stood up, pulled off the safety goggles and mask, and hauled his wallet out of his jeans pocket.

Tim wanted the money. But he realized that he wanted other things a bit more. "Look, it's fine. I had a great day, and I'm happy to do this anytime if you take me to sea."

McKay laughed, pulled money out of his wallet. "I don't go out fishing that often, Tim. Just when my friends come over from the mainland, really. But at the price of a flight over here, that doesn't happen that often. They'd rather go to Bali or Fiji with fifty thousand other people. Crazy. But you can come out someday when we go ab diving. It's pretty hard work, mind you."

"Really? Oh, wow! That'd be fantastic. I'd love that. I...I don't mind hard work." That was true...if it was doing this sort of stuff. "But you don't need to pay me." His grandmother's words about being useful and learning came back to him. "I need to learn."

"You'll go far with that attitude," said McKay, handing him the money. "Far, and stay broke. Take it. I can afford it, and we've got a lot done. There'll be other jobs if you want them. There's always work on the island if you're reliable and work hard. Now let's get you back. Your gran will be wondering if you've drowned."

Tim folded the cash carefully and put it in his pocket. "Anytime you need help. And anytime I can go to sea..."

The diver grinned. "Right. You really liked that, did you?"

Tim nodded. "It was the best ever." To his surprise, he wasn't just saying it. It had been.

He didn't say much on the trip from the boat shed

back to the farm. He was tired. Gran was pleased with the fish, though. "I get some off the beach, but not as big as these," she said, touching the fillets. "Yer thanked Mr. McKay?"

Tim nodded. "Yes, Gran."

"Not more than ten times," said McKay. "Right. I'll be seeing you, then."

And he drove off. "Fresh fish and chips for tea," said Gran.

Fish and chips had been fairly low on Tim's list of take-away meals, back in Melbourne. But this didn't taste even a bit like that. This would have beaten chicken tikka pizza, any day, hands down.

Tim had eaten, washed and fallen asleep, and the world, even Flinders Island, seemed a fairly good place.

It was too good to last, though.

CHAPTER 8

Being woken up the next day was hard enough. He'd have slept until midday if he'd been allowed to. He really didn't care if the cow needed milking.

Unfortunately, the cow did, by its bellowing. And his grandmother had decided he had to do it.

He resented that. He resented her holding his money a lot more. "Where did you come by this?" she asked.

"It's mine!" She must have gone through his pockets while he was asleep!

"And how did you come by it?" she asked, not showing any signs of giving it to him.

"Mr. McKay gave it to me for working on the boat. I told you I did that. Anyway, it's got nothing to do with you," he said crossly.

"You're in my care. It's got everything to do with me," she said grimly. "Well, follower, does he speak true?"

She wasn't even talking to him, daft old bat.

And then she handed it back to him.

"See you put it safe. That's a lot of money to be taking

from a man who did you a kindness. And the cow needs milking."

"I don't want to milk the cow."

"It's not what you want. She needs to be milked and her udder is sore. You're hurting her, and the calf, with her crying. What has she done to you? I don't want to make your breakfast but it needs doing. And breakfast needs milk."

So Tim had gotten up and put the money in his pocket again. He wasn't leaving it here. How could she go through his stuff? What did she think he was? A thief? A shamed part of himself said "probably" and knew that he had been one. He had just been lucky. He looked at the room, the non-working laptop, at his island prison outside the window, where the cow was bellowing. Sort of lucky. He was sore and his hands were stiff. But the cow was glad to see him. She had big soft eyes, with long eyelashes.

He was still resentful. Still angry, even if he had to be calm and gentle with the cow; you had to be, milking. He didn't want to be here, milking a cow. He couldn't hate the cow. The bull-calf was another matter, maybe, if it didn't shut up. McKay had said there were always jobs to be done. Well, he'd do them. Do the jobs, earn money that he'd have to find some way of keeping his crazy grandmother from knowing about, giving him a rough time about. He'd worked really hard for that money. If he got enough he could use it to buy a plane ticket out of here. His mother wouldn't actually turn him out again if he showed up at home, would she? And there were plenty of schools that weren't St. Dominic's. Otherwise, well, he could get a job...on a boat or something. He knew he couldn't really until he was sixteen. But he could tell them he was. Deep down he knew that wouldn't actually work. It was just a cool dream. But he wanted to have that escape possible, the minute that he could. Or...if the story of what happened in Melbourne all came out

at school, or something. Anyway, it might take him until
he was sixteen to save the money up. He didn't know
what the flights off the island cost. He just knew it was
a lot. He'd have to find out. Meanwhile, he'd just have
to pretend to be cooperating. Being good.

He didn't feel good.

Still, he worked on the farm that day and went meekly
off to school on Monday. He had to admit it wasn't actually bad at school among the zombies-of-the-island. He
could almost have been enjoying it a lot more than St.
Dominic's, if it hadn't been for the worry that they'd
find out about why he'd left there. It was just such a
different world here. They would never understand why
he'd done . . . stuff. Tagging. And the shoplifting thing.
They were all just so . . . good. Well, not really good, but
not the same kind of not-good. The sort of dangerous
side to Hailey that had attracted him just wasn't there,
in any of them.

At first he kept the money in his pocket. But he was
worried about losing it, as he didn't have a wallet, and
he wasn't going to spend any of the money on buying
that. Mum could have sent him pocket money at least.
It wasn't fair.

He found a little Ziploc bag at school. It had probably
had had some kid's lunch treat in it. He didn't care. It was
clean and was better than nothing. He kept it under his
pillow at night, and in his pocket during the daytime.

He was getting along better with Molly, too. They shared
the bus trip, and they were the oldest ones, on for the
longest. Only two of the littlies came from farther out
than they did. Molly read on the bus when they'd let her.
She was popular with the two kids from Killiecrankie,
and with Troy and Samantha Burke. She had looked
after most of them. "Babysitting is my pocket money. The
B&B doesn't make as much as Dad thought it would, and

there is only so much computer work going. Mum's been cleaning holiday houses to help. I felt bad after I heard them talking about it. It was awful. Besides, like, I want a new computer. I was collecting nautilus shells to sell before, but I've only found three, and no perfect ones."

They ended up talking about computers because it was easier than talking about money. "My laptop is on the blue screen of death," said Tim gloomily.

"Let me give it to my dad," she'd offered. "He fixes them. Well, he swears at them a lot."

So he'd brought it in and given it to her.

It came back the next day, which was Thursday. "My dad says how anyone had so many things unplugged in a laptop that still had all its seals intact is a mystery to him. He reconnected your power supply. There was nothing else wrong with it, besides an old battery."

"Wow. Thanks! Yeah, it doesn't hold a charge for long," admitted Tim. "But now I can at least plug it in and play a game on the weekend. My gran doesn't even have TV. She listens to ABC on this old radio."

"We get really bad TV reception anyway. So are you going to the show tomorrow?" she asked.

"No. What show?"

She stared at him like he'd turned green. "You really mean you don't know? It's the Flinders Island Show. Everyone goes. There are, like, art competitions and veggies and wool, and there are a load of stalls from off-island selling things." She colored slightly. "I've got a painting entered in the landscape section. Mum bought me the painting stuff out of her cleaning money." She giggled. "Dad wanted to enter his broccoli, but it all started flowering. He's not much good at gardening really. Great with computers, but he wants to grow veggies." She bit her lip. "I could ask my parents if they could give you a lift. You can't miss it. It only happens once a year."

"I could ask my grandmother. But she'll probably say no."

"Well, if she doesn't...look, I'll phone if they say it's okay. Or get my mum to call. That might be easier. They always like to interfere anyway."

"Well, she'll say no. But thanks. Have you finished the Wheel of Time books?"

She nodded. "It's just brilliant how he put it all together. He must have planned it all before he even started."

"I kind of lost it at book six..."

And they got involved in talking about books, until they arrived at school.

Tim wondered, that day, how he'd missed knowing about the Island Show. No one did much work, and he heard quite a lot about it.

And to his surprise, Molly's father phoned Nan. And she said he could go. She even gave him five dollars from the tin box under her bed. Tim saw her pulling it out as he walked past.

Tim's first take on the Island Show had been dismay. Five dollars to get in! He hadn't known there was going to be an entry charge, and all the money he could get was for getting off the island...and then Molly's mum had paid it for him so casually, while he was still feeling the blood rush to his face.

He gritted his teeth. Dug in his pocket. Nan obviously hadn't been anywhere for so long that she still thought five dollars was a fortune. He'd planned to put it with the rest of his money. Just look around. He held out the note. "Here's mine."

"Oh, don't worry about it," Mrs. Symons said.

Like he didn't know they were scratching the bottom of the barrel a bit to survive. "No. I must. Really."

"Call it payback for . . . for keeping me calm on the plane," said Molly.

Tim had been getting quite good at reading her voice. She understood his embarrassment, and that was worse. "Thank you," he said, awkward and gruff.

It was odd walking across to the buildings from the car park. Tim realized he wasn't used to . . . the sound of so many people. Yeah, the kids made a noise on the playground at school. But other than the teachers and Nan, and Mally and McKay, he hadn't really heard a bunch of adults talking since he left Melbourne. Noisy mob, he thought, smiling to himself at his own reaction. Compared to Sandring Mall, which he'd never even thought of as noisy.

"Hi, Tim!"

It was one of the younger kids from school. He thought Tim was smiling at him. Huh. Tim started to scowl, and then changed his mind. "Er. Hi."

The kid didn't notice. "Have you seen those big ball thingies you can get into? They're so cool! Yeah, Mom. I'm coming."

The last part wasn't addressed to Tim, and the kid ran off. But it was just the start. Everyone greeted them. And half of them stopped to talk. They all seemed to know who he was, and several of them asked after his nan. They hadn't even gotten halfway to the big old sheds that everyone was heading for. Their familiarity left Tim feeling even more uncomfortable. And yet . . . no one treated him like dog mess under their shoes. "Takes a long time to get anywhere," he said, after the fourth stop.

"It's strange, knowing everyone," nodded Molly, understanding. "I felt like I was getting inspected at Customs at first. I didn't like it much, but you get used to it."

"I guess." He'd realized that in two weeks he'd gotten used to quiet, to the noises of the bush on the farm. He'd never thought that would happen.

"And then when you go back to Melbourne and greet people and they look at you like you're about to mug them," she giggled. "Daddy nearly caused a couple of crashes, waving at cars over there."

They'd arrived at the door to the first big shed. The Lions Club—so the sign read, were frying donuts. And the smell of hot oil, the hiss and pop of frying, and the prickle of cinnamon took him back. He blinked. He hadn't realized how sharply smells could poke your memories out from where they were hiding. He hadn't even liked the movies, but Hailey had.

And as if it had all been some kind of magic spell, there she was. Looking bored, with that expression that Tim had learned meant he should avoid her...if he could. But he'd never been able to. "Uh. Hi, Hailey."

Her expression changed. She smiled. The same teasing smile that had made him take that DVD and hide it under his jacket. That had made him try that spliff. And, just then, he'd have done it all again.

Except...she wasn't smiling at him. She was smiling at the big guy with the tattoo on his shoulder and the earring who was sauntering through the door, his jeans fashionably low. She walked past Tim, as if he wasn't there. "Hi, Justin. Daddy flew me over for the show..." They walked off.

Tim knew then that it wasn't enough just to get together the money to leave the island. He needed to do more. He just wasn't sure what.

In the vast and misty halls under Cnoc Meadha, where the rules of time and space are quite different, King Finvarra's host feast, drink, dance. Sometimes they will ride and sometimes they will hunt. Sometimes they will fight too. To the high ones of the Aos Sí, this

is life. Sometimes in their timelessness it palls a little. They will intrude on the human world. Humans are amusing to them, in the way humans find pet monkeys amusing. Monkeys that could be enchanted.

It is a rare human that finds the charms of the hollow lands of the Aos Sí pall on them. But then, their lives are short.

Áed did not miss it much. But then the feasting, womanizing and finery were not for the lesser spirits such as Áed. They were bred to work, much as sheepdogs are, and while the great ones could weave glamour and work spells of power in the underworld, Áed liked the change and the challenge out here, and even the weakness of his master. Given a choice, Áed would remain in the wind and wild of the world above.

Few humans, though, once the magic of Faerie had touched them, were strong enough to make that choice.

Molly had met Hailey Burke before, introduced by the delusion that some adults had that because you were both girls who were not too far apart in age, and who lived near to each other out in the Whoop-Whoop, you'd naturally be the best of friends. It had been dislike at first sight from Molly's point of view. They had almost nothing in common. Molly had decided Hailey was a horrible little airhead who had never read a book in her life, but was a faithful follower of fashion and celebrities. By the way they'd never met up again, it seemed Hailey hadn't liked her either.

Watching Tim's reaction to meeting her here, and Hailey ignoring him, just made her feel sorry for Tim and want to slap Hailey. He just looked like such a hurt puppy. But he had seriously bad taste.

They'd walked around the photographs and painting

and embroidery. He'd emerged from his dismals enough to tell her that he really loved her sea picture, and his gran's veg would lick anything they had here.

But she could see that his mind, and his heart, was elsewhere.

It was pretty irritating, really.

When Tim got back to the house, his grandmother was out somewhere. He was glad of that. He was glad of the silence of the farm. He didn't want anyone. He didn't want to talk either. He'd done that. Made polite conversation. Molly's parents were okay. A bit weird, and asking far too many questions about his family. He didn't have a clue how long there had been Ryans on the island. What did it matter, really?

At least they'd stayed off questions about his mother and father. Or too much about Melbourne.

He sat disconsolately on his bed for a bit. Then thought he might as well play some computer games. His head was too all over the place to read. What he really wanted to do was to go fishing or to do something exciting...but he'd play a game or two. Starcraft just didn't grab him right now. He had a CD of stupid old first-person shooter games in his bag that he'd been given for his birthday by his mother, who didn't understand games and had found these really cheap. A couple of them were quite good, even if they weren't new. That might do.

He took the old Spiderman II bag down from on top of the cupboard. Feeling for the CD, he found his passport instead.

He'd forgotten that he'd taken that.

He sat and stared at it for a long time.

That might be far enough, if they didn't just send him back.

Only it would cost a fortune.

And right now he only had thirty-five dollars.

Thirty dollars he'd worked for. Five dollars Gran had taken from her tin box, and he hadn't spent. Like she could only give him five dollars!

And now Hailey was ignoring him. And she'd probably tell everyone he was a thief. Like Gran thought he was, when she found the money in his pockets. What had she been doing in his pockets anyway? A reasonable part of his mind said, probably emptying them before she washed your jeans. He ignored it. If she could look in his stuff and take, he could look in hers. If she thought he was a thief, he might as well be one.

He went to her room and pulled the small old tin box from under the neatly made bed. He had a big twinge of "you shouldn't be doing this," but he did it anyway. The box wasn't even locked. He put it on the bed and opened it.

Thousands of dollars did not spill out. There was a thin little sheaf, mostly of five-dollar notes, on top of a pile of slightly yellowed envelopes. During the week, in conversation, he'd fished from Molly the cost of a flight to Melbourne. Without even counting the money Tim knew that it wasn't enough. The paper clip holding the notes together was rusty and old.

Tim picked up one of the envelopes, the top one. It was addressed to Mary Ryan, care of Whitemark Post Office. It had been carefully opened.

Feeling decidedly uncomfortable... but now that he'd come this far, Tim took out what was inside. It was just a letter, the folds cracking slightly.

In spite of himself Tim couldn't help but read part of the first page. It was very neat, round-lettered upright writing, as if written by someone trying very hard, who hadn't done a lot of writing:

My Darling Mary,

Here in Saigon it is so hot and sticky it's hard to breathe. I miss the Island and the Cuckoo's Nest nearly as badly as I miss you and my boy, my love. I just hope you've got enough money for...

Tim stopped reading, put the letter carefully back in the envelope. On the back in the same big, round hand was the sender's address. It started with "Private JM Ryan" and a number. Shaking himself and feeling creeped out and guilty, Tim carefully put it back, and put the box under the bed again.

He went back to his room, chewing his bottom lip. That must be from, like, fifty years ago, and she still kept it.

The phone started ringing. It didn't do that much. Tim went and answered it. It was McKay. "Hello, Tim. Sorry, not going to sea, but do you want some more work on the boat?"

Tim heard the kitchen door open. It was obviously his grandmother back, and he did stammer somewhat, thinking what could have happened if she'd come back two minutes earlier. "Uh, yes, I...I have to ask my grandmother. She's just come in."

"It'll be about three hours tomorrow afternoon."

So Tim held his hand in front of the mouthpiece, and asked. His grandmother nodded. "There's a bit of work on the farm to do, a bit of fencing, but I can manage. I have, all these years."

"It's only in the afternoon. If you get me up early, I'll do it." Even as he said it, Tim thought he was crazy. Early? He was offering to get up early. But he was still feeling guilty.

It did get a hint of a wintery smile from the old woman. "Go. I'll cut yer lunch."

So Tim confirmed, arranged a time to be at the corner, as his grandmother made a pot of tea.

"So how was yer show?" she asked, pouring the tea. "I used to go every year, but I haven't for twenty years now."

"You should. Your veggies would win, hands down." Tim stuck his hand in his pocket and pulled out the five-dollar note. "I didn't spend it."

She didn't take it. "I gave it to yer to have some money to spend there. Buy some stuff."

Tim shrugged. How could he explain that most things cost more than five dollars unless he wanted food or junk, and that anyway he had been hoarding it...and that having looked in her little tin box...he couldn't keep it now. "I just looked at things. I...I didn't want to waste money. And I'm earning some money."

His grandmother took the note. "You're a different boy to yer father. I'll put it back with the emergency fund then. My John always said I must put a bit there for a rainy day. Money does seem a bit tight, Tim. Stock prices have been terrible."

Tim blinked a bit at this. Several of the kids in his grade were farmers' or farmworkers' children, and beef prices had been mentioned. It sounded like a lot of money to him. "I'm sorry."

She shrugged. "We'll manage. This is our place. Been through tough times before. Yer granddad's family were some of the first people to farm on the island."

"Molly's dad asked."

"There's a lot of history here, some of it best forgotten," said his grandmother, in a way that said parts of it were best not asked about. "But yer belong here. This is yer place. Now we need to move them sheep."

No, it wasn't his place. His place was Melbourne, thought Tim. A place where you didn't spend hours chasing sheep through the bush. But at least the next day he'd get out, earn some more money.

Better yet, the next day after McKay had picked him up, he was sweeping out the sawdust inside the boat's new structures, when he came across an old bag, about the size of his fist. It was a neat leather pouch with a drawstring. He'd almost swear it had just appeared among the sawdust and shavings, but it must have been lying under something. There were a couple of coins in it—black and green . . . but that was with age.

He showed it to McKay. "Right. I wonder how long that's been there. It's someone's little change pouch, I reckon. What's the date on the coins? Must be before the 1966 changeover."

Tim peered. "The black one is 1945. The other . . . It's quite worn. Nineteen thirty-something."

"Right. Well, it's been around a while! Nice little oilskin bag, too. It's a real sailor's thing. Quite a find for you. Wish I was that lucky."

Tim held it out to him. "It's your boat."

McKay shook his head. "It's some long dead fisherman's lost property, and you may as well have it. You found it, after all. I was working there yesterday. If I'd cleaned up after myself, I would have found it. So, there you go. A start to your fortune. Your first piece of silver. I think it's probably worth about five dollars by now."

"Wow. Thanks!"

Tim hung the oilskin bag from a piece of old hand-line cord around his neck, and added the rest of the money into it, in the Ziploc.

Áed had found the old pouch and its coins between two floor planks. It had been dropped there when the board had been nailed on, and no human could reach

it. He understood his master wanted money. Why he was collecting paper, though, was beyond him. Real wealth was copper, or silver, or gold.

His master was still largely unaware of the sprite of air and darkness that was loyal to him. But he'd taken to the old ways and courtesies taught by his grandmother. And sometimes he blinked as if he almost saw Áed, but refused to believe what he saw. That was quite a common problem for humans.

CHAPTER 9

During the next few weeks, as school trundled on its slow way towards the summer holidays, Tim gradually learned more about the bounds of his prison and how to use what it had. He could go online at the library. His Facebook reminded him of what a quiet desert his life was. He didn't want to update his status, in case anyone back in Melbourne asked him why he was here. He looked to see how Matthew, the guy from junior school he'd been best buds with, before, well, before they'd moved, before Dad had gone to Oman. Before St. Dominic's. But he didn't comment, because he didn't want anyone to know where he was. Or in case someone from the island friended him or something. It was like a lingering toothache that sneaked up on him when he'd almost forgotten about it.

He found the more he knew of the island kids and adults, the less they were like the zombie horde. They didn't know anything, of course, not about real stuff in the city, but some of them were actually pretty decent. A couple of the kids said he must come fishing sometime, or on a quad-bike trail. It hadn't actually happened yet, but they had offered. He hadn't ever wanted them to know why he'd come here. Now he really, really didn't.

Things people had said made him realize they thought he was here because his parents had divorced, or were getting divorced.

That story suited Tim just fine. It had a bit of truth to it.

While online, he also looked up the prices of flights. That suited him a lot less well. He'd set quite a high bar for himself, he thought, sitting on the ground, weeding. At Gran's, there was always weeding to do. And digging his fingers in the dirt...it left him feeling stronger for some crazy reason. Well, "stronger" in "the more able to cope with all of this" sense of "strong," not in the "picking up stupid sheep and putting them over the wonky fence" sense. That, he still struggled with. There was just such a lot of heave and carry and lift about the farm. Even the carrots he'd taken as just orange things at the supermarket took a lot of pulling out of the ground.

He'd found a shortcut across the fields, and he could walk fast and catch the bus in twelve minutes now. And he'd found his way down to sea. The day after a storm, when they'd had enough rain to make it a dripping-wet walk back through the bush from the school bus, Gran had taken them down there in the ute from the shed. The ute was a very old Ford pickup with a tub-tray, growing cobwebs. He hadn't even known it was there for the first few weeks. Gran's method of driving seemed to be to get into the wheel-ruts and look at the paddocks. She drove completely in first gear, so it was only mildly terrifying. She yelled out the window for directions, which was a lot worse.

"What are you doing?" he asked, clinging onto the dashboard.

"Don't backseat drive!" she snapped, peering sideways.

"There isn't a backseat. Mind that tree!"

She swung away from the fallen ti-tree and they scraped past several other trees and then back to the track. "Yer drive on the way back," she said.

"But I can't drive!"

"Yer better learn then," she said.

"But I am not allowed to drive. I'm too young."

"Not on the road. On the farm."

She turned the ute at the last dune just before the sea, and faced it more or less back down the track.

Tim rapidly discovered this hadn't merely been a scenic trip, or just to get his knuckles white clinging onto the window frame.

"The storm washed the weed up, and the rain's washed the salt off. It's good for the garden."

She looked at the sea. Shook her fist at it. "And yer be off. Don't yer be coming anywhere near here, or I'll stick a pitchfork in you."

"Who? Who are you talking to?" asked Tim looking at the gray angry water.

"The seal-woman. She's nothing but trouble." She pulled a face. "Have you got a knife?"

"No." Knives had caused one of the boys at St. Dominic's to get expelled only the term before. Pupils were not allowed to carry them, and while it had been tempting... It had to be something cool, not like a kitchen knife or something. Tim had never had the spare money, or really been... well, bad enough to get one. He'd wanted... sort of, to be bad, to get a bit of respect and to make up for being small and really not much good at ball sports. Now his life was too full of people who thought he was bad, and trouble, and who still didn't give him any of that respect, back in Melbourne anyway. Did his gran think he was a mugger *and* a shoplifter? Why did she think he had a knife?

"Yer need one. Yer never to go near the sea without steel. I'm a fool. I didn't even think of that," muttered his grandmother. "Well, she'll not come near while I'm here."

They gathered armfuls and then carried loads of stinking seaweed up to the ute. Crabs scuttled away. Little bugs ran out of it. March flies bit at them if they stopped...

And then, when the ute tray was full, piled high, his grandmother said: "I hope yer can move the seat. It hasn't bin moved since yer father was a boy."

Tim noticed she never mentioned his father's name. Hardly ever even talked about him. If she did talk about anyone, it was "my John," and even that didn't happen too often.

They wrestled with the seat and got it to move slightly. Then it stuck. "Can yer push the pedals all the way down?"

Tim tried. The ute lurched forward. "Foot off the clutch, on the brake," said his grandmother.

He got the part about taking his foot off the pedal. "Which is the brake?" he asked in a panic.

It was rather a long trip back with the seaweed. Tim was exhausted, but quite pleased with himself. He'd found the concentration of driving a strain. He'd stared hard ahead so much that he imagined he saw all sorts of things out of the corner of his eye that just weren't there when he looked properly: Potholes, logs, a small hairy manikin in a hat clinging to the outside mirror. That, which nearly sent them off the road and into the bog, was on second glance a bunch of weeds.

When they got home his grandmother said, "I need a pot of tea. And they deserve some beer. I don't think we're ready to try taking the ute into the shed yet. Just stop."

Tim had gotten used to his grandmother's ways by now, or at least the beer for the fairies idea. He set out the bowls. There were two of them to be put out, one in the barn, and one in the corner of the kitchen, each with a half-centimeter of beer in them. A bottle lasted a couple of weeks or more. He figured the mice or something must love it.

Only this time, he was tired enough to just sit there in the kitchen, and he happened to be looking at the bowl. The flat beer was a limpid brown pool in the bowl... and then it began to ripple, as if something was lapping at it. And then, all by itself, the bowl tipped a little. Tim blinked. Rubbed his eyes.

Looked. Rubbed them again.

The bowl was empty. Drained of the last drop.

It must have been a mouse he couldn't see at this angle... or something. It was enough to creep him out. But Gran decided they'd sat about idle for long enough, so she said, "Come. We've got a ute to offload." She hesitated for a second, went to the drawer of the kitchen dresser, and rummaged about. "Here," she said, holding a flat, yellowed object out to him. "It was yer great-granddad's penknife. Useful on the farm. I thought yer must have one."

It was a solid, heavy piece of steel, with the outside casing made of a yellow, scratched... something.

"It's supposed to be walrus tooth. Sailor's knife, been in my family a long time. Must have come from Scotland, somewhere. We don't have walrus here."

Tim opened the knife warily. It had obviously been sharpened many times. Once it must have been quite a broad blade. Now it was narrow. He tested it against his finger, and cut himself. "Ouch. It's sharp," he said, looking at it.

"Yer keep it that way," said his grandmother. "What use is a blunt knife? It's not this new stainless steel, boy. It'll rust. Yer oil it, clean it after yer use it, and keep it sharp." She took a deep breath. "And yer keep it with yer all the time. Especially at the sea, or near it. That seal-woman doesn't like iron. I didn't know she was still around. Yer don't ever go into the sea without a knife. You wash it in fresh water and oil it after, as soon as you can."

"But... it's dangerous. I... I'm not allowed to have a knife." He could just imagine his mother finding it. Or someone at St. Dominic's. Or the store where he'd been caught.

His grandmother snorted. "Townie nonsense. They got nothing they need a knife for, except to try and pretend they're tough, and cut each other. It's different here, Tim, working on the farm. A knife ain't dangerous, any more than a spade. It's laid there in that drawer for forty years and not hurt anyone. It's what you do with it that's dangerous, if you're a fool or a little child. It's a tool, not a toy. Don't play with it. And never test it on yer thumb."

Tim felt quite peculiar about the old knife. He wanted it. But he was scared about being in trouble because of it. "They won't let me have it at school."

His grandmother rubbed her chin, a sign, Tim had learned, that she was considering something. "Fair enough. It's far from the sea. But the minute you get back here it goes in yer pocket. No going near the water without it."

That was rather different from the warnings his mother had given him.

Áed saw the knife and, because he was a creature of air and darkness, saw those aspects to the piece of steel too. It had the marks of blood on it. Fae or half-Fae blood, which left stains that did not wash away. The marks were old and fading, but it was ironic that this knife would come to the child-of-the-child-of-the-child-of-the-child... many times of the changeling blood spilled on it. In the distant past... it had killed

Finvarra's half-human child, here. It was appropriate, a repayment of a kind, that it should now be the defense against Finvarra's sendling. It would be effective on the selkie too, and quite possibly kill her, if the master had the sense to have it with him, and to use it.

Áed made a point to tell the selkie about it that night, while the young master slept, exhausted by his labors. "An iron tooth he carries. It's had the lifeblood of one of the Aos Sí gush over it," said Áed. He relished that part. "He keeps it next to his skin, seal-woman. Neither your art nor all the water in the sea will save you, if he wields it against you in fear."

The selkie smiled, showing her tricuspid teeth. "It's first that I'll bargain for what I want, little one. I always bargain first... after frightening them a bit. Forewarned is also forearmed, though, if bargaining fails."

Áed knew he'd at least made her wary. He was not sure that was a good thing.

Tim found the December holidays had sneaked up on him. To the other kids, school might drag, but although he would rather have died than admit it, he quite liked going there. One was supposed to hate school, and long for the holidays. However, the holidays were a big uncertain area, and Tim knew it would be majorly uncool to admit it too, but tiny classes and fairly flexible work suited him better than the "you are just a number to pay the fees" attitude at St. Dominic's. There, money, and how you dressed, and how good you were at ball sports counted. He didn't drip money, couldn't get his mother to buy the right clothes for him, and was never going to be any good at ball games. He'd been left out. Here... well, it was difficult to avoid being involved. Besides, he'd found he was good at swimming, at least by local standards. The school pool was a place where he felt a bit of a champion, and where swimming lessons back in Melbourne paid off. There was nothing like winning a race to make you feel like taking part in the other things, Tim found.

Term ended. Tim waited for the call saying he was heading back to Melbourne for the holidays.

So, plainly, did his grandmother. "Yer better call yer mother," she said, on the second night of the holidays. It hadn't been much of a holiday, so far. They'd been fixing the troughs and fetching in the hay. Tim was a much better driver by now, but the hay was hard work. He hurt and itched and sweated and sneezed. And Gran just kept going. "Yer've come on, boy," she said at the end of it all. "Yer couldn't have picked up a bale when yer come here."

It was still heavy enough, like the telephone in his hand. He dialed. It rang. He tried to think of what he'd do, back in Melbourne. Who he'd go and see. Who he'd hang out with, and... and...

The phone went on ringing. Eventually the answering machine cut in, with his mother's lilting voice. "I'm sorry, I'm not home. Please leave your name and number and I'll get back to you."

He hadn't thought of what to say.

"Uh, Mum. It's me. Tim. I was just wondering, um, about the holidays..." He realized he had no idea what the phone number was here. His grandmother hadn't been about to give him any privacy for this. She was standing right there. He put his hand in front of the mouthpiece. "What's our number? I'm leaving a message."

"Our number..." Nan told him, and he had to put the phone down. He wondered where his mum was? If she was all right... What if she was dead, or in a hospital or something? Would he spend the rest of his life here? He felt the little bag hanging around his neck. Not a chance. He was 17.4 percent of the way to Melbourne already.

"Out gadding," said his grandmother, disapprovingly. "Looking for another man, probably. We'll try in the morning. Bet she will be in her bed when the cow is being milked."

Tim had gotten more or less used to that by now. That would be something he could do in Melbourne. Not get up and milk the cow. The cow would just have to cope with Nan.

"I didn't think. I could call her mobile."

"It costs extra."

"Please...I want to know," he asked, worried now. "She might have had an accident or something."

His grandmother rubbed her chin, then nodded. "Tell her to call you back on the landline."

He dialed the number. He had to think to remember it...It had been a while. Hailey's number, he had down pat still. Not that he would call it after the Island Show! His mother's phone rang twice, and she answered. There was laughter and music in the background. "Tim? Is something wrong?"

"No. I just wanted..."

"I'll call you in the morning, dear. I got your report. You have done well, but I can't talk now. Bye-ee."

"Well, at least you were quick," said his grandmother. "Is she calling back?"

"Tomorrow. She's out somewhere. She says she got my report."

His grandmother gave him that sideways stare of hers. "And?"

"She says I did well," said Tim, feeling a little defensive about it.

"An' so yer should. Yer can do computers and things. I reckon yer teacher should have sent it to me, not her," said his grandmother. "Now, we've got nearly no wind, the tide will be full about an hour after dark. Yer eyes are good enough, and the water will have warmed up. We'll go spearing flounder. Get yer shorts on."

She fetched out an old inner tube that had a cut-off twenty-five-liter tin jammed into the middle of it, and a barb-pointed fork on a pole, and a spare car battery from the shed, and a light on a pole. Minutes later Tim drove them, bumping down the track to the beach. The sea was mirror-calm, still and, in the shallows, not too cold.

The light was waterproof and pushed underwater. Shoals of tiny silver fish schooled to it, and then, in sudden alarm, darted away. "I can't see well enough, Tim," she said, as they waded in the knee-deep water. "You'll have to look for the fish. They're diamond shaped an' you'll see their eyes. They hide in the sand. You'll see squid and flathead sometimes too."

Tim looked. He saw the tiny silver fish, and a curious slim long-beaked garfish, skipping away...and nothing else, until he stood on a flounder. He screamed and fell over as it swam off.

"What happened?"

"I stood on something that squirmed under my foot and swam off."

"Quick," she said eagerly. "Up you get, see if you can follow the dust to where it settles."

All Tim wanted to do right then was run for the shore, but she was so urgent, he stood up and looked around. And sure enough, there was a trail in the still water of the silt that the fish had stirred up. He walked closer... and nearly stood on it again before he saw it. It camouflaged well, and the edges of the fish were blurred into the sand. "I can see it. What do I do now?" he asked, looking down at it in wonderment, seeing the two small eyes looking up.

"Walk really slowly and quietly until it is less than an arm's length from yer feet. Take yer time. Then lower the spearpoint into the water, until it is maybe a hand-width above it. Then yer push it down, hard, fast."

Tim did as he'd been told. He couldn't believe the fish wouldn't swim off, but it didn't. It just lay there as the spear point got closer. He couldn't breathe and it felt like the weight of the whole universe was pressing on him. Why should he care, a part of him demanded? But he did. He had to. He was sure he was going to miss...

He thrust the spear down into the water as hard as he could, and felt the sudden quiver and thrash as he lifted the fish. "I got it! I got it! I got it!!!" he yelled.

It was really weird. It sounded like a thousand people were yelling with him too, drumming their feet on the hard sand. Shouting in triumph, not in English, but he understood them anyway. And just then he felt like he was one of them. Like part of some huge family, generations of them, looking at him, and yelling in delight. The fish was beautiful and he was enormously grateful for it, that it had been there to be speared. To be food. That feeling was strange as an idea in itself, but right, somehow. He rocked on his heels in the sand, giddy with the adrenalin rush, as he stood there, holding the speared fish up to the star-patterned night.

"Well done!" said his gran, her voice full of pleasure too. "Hold him over the box, Tim."

Tim did, and his grandmother worked the fish over the prongs with her knife. "Yer first fish. You done good, young man," she said.

She'd always called him "boy" before. "That was just like...amazing!" He meant the way it had stayed still, and that really odd feeling he'd had when he'd thrust the spear through it. He was still shaking from it all.

And for once his grandmother seemed to understand

without him trying to explain. She put a hand on his shoulder. "It's in yer blood, Tim. My people have always done this. Always and always. This is our place. This is what we do, this is what we are. Without it, we're just leaves in the wind. I'm glad yer here to carry it on." Then she shook herself, and said gruffly. "Well, don't just stand there. Get on with it. We need another one for our tea."

Tim was thoroughly wet, and the air was cool, but absolutely nothing could have stopped him from getting on with it. And now that he knew what he was looking for, he saw the next fish, about twenty meters away. And then, a little farther on, two more close together.

"That's enough for us. We can't keep 'em," said his gran.

Tim was still too fired up to want to stop. "But..."

She shook her head. "Yer don't kill what yer don't need. Other people will want a fish too."

She sounded a bit like McKay about the flathead, thought Tim, as they walked towards the shore. And there, lying against a trail of weed, was an enormous flathead in his grandmother's light. Tim didn't care if they didn't need it. He wanted that fish. He stalked forward, spear ready. Only this fish did not stay still, but swam off into the dark deep. He turned to follow.

"What is it?" asked his grandmother.

"Flathead! A really, really big one."

"Yer won't get it once they start swimming away. Yer came up in front of it, didn't yer?"

"Yes. But I was careful. Slow."

"Come up from behind next time. And don't try to follow it. They'll lead you out. I thought I saw that dratted seal-woman out there. She means no good to yer. Drowned a few of your ancestors and left their widows to raise the child on their own."

"I don't have any children."

"Then maybe she won't drown yer, yet."

His grandmother was weird. Couldn't see the fish, but thought she could see imaginary seal-women.

By the time they got to the beach, Tim realized just how cold and wet he was. But he was still full of the hunt. He felt...right. His ears seemed still full of drumming, and his body was tired, but oddly full of energy.

He had strange dreams that night. Strange, but good. Full of smoke and drumming of heels on hard sand, and people dancing in the firelight, and he was there with them, dancing too, passing through the smoke.

Áed saw the spirits of the old ones weave and stamp their dance through the smokes of their spirit fires. They were a hunting people, and a young man's first blooding was a very important matter to them. They had lived far more as part of the land, and the hunt, and the prey, had their love and respect. To hunt was what a man did. He brought food from the land—and the water—for his family with his spear and throwing sticks.

The seal-woman had been out there too, farther off to sea and hidden in the dark of the water. Her guile would have to be greater now. His master belonged to this land and it to him. They were part of each other, rock, sand, water, bush and blood. It would give him strength, if he learned to use it.

Tim was rather surprised to find, the next day, that he'd actually forgotten that his mother had promised to call. It was just as well, because he would have had to be patient, instead of being busy with the jobs on the farm, and thinking about the flounder-spearing. It was just so...more than cool.

When the phone rang he had a faintly guilty start.

Melbourne, yeah. It would be good... Except it was Jon McKay and not his mother. "Yes," said his grandmother. "He's here. But I don't know yet for how long."

She put her hand over the mouthpiece. "He's asking if yer want a job. His deckie is away for a couple of weeks."

"Oh, wow!"

His grandmother gave one of her rare smiles. "We'll talk to his mother, 'n' get back to you."

McKay obviously said something.

His grandmother nodded. "Right, then. Later."

She put the phone down. "He says it'll be hard yakka. Yer can go along with them tomorrow and see if yer want to do it, and he can see if yer up to it. Are yer?"

"I'll try. No. I won't just try. I will be!"

"Then we better call yer mother. Yer probably won't be able to."

Great. I've spent months wanting to get out of here, and just when I've finally got something here I really want to do, I am going to leave.

Tim called his mother. "Oh, Tim dear," she said, before he got a word in edgeways. "I am sorry. I've sent your father three texts. And an e-mail. He's supposed to pay for these things. I really can't afford it."

"Well, um, would you mind if I... only came a bit later? It's just I've been offered a job I really want to take... if I can."

He was surprised at the relief in her reply. "Oh, that would be fine. You'd just be sitting around in the flat here. I had been thinking of taking some time off. I really could use a holiday, and Mar... Mary-Lou invited me to go to Queensland." There was an awkward pause, and then then his mother continued hastily. "Um. She's found a great package deal, only a thousand five hundred for the week, but it is sharing a room."

That would have paid his flights a few times, thought Tim

crossly, before a thought about going to sea with McKay pushed it away instead. He was thinking about that, as Mum rattled on about manicures and stuff. It might as well be in Latin for how much of it Tim understood, but then she said, "Oh. I met that girl from the island, Hailey, when I was having a pedicure. She said she had to go over there for a week or ten days before they fly to Switzerland for some skiing."

Tim didn't actually know quite what to say. Or quite what to feel.

Then his grandmother took the telephone from his hands. "I want ta see his report," she said curtly. Tim hadn't realized how much Nan really didn't like his mum until he heard her speak. "I'm looking after him. If anything needs to be done, I'm going to need to see to it."

"I'll post it," Tim heard his mother say. "But he's done fine. Better than at St. Dominic's in fact."

"Yer do that. Goodbye."

She put the phone down. "I guess you can work for McKay tomorrow. But yer to promise me yer keep that knife by you. All the time. That seal-woman is scared of it."

Tim nodded, even if the "seal-woman" stuff was more of Gran's craziness.

"What's she up to?" asked his grandmother, in the tone that she reserved for Tim's mother.

"She says she's going to Queensland with ... with a friend."

"New boyfriend," said his grandmother with a scowl.

Tim had to wonder if she wasn't right. Something about the "Mary-Lou" had seemed a bit odd. For a few minutes he felt abandoned. Pushed out. But then Nan had him go out to the shed to try on some old oilskins that might do for wearing at sea if it rained, and got to talking about sailing herself, as a little girl. It was something she'd not done before, and it was different enough to distract him.

She plainly knew a lot about it, he realized, fitting his little experience into what she said.

The weeks leading to Christmas were something of a blur for Tim, looking back. He'd never been so tired in all his life. He just wasn't quite strong enough for a lot of what he had to do, so he made up for it with extra effort. He had to haul bags of abalone onto the boat, knock all the smaller shellfish and seaweed off the shells and at the same time move the boat after the man diving, making sure the air-hose was never dragging. He wasn't too sure what he was doing, so made up for it with extra concentration. And Jon McKay kept expecting him to learn new stuff. He started asking Tim tides, currents, and about where a good drift would be, from about the third day. Tim learned to spot the littlest things that could give him clues. He wanted to get it right. And it was really satisfying when he did.

By the time he got back to the farm every night it was all he could do to eat and wash before he fell asleep. Nan's ABC radio was something he heard for ten seconds before sleep. He'd thought quite a lot about Hailey the day his mum had told him she was coming, but, like his report card, after starting work with McKay, he forgot about her, and it.

He loved every moment of being out at sea, loved the boat, loved the way it responded to the sea, loved the sounds and smell and feel of it. He didn't really know why, but...it just felt good. But he was still glad for the two days when the weather was too bad, and work was merely three hours of boat maintenance and cleaning. He was so tired those were like a holiday.

Two days before Christmas, McKay stopped shipping, and Tim got paid. It added a lot to the neck pouch. "I guess you'll be able to buy a few more presents," said Jon, with a grin. "Speaking of which, I have one for you.

With my talent for wrapping stuff up, it's still in the box they sent it in. You can pop it under the Christmas tree. Don't get overexcited. I don't have much experience of buying presents. I always buy Rob and my dad a bottle of Scotch, and my mother chocolates. And Louise I just make a mess of." Louise was Jon's on-again-off-again girlfriend. She was an artist who spent most of her time in Hobart. She'd just come over for the Christmas break, and so far Tim had decided he really didn't like her. She was beautiful, he supposed. But she wore loads of tinkling jewelry and talked about opera, or ballet, or art, and not about fish and the sea.

"I really feel bad now. I haven't got you anything," said Tim awkwardly.

Jon just laughed. "Didn't expect you to. Rob's back after New Year, but he's prone to taking Monday off sick, and sometimes Friday too, so I might give you a call. And Mally is coming over again at the end of January. He'll want to go fishing again."

"I'd be keen!" said Tim, grinning. "We can teach him a thing or two."

"Heh. I know you would. You'll have to fish off the beach in the meanwhile."

Tim was thinking about this, about what he could possibly get McKay for Christmas, walking down the track to the farmhouse, when he realized there was a vehicle behind him.

It was a police ute.

CHAPTER 10

The holidays were Molly's parents' busiest time of the year and Molly had her bit to do too. Of course there was more spare time, and there was quite a lot happening on the island, from cricket matches to concerts, but as she couldn't drive alone yet, it meant someone had to take her, and she felt guilty asking. Still, with the long daylight of summer, and the water warming up, there was time to run Bunce on the beach and to swim afterward. The endless beaches and coves to yourself were something you took for granted, until there was someone else on the beach. Then it felt like they were intruders.

She ran into a sulky-faced Hailey Burke wandering around in the little supermarket in town when they'd gone in for their weekly shop. "Hello," said Hailey. "Are you stuck in this dead boring place too? Are there any parties I don't know about?"

"New Year's..."

"Oh, I'll be gone by then. We're going skiing in Chamonix. I hate this place. I wish I could have stayed in

Melbourne. My stepmother thinks I'm nothing but a babysitter."

Molly had to laugh to herself translating "Chamonix" back into the place Hailey was boastfully referring to. Cham as in "Charles" and nix as in "Nicks"—not "Shamonee," as Dad's climbing friend called it. It was going to be funny when Hailey tried that on the first bunch of other skiers.

"I wondered why I hadn't been asked to sit over there for a while," Molly said. "Oh, look, my dad's at the checkout. I have to go. He's waiting for the lettuce."

Molly made her escape. There were times when she thought the island boring too. But that girl made her want to defend it. And what on earth had a nice guy like Tim seen in her? Hailey was, Molly admitted to herself, what most guys would think was beautiful. And she was good at makeup, and at choosing clothes to make her breasts look like they were going to pop out the top of them. And she had enough to pop, not like Molly. But Tim could have found someone with boobs, looks and brains, or at least a nice personality, surely? Thinking of Tim, Molly wondered what he was up to. She hadn't seen him since school broke up. Maybe he'd gone back to Melbourne for the holidays. Just as well. She could see a bored Hailey using him for a toy to run after her, until she left again, or found something better.

Tim wondered for a moment if he should run. Naked panic nearly took him headlong into the bush.

Then there was a loud bang behind him. And he really did dive into the bush, squirming into its thickness, dropping the parcel Jon had given him.

They couldn't just shoot him! Couldn't! It wasn't allowed! He peeped back from the cover of the ti-tree to see which way to worm in its dense thicket. The vehicle had stopped; the driver was out of it. But the driver wasn't looking at him. Rather at his ute, and scratching his head. There was no gun in sight.

Tim put his head up a little more, just as the cop turned to look at him, his hands empty, and a rueful look on his face. "I really am sorry about that, son," called the big policeman. "Didn't mean to give you a fright. My tire just burst."

Tim stood up, too angry to be frightened anymore. "I thought you were shooting at me! If you broke my present, I'll . . . I'll . . ."

"Tell the coppers?" said the policeman with a smile. "Look, I really must apologize. If it is broken, well, I'll replace it. Can't say fairer than that, can I?" He walked forward, picked the box up, and handed it to Tim. "Tamar Marine, eh? What is it?"

"I don't know. I just got given it. It's my Christmas present."

"Well, if it is broken, really, I'll replace it. That tire-burst nearly gave me heart failure. It must have been even louder out here. I am sorry. Good thing it happened here, though. If I'd been on the road, driving faster, it could have been serious. I'm looking for the Symons place. I am supposed to inspect a gun safe there."

Relief washed through Tim, and without meaning to, he started to laugh. And laugh. He laughed so much he couldn't breathe, and had to sit down. The cop looked a little worried. "Sorry," he said when he could breathe again. "I don't know what came over me. I just got such a fright with the bang. Molly, uh, their place is about two kilometers further along the road. There's a sign."

"Ah. This'll be the Ryan place then," said cop, in a questioning tone.

Tim nodded, unease returning. A sudden angry gust

of wind blew in the police ute's open door and scattered papers out of it, into the bush. "Oh, my word! I need those. Give me a hand to catch them," said the policeman.

By the time they'd gathered the forms, and Tim had helped to change the tire, he was no longer quite so terrified of the big policeman. He wouldn't want to be on the wrong side of him, but he seemed more interested in fishing and boats than in Tim's past.

He put the ruined tire in the back and said: "Well, thank you. I'll give you a lift for your fright."

"I can walk," said Tim.

"Well, I can't turn around here, and I don't want to reverse back to the gate. So I am going your way."

So Tim got his second ride in a police vehicle. It was more pleasant than the first, but he still wouldn't have minded missing it. The policeman said he was new here and asked questions about the island, casually, but Tim would bet he was doing more than just being curious, by the too-casual questions about the neighboring farms and people. "I don't really know. I haven't been here long. I'm just staying with my grandmother," said Tim, quite relieved to give a true answer. He got the feeling that lying to this cop wouldn't work well.

"And there I thought you were an islander," said the copper.

"I'm from Melbourne."

The cop smiled and said, as if he was giving a compliment, "You look more like the son of a local fisherman than a city boy."

Tim's first take was to be a bit offended. But he was in his oldest jeans, and they were quite salt-stained. And he did like fishing. They'd talked about flathead, earlier. "Well, um, I'm not."

✧　　✧　　✧

Áed had not felt such a burst of fear and rage from his young master for many days now. This place had had a calming influence. He could have burned the vehicle, but Áed had worked out that the last fire he'd started had...caused complications. The ways of humans were strange to incomprehensible. So he merely settled for making the wheel lose its trapped air. Air did not like being trapped, and Áed was quite good at exerting his power over it. At the same time...well, this was the master's place and the land spirits welcomed him. They were powerful even if very, very old. "Help him!"

The answer was not quite in words, not even in the tongue of creatures of the air and darkness. But Áed understood it anyway.

The land would lend him strength. But this child-of-the-land would have to use that strength and be a man and deal with his enemy all by himself. The land would not do it for him. He would never be a man then.

This was alien to the little creature of air and darkness. They existed to do their master's will, to defend. Perhaps that was why Fae were not men.

He'd raised a little wind to help anyway.

They arrived at the farmhouse. Tim saw his grandmother come out. And with that odd sideways look... turn white and sit down on the step, clutching the rail. They both bailed out of the ute and ran to her.

"Tim? Is he..." she quavered.

"I'm here, Nan. I'm here," said Tim, taking her arm.

His grandmother pulled herself upright on his arm, and then to her feet. "He's a good boy," she said belligerently, as if she was going to take the big cop's head off. She held on to his arm, tightly.

"Yes, Ma'am. He's a very good youngster," said the

policeman. "He helped me out. I was lost and gave him a bit of a fright."

"Yer gave me one too. Now get out of here. You ain't welcome." Her voice would have frozen a volcano.

"I really must apologize," said the policeman calmly. Tim was surprised he could be so calm-faced with Nan like this. "It was an accidental thing, and I didn't mean to give anyone a shock, let alone both of you. I'll be off now. Tim, don't forget your parcel. If it is damaged, I'll replace it."

Tim went to collect it and the policeman drove off.

"Make some tea and tell me what's going on," said his grandmother, looking after the departing vehicle with grim satisfaction.

So Tim did, explaining about the burst tire. "He probably thinks we're criminals, shouting at him. He was just lost."

"Hmph!" snorted his grandmother. "Him. He ain't lost. He's just nosing about. Looking for clues about who is growing cannabis. Looking for signs of money."

Well, he wouldn't see it here, Tim thought to himself.

"And what's the parcel?" His grandmother asked.

"Jon . . . Mr. McKay gave it to me. He said it was a Christmas present. I dropped it when I thought I was being shot at."

"I haven't got much for yer myself," said his grandmother. "I ain't got a tree or anything." She sounded faintly guilty. "Good thing that copper didn't look in the fridge though, because I did get us a goose for our Christmas dinner."

Tim blinked. "A Cape Barren goose?" There were quite a few around the farm, big gray birds with pale green upper beaks. They fouled up the drinking pools on the lower paddock, and his grandmother did a fair job of cursing them for it. They were protected birds in Australia, but very common on the island.

His grandmother nodded. "My little helper caught him."

"Some people do shoot them. They were talking about it at school."

"Yes, but yer got to have a permit for that, an' that costs money, which we ain't got. I'll claim it's Aboriginal hunting if they asked me."

"But you're not Aboriginal," said Tim.

She snorted. "They say I am. So, so are you. Now drink yer tea, we got some cows to shift."

Tim was left to puzzle this out, as his grandmother was plainly not going to tell him any more about it. Her tone—and he'd gotten quite good at reading that—said he shouldn't ask. They moved cows, patched a piece of broken, rusty fence, and went back to the house. It was hot, but windy. "Pity about the wind. I'd love to go for flounder again," said Tim.

"It'll settle in a few days. Yer could try for flathead off the beach. There's an old rod of mine in the back of the shed yer could take. Call it an early present."

Once, not even that long ago, that would have not raised much excitement. Now it was different. "Really?"

"Yer looked after yer grandfather's flask well enough, and yer seem to have bit of common sense, when you're not driving," said his grandmother, dryly.

"I will look after it. I promise. I've never done any fishing, except on the boat with a hand-line. I don't really know what to do."

"Yer put a bait on and cast...oh, get it out. There's a canvas bag next to it with sinkers and stuff. I'll show yer quickly, and you can go and try. I've got to do some baking. You keep your knife by you, stay away from seals, and don't talk to any strange women."

So she showed him, and soon Tim was walking down through the paddocks and bush to the sea, a long rod on his shoulder, wondering just how many strange women his nutty grandmother thought he'd find down there.

The sea was a far call from the calm of his flounder-spearing night, but not as rough as on some days he'd been working for Jon out on it. He looked at the low-tide-exposed gleaming sand where his grandmother assured him there'd be pipis and nippers for bait. She obviously thought anyone who could breathe would know what those were, and Tim hadn't wanted to ask any more questions in case she changed her mind. It was good to be down here, with the wind and salt in his face, the beach under his bare feet. His toes would have to dig into the sand like roots to keep him from blowing away if the wind got up any more, thought Tim, burrowing them into the wet sand anyway, and feeling, somehow, like a tall tree, firm against the wind. He stood there for a while lean-ing into the wind, before walking toward the low rock that jutted into the water, that he'd been told to fish off.

And there was a strange woman... riding a surfboard, so it was kind of logical for her to be here. She was hot, and not just for her wave riding. Tim had fantasies about a girl that looked like Lorde, and this girl looked very like her. The black wetsuit didn't leave that much to his imagination. She waved. He waved back, more than just a little surprised.

There was obviously a deeper patch of water, there near the rock, because the waves were not breaking there. The surfer girl paddled into that and sat up on her board to talk to him: "Hello. You must be Tim Ryan."

She had a beautiful smile and long, dark wavy hair that hung down over her breasts. The wetsuit was unzipped enough to let Tim wonder what, if anything, she was wearing under it. He was trying not to stare, and fail-ing. "Uh. Yes."

"I'm Maeve," she said, giving him a little wave.

Her smile made Hailey's best try to be charming look like a candle to a searchlight. Tim swallowed, trying to find something not stupid to say, and to stop staring. She had a rich lilting voice...and his mother's Irish accent.

Áed had been afraid that the selkie would be in ambush. He'd been sure she would be waiting and watching, but Áed had hoped that he'd made her wary. Instead it seemed to have made the seal-woman determined to use her powers to the fullest. Because seals looked graceful and their little ones soft, because men and sharks had hunted them...men seemed to forget that seals too were relentless hunters. She was drawing on the human side of Áed's master, letting Áed master's own idea of beauty provide the magical glamour. She looked like the woman of his dreams, because she *was* what he dreamed, rather than her own more voluptuous self.

Áed searched desperately for some way to distract his master. But she was easily able to counter his small magics. She could probably kill him, if she chose, or get the master to banish him, he was that enthralled. Yet...Áed's poor master should have just rushed into the water after her...blinded by the charm and magic, not even aware that he was drowning. And he hadn't. She was trying to talk him away from the land that gave him strength. The land touched the master's bare feet, and he was a part of it, and it seemed its spirits, even if they would not help him fight men, protected him, at least from magics and enchantments. That... and maybe the Aos Sí blood that allowed him to look at her glamour, and perhaps see through it.

But would it be enough? She was clever, she watched humans and understood them all too well, and there was nothing a little creature of air and darkness could do against her power, drawn from the vastness of the sea.

Her look told him that he would suffer if he even tried.
Áed fled...
To find help.
Fortunately, it was on the beach, and it had very long
legs. Four of them, and when taunted by Áed, the huge
wolfhound could run faster than a stag.
The human girl who had been with the dog was left
far behind, even if she too had long legs and could run
well for her kind.

"I'd love to try it! But I haven't got any bathers," said
Tim. "Anyway, I've never surfed, and really I wouldn't
know what to do." A cautious part of his mind said he
would only make a complete fool of himself if he took
her up on her offer of having a go at riding the board.

"Oh, it's easy enough. I'll show you," she said.

There was an enormous splash. Tim turned and saw
what he first took for a sea monster, and then realized
that it was merely a huge brown coarse-haired whiskery
dog's head above the water—with the rest of the dog
submerged, but swimming, and barking.

Looking back along the beach, Tim could see Molly
pelting along the beach.

The surfer girl looked at the dog, at Tim, at the run-
ner...and said: "I see you have friends. Another time."
And she paddled the board away, far faster than the
swimming Bunce, who did a deep-throated woof at her
and it, before he turned shoreward.

"Bunce!" gasped Molly. "Come here,"...pant..."bad
dog!"

The bad dog in question surged and bounced out of
the shallows with a vast doggy grin, hurtled out of the
water to Tim, and leaned against his legs, wet and hairy.
Bunce looked adoringly up at Tim, tongue lolling, as if

he was best thing he'd ever seen. He didn't have to look that far up, either. He was a huge dog. It was a hard look to resist. Tim patted the big head, a bit warily. He hadn't had much to do with dogs, let alone ones quite this size. He got a big, sloppy lick of appreciation.

"Don't think you can hide behind Tim, you ... you faithless ratbag," said Molly, grabbing him by the studded collar. The collar was more imposing than the dog, who was pretending to be very small, and succeeding quite well, for a cart-horse. "Sorry, Tim. He just took off. I don't know what got"—she panted—"into him." She stared crossly at the large dog thumping his tail at her and panting back. "He always comes when I call him."

"He just can't resist surfboards," said Tim, mildly irritated that the gorgeous woman had paddled off, but still pleased to see Molly and her daft dog.

Molly wrinkled her brow. "What surfboard?" she asked.

"That woman on a surfboard. She was here when Bunce came to show off his moustache." Tim pointed out at the sea. And then blinked because neither the woman nor the surfboard was visible. "Hello. Where has she gone?"

Molly looked at the sea. Dug into the magazine pocket of her camo trousers, and came out with a book and a small pair of binoculars. She stared at the water, searching. "There's a seal. Did you think that was a surfboard? Maybe Bunce thought the seal was another dog. He's not very fond of other dogs."

Before Tim could tell her that he wasn't blind, didn't need glasses and did know the difference between a woman and a seal, the Irish wolfhound curved his back.

Molly let go of his collar and backed off, but not quite fast enough, as he shook himself, sending what seemed like half the ocean spraying over the two of them. "Oh, Bunce! If you've damaged the binocs I'll kill you, and Dad'll kill me!" shrieked Molly.

By the time the binoculars had been carefully dried of the few droplets, inspected and the end result greeted with some relief, with an apologetic dog trying to lick them, the surfer had been momentarily forgotten. The two of them were talking with the ease that bus journeys together had brought, about how the holidays had been so far, and that had led into books, and the folly of parents, or in Tim's case, a grandparent. "She says I am to take this old knife with me everywhere. And not talk to strange women."

Molly stuck her tongue out at him. "I'm not that strange."

Tim laughed until he had to sit down on the wet sand. It was neat to have someone like himself to talk to. He hadn't realized he'd missed it so much.

He was a lot different from the miserable kid who had been kind to her on the flight over, thought Molly. That kid had been pale and a bit weedy, and had looked out of place. Tim was tanned to quite dark-skinned now, and his shirt looked too tight for him. And he looked more comfortable here even than he had been on the bus or at school. More confident. Telling her about how cool it was to go spearing flounder in the dark. Very full of his adventures on the boat with Jon McKay. Other than the fact that he was an ab diver, Molly didn't know much about the guy. Tim plainly thought his word was law.

It was strange that Tim had been here for so long during the holidays without showing up at the island's functions and parties. But then, his grandmother never seemed to go out.

Talk went on to fishing. "I'm supposed to find nippers or pipis," admitted Tim. "Gran seemed to think I'd know what they are, and how to find them. I have used squid and a hand line, but not this stuff." He pointed at the rod.

"Dad fishes off the beach. But he mostly catches little flathead, too small to keep. I've helped him collect bait. If you want pipis, they're just about wall-to-wall in the next bay. We've got a sort of pump for the sand-yabbies. I don't think you can catch them with your hands."

Soon they had their trousers rolled up and were collecting the little shellfish, "helped" by Bunce's earnest digging, and then trying to work out how to put a shell on a hook. It was, Molly admitted to herself, more fun than she'd had so far that holiday. And fishing with Tim was more exciting, too, because it was not like with her dad, standing around waiting for something to happen, getting bored. Things happened, and fast. They had only managed—as a team effort—to cast out the broken shells on a hook on the third try, and that had barely had time to get wet before they had a fish on the hook, pulling the line, and jerking the rod around, bending it like a grass-stalk in the breeze.

"It's a big one! What do I do now?" asked Tim, clinging onto the rod, as the reel screamed.

"Wind it in! Keep the rod pointed up," said Molly. That was the extent of her knowledge.

The reel screamed again. "It's heavy! It's pulling like mad. I'll keep the rod up, if you wind the reel. I need two hands."

Bunce started barking and prancing around them with the excitement. Eventually they had to run backward up the beach—and fall over Bunce—and get up and run again, to pull the fish up onto the shining wet sand.

It was a mammoth-sized flathead, yellow with leopard-pattern brown spots and dots of red, and a huge, wide, flat mouth full of sharp teeth, and eyes with a golden iris that formed an odd crescent. It looked like a fantasy book's dragon's eye, staring at them.

"Watch it! The gill-covers have nasty spikes," yelled

Tim as she bent to try and pick it up. "Here, hold the rod. I'll kill it."

He did, stabbing it neatly through the head with the knife from his pocket. "Quick and clean, Jon says."

Molly was glad he was there to do it. Bunce growled at the fish and sniffed it. "Don't you dare eat it, you menace!" said Molly. "Boy, my dad would be green with envy!"

Tim laughed. "We'd better catch another then, so you can take this one home. Nan told me she was expecting fish for tea."

"We'll never catch two."

But they did, the second not quite the size of the first, or quite so difficult or so mixed up in their efforts, but still a big fish. And then Tim...stopped. Put the reel down carefully on the bag. "I suppose we'd better fillet them and clean the guts out. Only I am not too sure how to do it...I was just doing the skinning with Mally. How can we carry the fillets? I haven't got a plastic bag or anything."

"Aren't you going to try again?" asked Molly.

He shook his head, looking a little regretful. "That's enough. Jon says you always leave fish in the sea for tomorrow, and we don't have a freezer, and we've got a goose for tomorrow..." He colored. "Gran caught it. She thought the copper was on to her."

"The copper?" asked Molly.

Tim looked uncomfortable. "He wanted to know where your place was. Something about a gun safe. He was lost."

"But he came and had a cup of tea back in November. With that nice guy you went fishing with."

Tim bit his lip and stood silent for a moment. Then he looked at the fish. "Well...I suppose I'd better try to deal with these."

Molly wondered just what it was about the policeman that had made Tim so uncomfortable. She nearly asked, but then a tangle of blue baling twine and bits of dry seaweed, which had obviously been cast up by the tide, blew along the beach and nearly hit her in the face. It would have, if she hadn't caught it. She held it out to him: "Boy, the wind is getting up. We could put the fish on some of this string and carry them home. My dad knows how to fillet fish."

"I wish mine was around to show me," said Tim, quietly.

What did you say to that? You could hear it hurt him. "We could at least take the guts out. I know how to do that from catching wrasse," she said, changing the subject.

Tim grinned, obviously making an effort to pull himself away from whatever he'd been thinking of. "Here's my knife," he said, holding it out. "Just don't tell Gran. She said I was never to let go of it."

"She sounds, like, really weird," said Molly.

"No!" he said defensively, and then pulled a face. "Yeah, I guess she is a bit. But she's, well, I guess sort of living in the past or something. Like we don't have TV, let alone the Internet. I didn't think I could live without it."

"I don't think I could," said Molly, cutting the fish's belly open. "You can haul out the stuff inside. So, like, what do you do? I mean, no Internet, no TV . . ."

"Pull out fish guts," he said, waving them around. "I've been working during the holidays, and Gran has always got jobs for me to do when I get home. I read. Play Starcraft. It's a bit dead, but I've been so tired after being at sea. And I might be going to Melbourne later in the holidays. Or Jon said he was going to organize for me to take a motorboat handler's ticket. That'd be cool. He's a good guy, Jon."

"I can lend you some books," said Molly. It all sounded fairly dreary to her. Well, the motorboat part might be all right.

"That'd be great! I was wondering about the library, but it's a long way to town."

"We go in to fetch guests, and on Wednesdays when the ferry comes in, to shop."

"Ah. I might scrounge a lift sometime. Nan gets Hailey's dad, uh, Mr. Burke to collect our post and stuff." He pushed a strand of the blue baling twine through the fish's mouth. "There you go. Bunce will think you are carrying it for him." The wolfhound lolled against Tim, panting affectionately.

"He likes you anyway. You can't give it to me, though."

"Why not? They're too big for us to eat more than a fillet each," said Tim, taking the guts out of the second fish.

It would be nice to shock her father with it. And, well, she felt she'd been part of catching it, and he really didn't seem to be only being polite. "Um, like, if you're sure? My dad will be green with envy."

Tim nodded, waved at the sea. "Yeah. There are more fish out there, anyway."

A little later Molly walked home with the flathead. The string was heavy and cut at her hand, but it was still going to be worth it, just to show her father. She found herself grinning at the thought of their method of catching fish. It had all been a lot more fun than just a walk down the beach with Bunce. It must be so strange for Tim. She didn't really know a lot about him, about his family, or his weird grandmother. Why was he afraid of the cops? Why did he get miserable so easily? Maybe his grandmother was up to something. Or... were his parents really divorced? Maybe his father was in jail or something?

Áed was pleased with his work. He had made his peace with the Cu—the noble hound. It would seem the dog had the blood of the ancient hounds of the Irish chieftains in its veins, and was proof against most

magics. Too, the steel studs in its collar had protected it from the sea-dog, and it had driven her off. And the dog's mistress was helping to counter the selkie's charms as well. Young humans had more in common than an old fae and young human, no matter what magics she used to make herself beautiful and seductive.

He'd flung the sea-wrack blue cord at the Cu's mistress, set with the little charms that he had been able to add to it. She had taken his actions, as many humans did, for the wind, and "accepted" the gift by catching the tangle of twine before it hit her in the face. Such are the traps and gifts of Faerie. And she had taken a piece of it with her to string the fish onto. In way of such charms . . . she might try to throw it away, but it would fall into a pocket or end up being used for something in her home. The spells he'd placed on it would work, slowly, on her. He could summon her now. She would come and help to protect the master when Áed called.

CHAPTER 11

"Well, that's a good-sized rock flathead!" exclaimed his grandmother, touching it. "You were lucky!"

"I caught another one. A bit bigger."

"But it got away," said his grandmother, raising an eyebrow.

"No, I got it out. But I gave it to Molly."

His grandmother turned her head askance, her face setting in lines of anger. "I thought I told you not to talk to strange women!"

"She's not! She's a girl from school! She's on the bus with me every day. She's not a stranger or anything. I went to the show with her and her parents. You even spoke to her dad," protested Tim.

His grandmother had opened her mouth to start shouting...and stopped. "Oh. What was she doing on the beach?" It was still suspicious.

"Walking her dog. They live a bit further toward West End. She helped me find the bait, because I didn't know where to look. And helped gut the fish. I...I thought it was only fair and...and polite to give her one for her family. Good manners. They took me to the show, and I thought I ought to give her something to say thanks."

The last part was plainly the right thing to say. "Yer right. It was a good thing to do. Well done."

But Tim's curiosity, as well as some anger, was up now. "Why are you so worried about this woman? Who is she?"

His grandmother rubbed her forehead, pushing back a stray lock of dark hair. "I don't know the whole truth of it. But she's been botherin' yer grandfather's side of the family forever. I didn't believe it all, but yer grandfather reckoned his great-grandfather nearly got drowned by her. He didn't go near the water alone, and said you always kept iron next to your skin if you did. My family, we used to sail a lot, always been fishermen. But they farmed. Didn't even go mutton-birding."

She took a deep breath. "I didn't think much of it, but your father...he took to diving. He could swim like a fish by the time he was eight. He used to go and get us crayfish and abalone. I didn't think much about it, my brothers all did it; me, I collected muttonfish when I was littler than him. He used to go down most days...I was busy on the farm, I always said it was all right as long as there was two of yer. He would meet yer Uncle Dicky, and the two of them would go down to the beach and fish and dive and fool about. And then one day, when he was about thirteen, he went off to meet your uncle to dive. Dicky didn't show up, but he went anyway, even though he wasn't 'lowed to. And he had a run-in with a woman down there. He wouldn't ever tell me no more about it. Just that she nearly killed him. I tried to get him to talk to the cops, I tried to get his teacher and even that priest to talk to him. He wasn't talking to no one. But he never went back diving." She shook herself. "And yer to stay out the water. No diving. No strange women.

No going down on yer own again. That seal-woman is around, and she's bad luck—trouble, too."

Tim was seething with this. It was crazy and so unfair. Just because of something his father did. He was about to say something and then he remembered that well, actually, he had met a strange woman down there. One that looked a bit like Lorde. Maybe he should just let it blow over a bit. Otherwise maybe next she'd stop him going to sea with Jon, too. He had a bit of money in his pouch, but not enough to see the back of her and this place forever... and he liked being out on the boat. So he just kept quiet.

Maybe his quiet got to his grandmother, because after their fish tea she said: "Yer could open that present. It's Christmas Eve. Some people open them then. Yer could see if it got broken by that damned copper."

Tim didn't need any urging. He was feeling flat and depressed. He opened the box. On the top was a pack of what Tim assumed were fishing lures. Plastic fish with hooks, silver oblongs with hooks.

"What is it?" his grandmother asked.

"Fishing stuff, I think." He held it out to her.

She took it, and peered at it in her odd sideways fashion. "Wobblers. Good for Aussie salmon and yellowtail. He knows his fishing."

Tim pulled the plastic packet out from the lower section of the box. It was red. He shook it out, and a lifejacket—the kind with sleeves and an inflation cartridge, which doubled as a windbreaker and waterproof, the kind Jon and his deckie wore, fell out. Tim had to put it on immediately. It was so cool. Jon had even gotten the size about right! It fitted him much better than the boat-spare he'd been using.

He was surprised by a little whimper from his grandmother. She'd sat down on the hard kitchen chair, and was staring at him. Not her usual sideways stare, but straight at him. Her suntanned face was as white as a sheet.

"Are you all right, Gran?" he asked, hastily stepping over to her.

She grabbed his arm with that iron-hard grip of hers. Squeezed. Nodded at him. He noticed a tiny tear leaking from her eye.

She sniffed. Rubbed her eye and said gruffly, "Yer promise me yer will always wear that jacket when yer at sea. Always. Yer hear me?"

"Yes, Gran." It wasn't exactly a hard promise to make. It was just...brilliant! All he needed was a chance to go to sea with it now. It was kind of like designer label jeans, only better. You had one of those jackets...you had arrived. You were the real thing. You were an ab diver, or at least a proper deckie. He couldn't help smiling and standing up a bit straighter. Jon must have thought he did okay.

"Yer look like yer grandfather sometimes," said his grandmother, shaking her head. "Now off to bed with yer. We'll go down and try for some salmon tomorrow with them shiny new jigs of yours, after we have our dinner."

"How on earth did you get that? That's the biggest flattie I ever saw," exclaimed her father, when Molly walked in with it.

"We caught it," said Molly proudly.

"Of all the luck! I've never caught anything near that size." He paused. "Who's 'we'? One of the guests?"

"Tim from school. He was down on the beach. He caught two. Both whoppers, in, like, fifteen minutes, and most of that was bringing them in."

"Hey! Does he give lessons?"

Molly, thinking of Tim and the fact he didn't even

know what a pipi was, packed up laughing. "This was his first time."

"Whoa Nellie! Talk about beginner's luck."

"Yeah, he, like, has this old rod, and can't cast, but he can catch. You should show him how to cast, Daddy. He's a nice kid. He...was saying he wished he had a dad to show him."

"Divorce can sometimes be really hard on kids," said her father, nodding. "But it happens, Molly."

"Yeah, and on top of it all, his grandmother is, like, really weird. I mean, no TV, no Internet. Never goes anywhere. She told him not to talk to strange women."

"Sounds like good advice to me," he said with a grin. "But you're not that strange, are you?"

"That's what I said to him. I said I'd lend him some books."

For Tim, Christmas day might have been a different day from any other day. But to the cow it was still a day on which she needed milking. By ten o'clock, when his mother called, he'd been up for more than four hours, and had done all sorts of tasks, had breakfast, and had just come in for morning tea. As a sign that it was not just any other day, there were little gingery star-shaped biscuits. Nan believed in lots of ginger. Tim had read that it was good for keeping off zombies, and it must work because there had been no sign of even one so far on the farm. Until his mother phoned he would have said they hadn't even got to Melbourne, but obviously they'd eaten the part of her brain that was arranging his trip home. She prattled on about her holidays, like his being here was normal.

Eventually he just had to ask.

There was a brief silence. "Oh, Tim. Your father is

being awkward about it. I asked him to organize it. He hasn't even gotten back to me."

Tim knew she wasn't telling the truth. Or not entirely. In the messy bit of his life where he'd realized that Dad just wasn't coming back, he'd learned to spot his mother's not quite revealing everything. Well, that was how she might put it. Lying was how he put it. "You didn't tell him, did you?" he said, crossly.

"I did, Tim. I did. You e-mail him. He sometimes listens to you."

Like "not unless he thought it would make you mad," thought Tim, glumly. He hadn't spoken to his father for months, even before he came to the island. But what he said was, "I haven't got the Internet here. That's just one of the other things you did to me. It's not fair."

"You did it to yourself, Tim Ryan."

The call didn't get any better. It didn't quite get to shouting and screaming, but when it got down to "you're ungrateful and didn't even say thank you for your Christmas present" Tim was actually quite able to say "well, I haven't got one." He hadn't got her anything either... actually, hadn't even thought of it.

That did stop the rise in temperature. "I posted it."

"We only get the post about every two or three weeks."

There was another silence. "Then it's waiting for you."

"Well, thank you, anyway," still resentful. At least she hadn't forgotten.

"Yes, um, I am sorry it didn't get there. And contact your father. Now, love, I really must go, I'm going out to lunch with...with Mark. Goodbye, be good and take care."

Tim was left holding the sound of long-distance silence before he could ask just how he was supposed to contact his dad. He couldn't phone on Nan's phone. And who was Mark? It looked like Nan was right about the boyfriend. No wonder she didn't want him home.

His grandmother put a hand on his shoulder. "Just so yer know, I asked Dicky to check the post for us yesterday. He said there was nothing, but yer can't always rely on him." She took a deep breath. "I got nothing for yer, really. Just some chocolate. There's not a lot of spare money. But I'm hoping we're going to do better with those steers at the next sale. Prices have been bad."

That was puzzling. "People at school were saying the price was up. They talk about it. And Gran...I got my present early from you. You let me use the fishing stuff, and...and I enjoyed that so much." He knew he was being a little devious, but he wanted the freedom. "If I got hold of Molly, and she and her dog met me at the beach paddock...could I go fishing again? She's older than me. I wouldn't go down alone." He felt like a baby saying that.

"Hmph. I'll see." With his mother, that meant she was giving in. With Nan it seemed to mean "no." "Now I got to finish our dinner. You check the sheep near the road for me. My little helper is worried about the water."

Tim was glad to go out to walk through the bush and tussocky paddocks, to be alone with his head for a bit. Just walking along, barefoot, because he was too hot to put boots on, did seem to make things seem well, less unbeatable. If neither his mother or father were going to lift a finger to get him out of here, he'd just have to get out himself. He just needed somewhere to go. He was thinking about that when a big copperhead slithered across his path. By now, he knew better than to jump or run. He stood quietly and watched it slide away.

The dancing and feasting continued here beneath the hollow hills, with the Aos Sí lords and ladies on a wide and a level place, where the sun never shone

but somehow the grass grew green and long nights followed long warm days. There was a tenuous connection with the world above, and the things that moved and changed there, but this place did not change with them. The great lords of the Fae seldom walked or rode the lands of mortal men anymore. The tracery of steel spread across the land with the railways had set bounds on them, and they did not like to be reminded of the loss of their dominions.

Humans came to Faerie—but far fewer now—and were bound to Faerie lands, with the eating or drinking of the produce of Faerie. The Fae knew how food and drink were a part of the land and place, and that by consuming them, those who ate and drank became part of the place.

Most humans seemed willing to be thus entrapped, and loved the life of Faerie.

But they did not flourish there.

The selkie, Maeve, did not know or care how well they did. But she herself was entrapped and needed to free herself from the ancient obligation, the geas laid on her. The king under the hollow hill at Cnoc Meadha needed to be repaid before she could be free.

The young man had proved stronger than the last one she'd hunted. The bloodline had always been hard to catch, with the magic of the Aos Sí helping them and the spirits of the land binding them. Her last prey, this one's father, had escaped her by chance and luck, a piece of scrap iron from an old mooring that his desperate hand found as she'd held him down. It had been a bad mischance. She'd planned to frighten him witless and get him to agree, and instead he'd never come near enough to the water to be caught again.

The first changeling and his lesser spirit had fled Ireland long before she had been summoned to the court of King Finvarra. It had taken her some years to track him down, across the wide and wasteful oceans... to find him dead. Killed in a fight over an Aboriginal woman, his half-Aos Sí blood soaked into the sand, leaching down into the water, to the sea, to her.

The key remained, somewhere, hidden on the island where he had died. Not easily found, either, to one who had no claim to it.

There was, however, an heir to the changeling's birthright. A child carried by the woman. Maeve had planned to search for the key, or at least steal the heir-child... until she slid out onto the beach.

And found that this land had its own hold on the child.

If she was going to catch one of those who had a claim to the key, she needed them in the salt sea.

She'd tried, when the changeling's heir moved to the bigger island. There, the child had had defenders, besides the land. She still carried the scar.

But she was nothing if not patient. Long generations passed, and still she hunted the changeling-heirs.

This one... she hadn't gotten him into the water, but her spell-hooks would at least draw him back. She'd felt the lust in him. Humans were like that, and her kind were good at using it against them.

CHAPTER 12

Tim had been wondering about how he could get into town to e-mail his dad, when that became something he didn't have to do. His father called. At eleven P.M. on Boxing Day, which was probably a reasonable time of day in Muscat. A half-asleep Tim got to the phone first. His father's voice woke him like no cold water could have. "What's wrong?" he demanded.

"Nothing. I was just calling to find out how you're doing. You don't sound pleased to hear from me." His father's voice was guarded. Wary, the way it had been when he'd come home late and there'd been one of those fights with his mother. Tim had not really understood what had been happening back then. Now, a couple of years later, he had a better idea. He loved his dad. But ... well, in a way his mother was right. He was Mister Unreliable, especially if someone offered him a drink and company. His mother said he'd rather be with people he didn't like than alone. But then she'd also said that if he ever wanted to come back to Australia he could either pay child support or go to jail when he did come back.

"It's the middle of the night! You frightened me, Dad."

"Oh. I messed up the time difference. Don't bite my head off, you sound like your mother. So, how are things going there?"

What was he supposed to say, with Nan hanging over his shoulder? "Okay, I guess," he said, trying to keep the resentment out of his voice.

"Good. Good. Glad to hear you've settled."

"I haven't!" Tim drew breath to tell his father what he thought about "settled."

"Well, um, your mother said it would be best," said his father, awkwardly. "Look, I've had a couple of deals fall through..."

Nan took the phone from Tim. "Tom. What do yer mean frightening the boy out of his wits like that?"

Tim couldn't hear the other side of the conversation. He was too angry and still shocked by the fright he'd had. He just heard his nan say "Well, at least he's got a caring home with me." And then, "No. I told yer then, and I'm telling yer again now. It's out of the question. It's not happening, Tom." And then: "I'll look after him. I told you that."

Eventually Tim got given the phone back. "Look. I won't talk too long," said his father.

Gee. Like he called every day. "You never do," said Tim crossly.

"Well, you'll understand one day," said his father. "It's...it's complicated, son. I won't be back in Oz for, well, probably a year. And your mother has custody. So, um, she thinks you need to stay there, for now."

"You could have told her no!" But Tim knew he never would have.

"Yes. Well, I tried." Tim knew by his voice that that

wasn't really true. "And your grandmother will take care of you."

Tim swallowed, not really knowing what to say. "Why can't you come home?"

"Um. The business really won't allow for it," said his father. "Look. You'll be all right. I'll...I'll give Dicky a call. Ask him to keep an eye on you."

When Tim worked out who that must be, he managed to say: "Don't. I'll be fine. Just...go and leave me alone."

He put down the phone.

Nan put her hand his shoulder. "I need some tea. I reckon you do too," she said with a rough kindness. "This is your home, Tim."

The lump in his throat only let him nod. But Nan seemed to understand. She made tea. And started telling him a long story to distract him—about mutton-birding and the guy who found shipwreck loot in a hole—and somehow he got over being mad and disappointed, and dozed off. Nan sort of led him to his bedroom, he remembered. He had to ask about the end of the story in the morning.

She snorted. "He didn't want to share the find. A silver teapot, candlesticks...he pushed it back down, thinking he'd come back alone later. But he never did find it again, or so the story goes."

Christmas was over in the Symons household. The mince pies had all been eaten, the turkey had taken up its long, drying-out residence in the fridge. Molly had wondered about phoning Tim. She had a pile of books she thought he hadn't read, and that seemed a good excuse, better than "I'm bored with no company but my parents, their guests, and Facebook." She'd been down to the beach with Bunce several times, but he hadn't been fishing.

Her father solved her problem, partially at least.

"About that spot you caught those big flathead with the boy next door."

"He is not next door. There's like, two properties between us."

"They're holiday places. Unoccupied most of the time, and it is actually four, but anyway, what I wanted to know is if you'd show me the place. I've got this afternoon free, and I thought I might do some fishing."

"You'd have to ask Tim. I'm not sure I could find it, anyway," she said, which was not strictly true. But it was Tim's spot.

Her father grinned. "I thought you'd say that. I've got the rods on the ute. I'll go over, unless you want to come with me. There's a track down to the beach there."

"Might be better to phone," said Molly, thinking of what she'd heard of the grandmother.

"They were out with a mob of cows when I drove past. Tim gave me a wave."

"I guess I could come along. I've got, like, a pile of books for him. And Bunce needs a run."

Her father gave her his most annoying smile. "What a favor you're doing me, coming along. But I did put a spare rod on, in case."

"I don't like fishing much."

"I thought you said you had a lot of fun?" he said, grinning.

"Yeah, but that was catching fish, not fishing."

He laughed. "Fair enough. That's why I am going to consult an expert."

"Okay. Can we take Bunce?"

"I suppose so. You just need to keep him in the van if there is any stock about. We can't afford to pay for sheep he might play with."

Molly knew that. She also knew they shot dogs that

worried sheep here. Enough people had told her that. She collected Bunce and the pile of books, and they drove down the road to the unmarked gate.

They hadn't gone very far down the track when they saw Tim and what must be his grandmother and a small mob of sheep on the far side of the field. Tim waved.

"Who is this now," snapped Gran. "More blooming blow-ins wanting to use our place to get to the beach? I'm gonna..."

"It's Molly. The girl I'm at school with, from down the road, and her dad," said Tim, hastily.

"Oh." That was a gentler tone, anyway. "What do they want?"

"Molly said they go into town to collect guests for their cottage. She said I could have a lift in to the library..."

"Huh. Always got yer nose in a book. Well, we got to catch and treat that fly-struck sheep, Tim. It'll die on us otherwise."

It probably wouldn't—or not for a few days—but Tim couldn't have left a fly-struck sheep, either. The maggots burrowed into the living flesh, eating their way into the poor animal. "I'll go tell them, then see if I can come at it from the top corner." The problem with this paddock was that there was too much bush and scrub. The farm was understocked, and the bush was growing faster than the sheep and cattle could keep it back. Tim had seen other farms where they had to fence the stock out of the shelter beds. Here, well, the fencing was too expensive and they wanted it kept down.

He jogged over to the track. "Hi."

"Hi," said Molly's father, smiling and waving a hand. "I came to ask some advice on flathead fishing, and if you'd like to join us."

"And I brought you some books," said Molly.

"Thanks!" said Tim, delighted. "But I have to catch a fly-struck sheep. Maybe...maybe you could just leave the books for me at the corner post...I'll take good care of them, I promise."

"We could wait a bit. I'm in no hurry," said Molly's father.

"It might take a while. There's too much bush in this paddock, and the stupid thing doesn't know that we want to help it."

"Can we help?" asked Molly.

Tim blinked. Them catch sheep? Well, it wasn't that long ago he'd never caught one. And it could be quite funny, a part of his mind said. "Sure, I guess. See that mob of sheep there? Well, I need to catch one. Gran's pushing them this way. If you can, like, help box them in? I've got to grab the one that's got wool coming off its neck."

"What?"

"You'll recognize it when you see it," said Tim, to avoid describing it. They would. He'd nearly been sick the first time.

"That kid can run," said Mike Symons, wishing he was wearing something besides thongs on his feet. His daughter could run, too. And so could the sheep, breaking away through a copse. He was the only one out of breath, as the old duck had plenty to yell at them and the sheep, and still move through the tussocks. "Get around them, boy!" she shouted.

Bunce responded to the yells and the running with a deep-throated bark. Thank heavens he was firmly shut into the SUV, though heaven alone knew what he'd be doing to the upholstery.

And then...just as the sheep broke away again, he wasn't. Bouncing and leaping through the scrub and tussocks, the wolfhound had joined in the chase, ignoring their yells...

Mike braced himself for trouble, his mouth dry as he yelled "Bunce!" again. In his mind he was already seeing killed sheep, furious people, and a weeping daughter.

Whether it was their yells or that they'd stopped running, the wolfhound bounded wide of the small group of sheep, sending them running back to the human chasers, straight at Tim. The boy sidestepped, and then ran into the midst of them, grabbing one by the hind leg. Bunce, either thinking he'd caught one, and now they'd all feast, or just wanting to be part of the action, bounced around him as the rest of the sheep ran off. In the fashion of sheep, they didn't run terribly far before milling in a confused mob, going in circles.

Tim wrestled with a sheep that looked nearly as big as him. Mike ran up to try and grab the dog before it all turned into the disaster he'd foreseen. He was slower than the old lady, though. Her voice got there first. "Get in behind!" It was like a whip crack, that voice, and Bunce...stopped his cavort, put his tail down, and slunk away, behind her. Mike grabbed him by the collar as his daughter came running up and helped...to hold the sheep. "Oh, yuck!" she squalled, as the old woman arrived with a tin and a brush. "It's all full of maggots!"

"Have it dosed in no time," said young Tim, confidently. "Just hold her still for a minute." And to Mike's surprise, his daughter grabbed the sheep and held on.

Tim dabbed the liquid from the tin onto the place on the sheep's neck where the wool was blackened and spinning off.

"You can let her go now," he said.

The sheep gave a plaintive "baa," stood up and limped

her way toward the others—who had stopped running in circles now.

The old woman looked at Mike and Bunce, in a sideward fashion that Mike remembered all too well. So that was the issue! "Is that one o' them New Zealand Huntaways? He needs a bit more training. Big dog, but good for some work, I reckon."

She couldn't see much, Mike knew then. "No. I'm afraid not. He's a wolfhound. I thought he was going to savage the sheep. I don't know how he got out, and I promise he won't come here again."

"Ach. The wee folk think he's all right. I haven't had a dog for years. They don't usually like them much."

Mike noticed she wasn't looking at him anymore, but staring intently at his daughter, eyes wide. He wondered, briefly, if he'd been wrong. Then she turned her head sideways slightly, just as his mother had in her last years. She stood very still, and then shook herself, brushing her hand over her eyes. "Well. Thank yer. It would have taken us a while without yer and the dog," she said.

She sounded quite mild and reasonable, and if it hadn't been for the tone she'd used on Bunce, who was now lolling peacefully against his side, it might have fooled some people. Mike wasn't easily fooled anyway, and he'd had some advance warning. His intelligencer had indeed said the old woman was a real tartar, and he wasn't wrong. But it appeared she was disposed to be pleasant. Mike had to wonder why. "I was going fishing," he said, "And I saw you with cows earlier, and it struck me I hadn't said thank you for the fish."

She nodded. "The boy said it was a good flathead."

"Biggest I've ever seen! It must have been nearly two feet long. It weighed six pounds." He guessed that, like his mother, she wouldn't do kilograms and centimeters. "It was really good eating. Thank you."

She gave a little snort of laughter. "Yer new here? I've seen a few of them rock flathead that'd reach the ground from a man's waist. A big man, mind."

"We've only been here two and a bit years, and the ones I've caught wouldn't reach the ground from my knees. I'm afraid I don't know much, but I love the place."

"Yer do, do yer? Yer bought that block up Pine Scrub way?"

"Yes, the old Masterson place." Mike had learned by now. That was thirty years and three owners back, but that was how islanders knew the place.

She looked at his daughter again. "Well. Yer like a cup of tea, after that? Yer can take the track down to the beach. Good fishing down there."

Mike had heard enough from the friends he'd asked to know that was an almost unheard-of offer. Was the old girl looking on his daughter as a favorable catch for her grandson? Mike wasn't ready to agree, but... his mother had had macular degeneration too. It was hard not to feel some sympathy. And the kids would do exactly what they pleased, anyway, if he'd been anything to go by. Tim was a good year or so younger and half a head shorter than his girl, not a likely candidate when they were that age. "That'd be really nice. Let me just put this menace of a dog back in the car, and I could give you a lift down."

"We've got the old ute in the corner of the paddock. Brought some fencing up here. Yer can follow us down."

So they did. They got into the vehicles. "I thought I was going to die when Bunce came running. I don't know how he got out, Daddy," said Molly, when the door closed.

"I think your Bunce just used up a lifetime's luck, Molly. I thought it was going to end badly, myself."

"Tim's gran is strange. Like, why doesn't she look at you when she's talking to you?" she asked.

"Because she's trying to see you, Molly. I think she's got macular degeneration."

"What?"

"Macular degeneration. Like Nan Susan had. You probably don't remember. You were only seven when she died."

"I do remember her, sort of. She used to touch my face." His daughter was silent for a while as they drove down the rutted track. "Like, you mean she's blind, Daddy?"

"She can't see too well. She sees better out of the edges of her vision. In the center it's a blur, from what I recall."

"But...but she's, like, out chasing sheep. And driving!"

"She's a tough old woman. From what I've heard she's run this place on her own, and raised her son, with not much help. And there is nothing much for her to hit, except us. And they're in front of us. I wouldn't say anything to her about it; she's probably very touchy about the subject. Your Nan Susan was. She was a very independent woman, and I'd guess Tim's grandmother is the same or worse."

The elderly ute was in front of them, driven, Mike thought, quite fast for someone with vision problems. They stopped in front of the old house, and Tim got out of the driver's seat. Ah. That explained it.

They parked in the deep shade and opened all the windows enough for air for Bunce, without letting him out.

The house was what real-estate people called "a restorer's dream." Having restored a Victorian terrace house long ago, Mike Symons could see there would be a little truth in that. Parts of the building were stone, and old. But it had been built onto, added to as needed, and not with any thought about preservation, just about extra rooms and an indoor toilet. There wasn't much of a garden...for pretty. A little grass, and a few belladonna lilies next to the veranda, was about it. A huge veggie garden, though, dominated the side of the house. The other side was an orchard, and behind that, rather tumbled-down sheds and a barn. It all said "been here forever," and the garden filled Mike with envy. He said so. "We try to grow our own veg," he said rather proudly.

That got a wry snort. "Funny how things change. When I was growin' up buying yer veggies from the store was real posh. For the rich people. And they was old cabbage and carrots, come over on the boat, mostly. Now they fly them in, and growing yer own is suddenly the thing to do. We always did it because we had to do it. You want some spuds?"

"I'd love some," said Mike, seriously, knowing he was treading on dangerous ground, but also seeing signs of a struggle to make ends meet and knowing what that meant. He wasn't going to take food they couldn't spare just because he was a lousy gardener. "But my parents were real battlers, and the old man never let us take anything from anyone without giving something in exchange. That was just how he was, and it rubbed off a bit, I suppose. I still can't do it. Now if there is something I could do for you, that'd be fine, but it looks like you do everything better than I can."

She gave him that sideways stare he remembered so well from his own mother's later years. Nodded. "I don't take charity myself. But I've got a good crop not even the boy can eat us out of. I end up feeding a lot of it to the hens, the cow and the pigs."

"Well, look, I have to go into Whitemark once a week on Wednesdays, and often to fetch guests. If you ever need to go in, or get something brought from town, it's on my way. I have a trailer for wire and things. I'd call that a fair exchange for some potatoes."

She nodded again. "I don't ask no favors, but getting into town is difficult."

"I'm going anyway, and I can't grow things the way you can."

"Yer haven't got the soil out there. Now, the boy should have the kettle boiling."

They had tea in cups that were plainly old and cherished and hadn't been out of the dresser for years. The cups, the dresser and the table would have made an antique dealer quiver. Someone needed to make sure they didn't steal the old duck blind, thought Mike, as he asked about fishing, and learned a few generations' worth of information about time and tide and wind. "Yer wasting yer time this afternoon. It's blowing northeasterly and the water's low. Not when it's this warm and bright."

"Should change by this evening, Nan. Wind is going to shift. Fish'll feed on the incoming tide," said Tim, who just happened to be looking at the back of the top paperback.

"Get your nose out of them books! Time enough for that at night. We've got company, Tim. Where's yer manners? Yer learning the weather, though, boy, but we got them sheep to shift because of it. Going to take a while to get them out of the beach paddock and up to the sheds. We got crutching to do."

It was plainly an invitation to take their leave. "Well. I suppose we'd best get going."

"I'll get you a box for the spuds. How are you fer carrots and tomatoes?"

Mary Ryan was also treading on eggs. There was no getting around it, being able to get into town, and as much as she hated the very idea, go into the Centerlink Office and ask for some Social Services support, was becoming more important with each passing day. The boy needed clothes, and he...used things. Electricity. Soap. Toothpaste. Cooking oil. For him...she'd take their damned charity, just so long as they didn't take him away. If they did that, her heart was going to break, this time. She'd avoid having to ask for help to the last.

That was the least of it all, though. It was the girl. When the feller's daughter had spoken, she'd turned to look at her, and it had been another moment of the sight. Out of the edges of her vision, she'd been able to see the girl was slim and young, awkward as a young colt. But in what she'd seen...a woman, middle-aged, hair graying a little, and...changing the flowers on the grave.

That would have been terrible enough a seeing of the future if she hadn't recognized the headstone. She felt guilty enough that she couldn't tend it herself the last few years.

You'd best be nice to the girl who would tend your husband's grave. She'd never had anything much to do with these modern girls, and this one hadn't said much.

It was only while Tim was driving her down to the house that it suddenly occurred to her that it was a family lot.

She'd recognized John's headstone. But that might not be the graveside where the woman had been. Mary would be buried there too. It could be her own.

Or it could be her grandson's grave. Did she want anyone else to have that heartbreak? And did she have any choice? She saw what she saw. Could she change it? Could she ever have? That, too, was too terrible a thought.

It had taken all her strength to keep calm. The girl's city-feller father helped, talking about fishing and vegetables. She wouldn't normally have told a blow-in much—islanders kept their fishing secrets to themselves—but it could be a good thing. And besides, this blow-in was a neighbor, and, for all he knew nothing, he had manners, and seemed to love the place. One got to take it for granted, because that was the way it was. They still saw it with new eyes.

CHAPTER 13

Áed had gotten the fenodree to let the Cu out. Fenn was better with cold iron than he was. He'd ridden the great hound like a horse, clinging to the wild, rough fur, as it bounded through the tussocks. The beast was a better defender than a horse. But he'd felt the need in the land for these things. The old ones understood the hunter...the fenodree had threatened dire retribution if the Cu touched one of the sheep. That had been a matter of some concern to Áed, but the Cu...once the sheep milled, it was no longer a chase, and it lost interest. Áed knew various tricks to mislead the hound at need, if he'd had to.

Ah, but when the hound gave voice, it had brought back the running of the Faerie hunt to Áed. He'd nearly forgotten himself in the glee of it, and the land's hunter-people with him.

At the house, once the people were inside, they let the Cu out again, brought it water. It seemed to accept the small fae. Some dogs did. Others never could.

"Teach it to herd sheep, and save me some work," said the fenodree, using his strong, stubby fingers on the dog's hair, as he sometimes did to the cow, and often to his furry self. The cow liked it and so did the dog, thumping his big tail on the ground.

"It's a hunting dog. And it's the dog of the girl."

"The girl. Hmm. The old ones' women are out, gathering spirit honey. Means something."

The fenodree had many years of experience with them, and his kind remember well, even if they do not understand much. They love the tending of the land and livestock. Most Faerie creatures look down on them.

"How did he get out?" exclaimed her father, as Bunce got up from where he'd been lying next to the Nissan and bounded over to them, his long wire-haired tail flailing in delight at seeing them. "I locked the doors. We'll have to change his name to Houdini. Well, at least he didn't run off and chase sheep . . . I hope. I'll have to leave him behind if I'm coming here."

"The little folk let him out," said Tim's nan, just like Mum who was always blaming the fairies, when she knew it was Dad. Only the old woman sounded perfectly serious about it. "You bring him anytime." She paused. "You c'n come fish anytime too."

Something must have impressed the old dragon. Tim had said she was one, but you had to meet her to really understand it. But Dad was pleased. He said all the right stuff. Molly was still dealing with it all. Tim . . . he seemed so normal.

This wasn't.

When they were bumping their way to the gate, her dad said, "Why so silent, Molly?"

"I dunno."

"Give, girl. I'll pester you otherwise. Or I'll set your mum on you," he said, teasing, but somehow serious.

"Oh, Daddy. It's just . . . She's weird. The house is weird."

"In what way?" he asked, steering around a pothole.

"Like . . . I mean . . . Like there's no pictures on the walls. But you can see there used to be some. The paint is a different color. Now there's just those two old photographs on the mantelpiece. And it's . . . it's so bare. I mean, Tim said there was no TV. But I looked in the kitchen. There's, like, nothing. I think the only electric thing is the light, and an old fridge."

"Hon, I think she's pretty poor and had a tough time of it, and she can't see. Look, you know we battle a bit for cash, but I'd guess they're much worse off, and I can't take against someone for that. And those pictures . . . that's her wedding photograph, and the man in uniform in the other picture was her husband, at a guess. That's not a reason to take against someone, either."

"Yeah. Maybe. But she must have let Buncie out."

"Oh? Why? I mean, when?"

"I dunno. But there was a bowl with water in it. He didn't do that himself."

"So . . . does this mean you're not friends with young Tim anymore?" There was an edge to her father's voice.

She was silent for a bit. She hadn't really thought about it. It'd been more like backing away. But it was unfair, really. It wasn't him. "Of course I am. I just didn't know what he was talking about before. I thought he was just a bit spoiled and wanted to go back to Melbourne."

"Does he?" asked her father, sounding slightly surprised.

"He said so on the bus a couple of times."

"Oh, and there I thought he was doing well as a farm boy. He seems pretty good at it," said her father.

"You should see him fishing."

"What does he do? Look professional, unlike me?"

"Oh, Daddy...no, he just kinda looks so intense, sort of like a cat staring at a rat-hole. Or Bunce when he's sure you're going to throw the ball."

"Maybe I daydream too much to be a good fisherman, then," said her father. "But there are more fish here than in Melbourne."

They continued through the paper-bark thickets and out onto the road. "So...why are they so poor?" Molly asked. "I mean, like, not even a TV."

"I don't know, dear. Not my business. Maybe it's just not a very profitable farm."

"But I mean, cattle prices are up."

"I didn't know you were an expert," said her father with a chuckle.

"Some of the other kids at school were talking about it. Peter's dad is buying a new boat."

"I suppose it could be more complicated. I think how big the farm is, and how much debt it has, count for a lot. Farming has always been pretty tough. A bit like keeping a B&B out at West End." He sighed. "You know, the truth is there are also other problems sometimes. Debt. Bad investments. Gambling. Alcohol."

"There were old beer bottles outside the back door, in a crate. I saw when I went into the kitchen."

Reptilian eyes stared unblinking out of the dead understory of dry ti-tree leaves. The magical hold Maeve the selkie had on the creature was tenuous and weak. It would rather hunt mice than do her bidding, and it was too stupid to do much. But there were limits on her ability, and this land put more obstacles in her way.

The baby snake had washed down to the sea in a flood, some years ago, and she'd tossed it up on a raft of driftwood and old dry seaweed, bespelled it, and

planned to take the creature across to the place where the key lay. Cold-blooded creatures, especially fish, were hers to command. Snakes and other reptiles were harder to manage, but she had some power there, too.

But a savage westerly wind had foiled her plan, bringing up waves and pushing the sea debris back, and the snake had slithered out onto the large island, and not where she wanted it.

She had all but forgotten the useless creature until it came down to the dunes, hunting.

The copperhead was nearly the same length as the selkie was now. Fat, poisonous... and a set of magical eyes for her to watch the boy. When it was not distracted by prey, or lazy with digesting them, that was. She'd seen how the lesser spirits took delight in the great Cu. A defender they thought they had.

Land dog against water dog... in deep water, he would be hers. But he had big, sharp young teeth and a fearlessness about him.

Tim's mind was not taken up, much, with the happenings around the dog, and the strangeness of Nan actually inviting people into the house. He had books. New books. And as there wasn't a lot of other entertainment here, once the farm work was done, that was something to get excited about. Also it was kind of nice to see people. He'd had a call from Jon McKay and there was more work on the boat waiting for him, and a chance to be a deckie again.

At the rate his money was accumulating, he'd be able to fly back to Melbourne and still have a good bit left over. Maybe even take Hailey out somewhere... That made him scowl. He was still mixed up over her. He wondered if she'd be back on the island these holidays.

Mind you, he wouldn't mind seeing that surfer girl, Maeve, again. She'd said she lived somewhere nearby, too.

Michael Symons happened to almost literally run into his neighbor-but-one in the other direction the next day. Richard Burke was one of those "born on the island, I own it, and you blow-ins are second-class citizens" islanders that he'd found it difficult to get along with. The islanders certainly weren't generally like that, but there were a few. It wasn't that he was usually unpleasant. To your face he was always "hail-fellow-well-met-let's-have-a-beer," but he did tend to snipe at the other new islanders in the process. Still, he was sort of a neighbor, and Molly babysat there quite a lot. She said his wife was nicer. The wife came from "away" too, but she also seemed to spend quite a lot of her time off the island. They all did. Burke had a couple of farms and had done well out of selling real estate along the coast—parts of one of the farms he'd subdivided.

Burke drove out of one the little side tracks into the bush, obviously without looking, and Mike had to skid to a halt to not drive straight into him. He wound down the window. "Sorry, didn't expect traffic along here."

"I thought you were away," said Mike. Molly had said something about it.

"Nearly. I'm off to Europe tomorrow. Just sorting out a few things here. Laura and the kids are already in Zermatt."

"Lucky devil. The nearest I get to a holiday is a bit of fishing. Mind you, I have an invitation to a good spot near Marshall Rock now."

"Through the old Ryan place? I'm surprised. The old woman usually threatens to shoot trespassers. She's as mad as a hatter."

"She seems to be having a rough time farming it on her own."

"Yeah, but when I got onto Tom Ryan about getting the old girl to sell it, oh, maybe fifteen years ago—and I could have got them a good price—do you think she'd listen? All the bloody same, those darkies, I'm afraid. They think the world owes them a living."

Mike knew this was a neighbor, that he should at least not start a flame-war. "She seems to work hard and love the place," he said evenly, not rising to the darkie comment. It was something you really didn't say here, besides the reasons you might have on the mainland. A lot of the islanders were related, and some of them were descended from the first sealers and their Aboriginal wives.

"It's a dump. It could have been developed into something valuable. It's harder to get that kind of thing through planning now. Anyway, I got to scoot. You go past."

So Mike did. Looking back in his mirror, he saw Burke had gotten out and was hauling a dead branch across the track. It was probably his track to a secret abalone spot or something.

CHAPTER 14

The next weeks of the December holidays were so busy, Tim rather forgot about being bored. The summer days were long and his grandmother believed that daylight was the time to be doing things. Some of those things were fun, spearing fish, even beachcombing for paper-nautilus shells and other flotsam, trying to teach Bunce how to herd sheep... Molly was determined he could learn, but so far all that the big wolfhound had proved was that he had no interest in hunting or killing sheep. And he did come when called... but that was the limit of his natural sheepdog skills. He was almost impossible not to like, he seemed to feel leaning up against you and whipping you with his tail were his duty, and one he loved doing. But he just didn't quite get what they wanted him to do.

It made the two of them laugh until their sides ached a few times. Molly would get a bit defensive about her dog, but he was a big dork sometimes. He'd probably be really good at running down a wolf, but sheep-work was like another dimension to him.

It was a bit like Molly's dad and beach fishing. He was a nice guy, and had shown Tim how to cast properly, and how to fillet. And in a week Tim could do both better than he could. The guy was just like Bunce to sheep with the sea and fishing. Anyone could see where there was a gutter in the waves. The water was a slightly different color; the waves would be peaking and then flatten when they rolled into it... The foam and seaweed moved differently. It was so obvious that that would be where the big fish would move—to feed on the little fish, shellfish and scraps that washed off the banks by the waves—plain as the nose on your face, and Molly's dad would cast past it. And even when Tim put him on precisely the right place, he just didn't seem to get it. Tim knew when a fish was taking little pecks at his bait. How didn't you know? You could feel it... it was a very different thing from the movement of the water or the waves on the line. Molly's dad said he couldn't ever tell the difference. A fish just about had to commit suicide and jump out the water by itself before he caught it. It was kind of embarrassing, when Tim would have four fish and be ready to go home, and the guy didn't even know he'd had a bite yet, even though his bait had been cleaned out. After the first couple of times, Tim would catch two, gut and fillet them, and stop and supervise and chat with Molly, and stop Bunce from eating the bait or the fillets—or from getting himself spiked by a fish coming out.

It was still fun, even if it was really, really weird to realize that fishing was not like the rest of his life. He was sort of good at it. Better than them, anyway. Everything else he'd ever done, he'd been, well, trying to be good enough not to make a fool of himself. Not that it made any difference. It wasn't like being an ace hacker or great at footy or something. In the real world, back in Melbourne, being able to catch or spear fish would be unimportant. They'd care about as much about that as they would about herding sheep or growing spuds.

He'd been out a few more times with Jon, when his deckie had called in sick. That wasn't merely fun. That was just brilliant.

And then school came around, and he realized he'd never gotten back to Melbourne. Mum hadn't done anything more about it, and he hadn't chased her or his dad about it. It came to him one evening when he was sitting reading in his room, and Gran was listening to ABC in the dark, like she always did, that maybe his mother didn't want him back there, ever. Was she getting together with someone else, like Gran thought? He hadn't even gotten a Christmas call from his father. Hadn't heard from him again since the Boxing Day call. That was just too like his father: he'd promise, but never quite get to doing it, hoping it would go away before he had to. Had they all just written him off to Flinders Island forever? Like sending someone to Australia in the old days, and forgetting they existed. Even if he had enough money to get to Melbourne... where would he live if Mum didn't want him? The idea of living on the street scared him. And he'd never have enough money to get a place of his own. He wasn't sure how or if he could get some kind of job.

He wasn't wanted, and had no one who cared much.

It was a pretty miserable thought.

It was still bothering him the next afternoon after school, so when he'd finished fixing the water trough down at the beach paddock, the one that ran along the crown reserve and had next-to-useless grazing, he walked down onto the beach through the saltbush.

The sky was patchy with cloud, and the sea had that "warning" color to it. It wouldn't be much good for fishing. There was nasty weather coming soon, by the look of it. He wouldn't have known that three months ago. Now, he could look at the sea, work out that the tide had just turned, look at the flecks of white out on the blue-gray, and know that meant "southwesterly" and know what the swell would be doing.

And there, about twenty meters from the beach, was that gorgeous surfer girl in her skintight wetsuit, standing waist deep in the foaming waves. She waved to him. "Help!" she called. "I'm so glad to see you! I've got my foot stuck in a crack in the limestone and another rock has washed onto it. I can't reach down to move it. I think my ankle might be broken. I've been calling and calling. Scared the tide might come in before anyone came."

"I'll go and get help!" said Tim. "I'll run back and call..."

"Just come out here. I am sure you can shift it. It's just too sore for me to move the rock."

Tim was less than sure, and was going to go and get help anyway, when a furious wind gust tore along the beach. The weather change must be closer than he thought. He took his runners off and walked straight into the water, not waiting even to take his shirt off.

Áed summoned the girl desperately, again, just as he had when the master suddenly headed to the beach, using the power he'd put into that piece of blue baling twine on the beach when she and the master had caught fish together the first time. He'd felt the master was troubled, but the day with the other young ones at the school had gone well. The master was at ease with most of them, and they with him. That Maeve! She was too quick and too clever. She must have been waiting for this moment.

Áed had raised the wind, and that had made it worse.

✧   ✧   ✧

She didn't seem to be in that much pain. She was smiling. An odd smile for someone in trouble, thought Tim, just a second too late. She moved like oiled lightning, grabbing his hands with a viselike grip. "I've got you this time. Now I'll show you what I can do to you if you don't cooperate." And as he drew breath to scream, she pulled him under. He barely had time to close his mouth.

He was terrified... and then furious, even as he was desperate for air, as she towed him through the water. He kicked at her. What a stupid practical joke!

Briefly, he got a chance to gasp air and start to yell before she pulled him under again. Now the anger turned, at least in part, to fear. She was going to drown him! He began to struggle with every ounce of his strength. He had his knife...

He managed to kick himself free—to the surface. He gasped air and frantically tore at his wet pocket as she grabbed his legs again.

Opening the knife was an act of desperation, and he nearly lost it, but she let go. He thrashed in the deep water, a wave foaming and peaking next to him. So far from shore already—he must be seventy yards out now—and his foot kicked something that clung around it. His first panicky thought was that it was her. He reached under, stabbing in his fear... and came up with a broad strand of seaweed on the blade. He extended his foot that way and touched rock. A limestone pinnacle, a spike of rock that had not eroded away. Jon looked for them to dive on, and it was why the sea foamed here. Tim had even seen and noticed this one from the beach. He scrambled up onto it. The water surged up to his chest with the waves, but it was something to stand on.

He looked around for the madwoman.

The black shape torpedoed through the water, so close

he screamed. Came up, and the dog-face of the seal grinned at him, showing white teeth.

It was not a pretty-seal-at-SeaWorld seal's smile. Or a cartoon seal smile. This was a wild thing in command of its environment. And the wild thing rolled... and became the woman.

Now Tim screamed again, pure hysteria. He dug his toes desperately into the slippery, seaweedy rock.

After the third scream, when the seal-woman hadn't gone away, but was treading water about two yards off, looking at him, he managed to get some small kind of grip on himself.

"Found the rock, have you?" she said coolly. "Well, no matter. The tide and waves will get to you, if you don't do as I wish."

"Wh-wh-what are you?" demanded Tim holding the knife in front of himself in a shaking hand. "What are you trying to drown me for?"

"I won't drown you unless I have to, changeling-child," said the seal-woman. "I just wanted you away from the land that gives you strength, away from your little familiar. He's trying all sorts of small magics to help you, but here you are in my realm. King Finvarra wants the key back."

"What the hell are you talking about, you madwoman? What are you?" Fright or the cold made him shiver.

She turned into a seal again, swam around him, and then returned to looking human. She didn't look much like Lorde now. "That answers your second question. I am Maeve, and I can drown you. It's not me you need to know about to understand the first question. It is who you are and where your blood came from."

"What are you talking about? I can't believe this." He wiped his eyes with his hand. Not the hand with the knife clutched so hard his knuckles were white, but the other hand.

"Believe your eyes," she said, disdainfully. "Your kind, or rather your great-great-great-great-great-grandmother's kind, are good at deceiving themselves. Your male forefather's ilk were good at deceiving them. Which is how Finvarra seduced the silly girl and took her away to the hollow hills, to his palace beneath Cnoc Meadha. Your great-great-great-great-grandfather was her get, and like all of his half-blood kind, put out of Aos Sí lands to grow to manhood among mortal men."

"What are you trying to tell me? I don't believe this stuff." A part of him did, though. "Are you telling me that, like, I'm descended from some king?"

"A king of what you would call Faerie. There are many other half-blood children, many full-blood princes in the Hollow Lands. They ride and hunt and dance and feast, and are waited on by the lesser spirits and creatures of magic. Even as you are. Your birthright, the key, and the servant. The key will take you to Faerie lands. The door is closed, otherwise."

"I don't have any servants, and I don't have any keys. You've got the wrong person. I'm just Tim Ryan."

"I know your name, as I knew your father's name, and his father before him and his father before him, and indeed the two generations before that. You are all marked. And your servant . . . is frantically striving to bring you help from the beach. He is even calling the old ones of this place. They will not help you. You're not on their land anymore."

As she said that, Tim knew she was lying, because his feet told him so. It seemed to make him stronger. "I don't know what you're talking about. Go away or I'll stab you." If she was magical . . . "Cold iron. You can't touch me."

"I could command the sharks to do it for me. Their blood will just add to their frenzy. You would never reach the shore."

"Look, I don't have any keys. Just let me go."

"It lies hidden on that island out there. Your ancestor decided to flee Ireland, and brought it with him. He was shipwrecked, and took it and his few small treasures, and hid them. That much I have established. He joined the half-wild men there, the sealers, and took himself a wife, a woman taken from the Aboriginal people of Tasmania. He died there—his blood ran into the water so I knew of it—but not before he had fathered a son. The key is the birthright of the changeling, or of the eldest son of the changeling. And it has come down to you across the long generations."

"And you want to take it from me? I don't even know where it is, let alone want to give it to you."

"I do not want it," said the seal-woman. "I am a creature of the sea, not the endless lands of Faerie. King Finvarra wants it back. I am bound to see it returned to him. The Aos Sí do not cross salt water, or he would have sent his own warriors. The keys to Faerie lands are precious, and not to be left for any passing mortal to find. So I was sent. I need to fulfil my geas, and be free of the bargain I made. You are the last heir. You will not leave here without my consent, and the tide is rising."

A thought dawned on Tim, and with it a bubble of anger. "Yeah? Really?" he said sarcastically. "If you could get it without me, you would. And if you kill me, you won't."

The selkie tossed her hair back. Sighed. "Yes. But I can make you suffer. Or I can reward you. These lands protect you, but here in the water...I could take a leg off. Or both hands. You could still have children for me to get it from, even if I maim you and you still hold off. But I cannot find it without you. It lies on that island. The place protects those of the blood of the land, your great-great-great-great-grandmother's people, against my magic. It will not let me ashore. I would rather make a bargain with you than maim you. I wanted to frighten you first, that was all."

Tim didn't trust her. "Yeah. Like I'd believe you after what you tried to do to me."

"I was taking you to those floats over there," she pointed to a bunch of cray pot floats, all tied together, some forty or fifty meters farther out. "I wanted you away from the land. And we do not give our oaths lightly and easily like humans. There is no need for either of us to lose. You could take the key to Finvarra yourself. You have the right to enter the hollow hill. It is your birthright, your key, the birth-gift to your ancestor, and even though it has passed down to the oldest son, across the long generations, it is still your birthright. You would be welcomed and rewarded well. I swear this on my cape, that which allows me to change my form, and there is no more compelling oath I can give. The women of Faerie are beautiful, and willing and eager for young mortal lovers. They see few, now, and you would have the charm of novelty to them in their loving. There is feasting, and dancing and laughter, and there are great hunts across the endless fields of Faerie. I have seen the joy of the hunt in you, and you would love it. You would be a prince among them, not someone who labors, who chops wood, hauls water and shovels dung. You would be the darling and pleasure of the court. You would live out long days in happiness. What can this scrap of land offer you but hard labor and poverty? Look. I will show you."

She waved a hand languorously. A misty cloud appeared, and then the middle of it became transparent... and Tim could see a green, soft land. A huge pavilion was pitched on it, like a wedding marquee, only bigger than he'd ever seen. There was a long table set there, with, it looked like, everything that could possibly be roasted, from huge platters loaded with a circle of some kind of fowl, with smaller roasted birds speared on their own long beaks piled inside, to whole roasted pigs, and huge steaming platters of meat carved from a roasting ox over the fire pit just outside the tent. The table was full of platters of other things too, bread in twisted crusty loaves, pies, fruit—peaches and apples, huge clay bowls that steamed. On another table there were what had to be desserts. Huge fancy arrangements of tarts and cakes and what could be jellies. It wasn't like TV or a movie; he could smell the roasted meat, feel the heat of the fire, and there was a sort of real depth to what he saw. It was almost like he could just step into it. And there were people... well, not exactly like any other people he'd ever seen, outside of a movie or his imagination, talking and laughing as they dismounted their horses. They were dressed in bright, rich-looking clothes, clothes that looked like they belonged in a history book. The trousers were weird, and the guys wearing them tall, fair and handsome... but the women were all beautiful. Every single one of them was in the supermodel class. The horses—and the pack horses, which were loaded with different kinds of game—were being led away by little gnomelike creatures with dark eyes.

And then it all faded into a misty distance, and he was standing perched on an underwater rock as the cold sea surged around him.

"That is Finvarra's kingdom, beneath the mound of Cnoc Meadha," she said, matter-of-factly. "Time passes differently there, and the vastness of it is beyond any encompassment. You could go there, or stay here and age and die, in the endless toil of mortal men."

It was crazy... but hard to doubt right now. He had to admit it was sort of tempting. And... who wanted him here? Hadn't he come down to the beach mad as a cut snake because Mum and Dad didn't care about him? And hadn't the thing bugging him been that there didn't seem much sense in saving to go back to Melbourne... if he didn't have anywhere to go when he got there? "So, um, if I got this key... how do I get this key?" he asked.

"You would go across to that island there..."

"Prime Seal Island. Yeah."

"And command your lesser spirit to lead you to the hiding place. The little one can smell it out."

"Like some kind of spell? Sort of demons and stuff?" Tim knew enough to know he wasn't going there.

"No. He is one of the little people. You would reward him with a bowl of fine usque bagh or mead."

"What?" Mead was something he'd read about... some kind of drink made with honey, wasn't it?

"A little beer would do."

Tim began to connect the dots, from his grandmother's kitchen... to all of this. "Yeah? And then? I'd want to see this place. Like, actually see it. Not illusions or something."

"You go to Finvarra's mound and place the key on the enchanted ground, and it will open for you."

"Go to... where is this place?"

"Across the oceans. A place your one ancestor fled from: Ireland. In County Galway, near the town of Tuam."

That was enough to make Tim chuckle, despite the fact that he was out in the middle of the sea, talking to a seal-woman. "You have no idea, have you? I can't just go to Ireland. I mean I would have to fly, and it costs a fortune, and I would need a passport..."

It struck him suddenly that he actually did have his passport. Maybe this was all intended, all arranged? He'd go and be a prince. A prince in a place where no one would ever know he'd been caught shoplifting, ever been a kid in trouble. Away from that nagging threat of being shamed, forever. And it would be kind of cool to be important. And he hadn't ever really belonged in Melbourne. He was, sort of, a changeling. Really, he belonged somewhere else. He'd been left here to live a horrible dull life, where he was always a bit of a loser... It was a pity it was so far. It was tempting. Really tempting. "Kinda cool, but I can't get there. Not for years," he said, regretfully.

"I could swim you there," offered the seal-woman.

"No way! You nearly drowned me already. And I'd freeze, and starve. It's thousands and thousands of miles."

"Then you could fly in your metal birds," she said.

"I could. If I was that rich. It costs a lot, you know. And I'd have to fly from here to Melbourne and then to Europe. And they might catch me."

"Your servant, the lesser spirit of air and darkness, who is now fussing on the beach over there, can bring you the gold and silver from the chests of men. Áed will do what it can to please its master, and the locks and sealed rooms are no proof to the likes of it. Not even cold iron. It has helped you with your wishes before. They always do."

"Like what?" What was she talking about? The beer in the saucer in the corner?

"They are not strong, but he will fetch, carry, break, or use minor magics to summon wind...I am sure yours has done so."

"If it has, all it has ever done is get me into trouble!" said Tim.

She nodded. "There is often such a price on magic selfishly applied. But I can also provide. There is treasure in the ocean. Gold coins, lost long ago, jewels. Other things men find precious."

It sounded so good...only, if he was going to get out of here, that wasn't going to help much. You couldn't just walk into the airport with a bunch of doubloons or

something. They'd freak. Probably call the cops. And if
he tried to sell it to someone...to whom? He didn't know
anyone he could sell jewels to. There was a guy back at
St. Dominic's who Hailey knew, who bought car sound
systems and stuff. But that was in Melbourne. Anyway,
hadn't he gotten busted? "I can't use that. I need real
money," he said regretfully. "You know. Dollars. I'm earning some. I work for the diver...you leave him alone or
I won't even think of doing a deal with you. I sold the
souvenir shop in town some paper nautilus shells I found
with Nan; they'll believe that's okay. But if I show up
with gold and jewels...I reckon they'd take them away
from me. Want to know where I got them from."

"I will send such flotsam as may help you, and many
of the shells to the beach here, if you will agree to return
the key."

It might have worked better if she had just talked
to him, not dragged him out here. "It's my birthright,
you said. So I'll decide. And that kind of rests on you
behaving yourself. I think you did this to my father..."

"He escaped me, and I never had a chance to talk to
him," she said. She shrugged. "I have waited long. I can
wait longer. He fled me, but you won't. I have woven the
water-spell to bind—"

And she abruptly changed back into a seal, and turned
away, because coming out toward them was a large, hairy
dog, barking fiercely and swimming at the same time.

On the beach, Molly might have thought Bunce was
barking at Tim. Tim was closer, and he could see the big
head and what he was looking at. It was the seal-woman
he was barking at, and it wasn't at all his usual friendly
bark. It was a hunting cry, and the dog meant it.

The seal-woman seemed to get the message and dove
away. There was something very reassuring about the huge
dog, but Tim knew that Molly would never forgive him

if he let the seal-woman hurt her big baby. Tim called him, and Bunce swam over, climbed up on the rock next to him, and gave him an unavoidable lick. Well, at least there were two of them here now. He was still scared of sharks, after the seal-woman's threat, and it was quite a long swim...best to start in. He kept the knife in his hand, even though it made swimming harder, and headed for shore, hoping there were no currents...or sharks or... He just swam, trying to stay close to the wolfhound. The waves carried them inward. And then Bunce bounced. Tim realized the dog must be touching the bottom, and he stuck his feet down, to find sand. Together they surged toward the beach and Molly.

"Just what is going on?" she yelled. "Are you all right?"

"Just fine. Just wet, that's all. I, um, went in to get something. And then I got a bit far out. I was jolly glad to see Bunce. He really can swim."

"You and Bunce frightened me silly, Tim," she said, crossly. "Why have you got a knife in your hand?"

"Um, I was scared of sharks. There was a seal. It gave me a scare."

"Are you crazy, going that far out? And in all your clothes, too. What's your nan going to say?" demanded Molly.

"She'd freak out and ban me from the beach. So I guess I better not go home until I'm dry." It was a warm day, and now that he was back on the beach, Tim was shaken but felt oddly...triumphant. He'd always sort of felt he didn't belong in Melbourne, in a flat in Williamstown... without really knowing why he felt that way. But there was just a niggle that said he wasn't sure he belonged in Faerie either. "I'm sorry to have given you a scare," he said. "And I was really, really glad to see Bunce. He's a brave boy coming to rescue me!" He patted the dog, who leaned against him and waved a paw when he stopped.

"He's a brainless moo, just like you," said Molly, but not quite so crossly now. "Why did you call me, if you were going swimming?"

"Call you?" asked Tim, puzzled.

"To help with your math homework."

"I didn't." He shook his head. "On the phone, you mean?"

"Well, you couldn't have yelled, could you?" she said sarcastically.

"I couldn't have phoned either. Remember, we saw the Telstra guy working on the line. The phones are all out."

"Oh. Yeah. I had forgotten."

"And we didn't get any math homework."

She wrinkled her forehead. "That's weird. I was, like, so sure you called. And sounded, well, upset."

"Well, that's really strange," said Tim, thinking that she had no idea just how weird. "But I did want help. I'm not going out there again! So . . . now that you're here, I've got sheep to shift. How about giving me a hand for a few minutes, with our trainee sheepdog? The running around will help me dry out."

"You're crazy, Tim Ryan," she said, smiling and then hiding her braces behind her hand. It was a habit of hers.

"Yeah. Just let me get my runners."

The tide had come in since he kicked the shoes off to rush in to help Maeve. For a horrible minute, Tim thought he might have lost them. They were getting a bit tight and worn out, like his shirts and jeans, but, well, he didn't have any others, and he was getting used to the fact that Nan didn't buy anything she didn't desperately need. But there they were, just on the edge of the foam-line. Wet, and together, not the way he'd left them. With a paper-nautilus shell lying between them.

If he'd needed any more reassurance that it wasn't all some kind of hallucination, that did it. He carried it up to Molly, who was still half-frowning at him. "Present for you." He handed her the perfect, fragile spiral shell with a little bow, feeling a little stupid about it. But she and Bunce had come to his rescue, after all.

"Oh, wow!" she said, taking it, the half-frown vanishing as she smiled in delight, forgetting the braces for once. "I've never found a really big, completely undamaged one! But you can't give it to me, Tim. You found it."

"Ah, I've a found a few. You keep it."

She turned it over in her hands. "So that's what you were swimming after! Don't Tim. It's not safe on your own."

"I'm not going to do it again. No way!" He fended off her attempt to hand the shell back to him, stopped Bunce from bouncing it, and said, "Seriously. You keep it. A little thank-you present for the books and for coming to help. It's rude to give a present back."

She bit her lip. "Well...thanks. Thanks a lot. You're a star, even if you are crazy, Tim Ryan. Come on. Let's move those sheep."

"Crazy star, that's me!" he yelled, dancing down the beach and playing air-guitar just because he felt like it. Bunce thought it a wonderful idea. Tim tried a cartwheel and fell over.

So Molly put the shell down, carefully, in her hat, and showed him that she could do them properly.

CHAPTER 15

Molly carried her treasure back to her room, not stopping to show it to her mother, who was knitting, reading a book and watching TV, her way of saving time. It made for interesting jerseys.

She put the fragile spiral shell on the dresser, next to her mirror, and flopped onto her bed and looked at it. It gave her a bit of an odd feeling that she didn't quite know how to deal with, so she grabbed her current book and read. It wasn't quite good enough to stop her looking at the shell and smiling every now and again. Homework could wait a bit.

Áed knew both triumph and worry. Triumph that his master had escaped the clutches of the selkie, and worry as to how and why. She'd worked some kind of magic on the master, but these things didn't always come out the way the user intended. He had his strengths. And he built on other strengths too. Áed was sure the

master had not seen the spirit dancers leaping and prancing and waving their spears with him when he danced on the beach. But the strength of it had been almost intoxicating. The land was still throbbing with it, plants growing, animals flourishing.

Tim had come out of the water with a lot to think about...and a lot of weight falling away from his shoulders. It did make him feel like acting a bit of a joker. They'd ended up—and he would not have thought this possible a few months ago—having a lot of fun moving sheep. And learning to do cartwheels on the beach.

He'd walked back to the house, clothes mostly dry, and whistling cheerfully. "Something's makin' you happy," said his grandmother. "Lend me your eyes, Tim." She handed him an envelope. "Mr. Symons brought it. It'll be the rates bill from that blasted Council. I need to know how much money they want this time."

Tim opened the bill, and read the figure owing. His grandmother sighed. "Always bloody more. And for what? I'll have to get onto Dickie Burke about taking some stock to the sale."

"They're not back yet. Or at least the kids weren't on the bus."

She sighed again. "I don't want ter pay transport on top of it. I'll say this for Dickie. He doesn't charge me to take them in, and he deals with all of it."

"They've got to get back soon," said Tim. "The school will fuss."

"Ought to be there already," she said grumpily. "Now, is that woodbox full?"

So Tim went off to the chore of splitting the logs they'd sawed up a few weeks before. He found himself thinking about what the seal-woman said about chopping wood.

It was a little odd, because it was probably the chore he enjoyed most. It took a little bit of aiming and effort, but seeing the pieces fly was satisfying.

If he hadn't been dead tired, what with swimming, and running after sheep, he might have lain in bed thinking about it. Instead he slept. He dreamed about some of it, though. The hunt, and riding across the green, misty fields, only somewhere down the line it changed into hunting wallaby with a bunch of black men, on foot, through the grasstrees and the tussocks. It was, oddly, a good dream. He remembered it quite clearly when he woke and went to milk the cow.

The next day he spent some time on the library computer, looking up Finvarra. That took him to Cnoc Meadha, which he would never have spelled like that from hearing it.

He didn't look up flights to Ireland for a week, until he got onto the library computer in town, which was a bit more private. He was glad he was sitting down when he did it. That was a lot of money, even to someone who had just sold twenty-three paper nautilus shells and had arranged a day's work on Jon's boat for Saturday.

Still...it was building up in the pouch around his neck. Building up to the point where it was kind of tempting to spend some money on some new jeans. And a bit of conscience was pricking him about Nan. She hadn't been herself since the rates bill had arrived. She always made decisions quickly. Now she was dithering about them. She had even dithered about whether to go fishing with Molly and her dad the day before. Finally, she'd come down to the beach, and it looked like she'd had a good enough time of it. Tim had learned a whole lot more about where and how to fish, and she'd obviously been trying not to bite anyone's head off. But Tim, by now, had learned to spot the signs. She was waiting for Hailey's father to get back, waiting to arrange to sell some cows, and worrying about the price she'd get.

He'd told her. He'd heard what Mark's dad had gotten at the last sale. Tim got an irritable "Don't be stupid boy. No wonder you need help with yer math."

"Help with math" was Molly's excuse for coming over. Tim grinned. She was good at it. He pretended he was worse than he was.

In the meanwhile he'd been doing some thinking about the whole "lesser spirit" thing. And the beer in the saucer in the corner of the kitchen, and the trouble he'd been in, and how he'd gotten out of it, sort of.

He was watching it, having just finished his tea on Friday evening, and waiting for the kettle to boil, determined to see whatever it was. And Gran hadn't actually told him to go and do anything . . . that was in itself odd enough to be a bit worrying, when the phone rang.

Tim went to answer it, expecting it to be Jon, hoping it didn't mean that his day of work on the old boat was off. It wasn't. It was Molly's dad. "Hi, Tim. Mind if speak to your nan?"

So Tim called her. Of course he listened in as much as he could. It was all very well saying it wasn't good manners, but it would probably be about him. He hoped Molly wasn't in some kind of trouble. He couldn't think of anything he could have done . . . on purpose. Of course he could only hear half the conversation. "Yes. He isn't back yet." A pause. "Oh. Well, it'd save me transport." Gran sounding just slightly pleased. "No. It was good of you to think of it. His uncle was a decent feller. Me and my man, we liked him. Well, thank you very much, Mister. I'll have to show yer a few more fishing spots. There's a good corner for gummy shark on a no-moon night."

And then the polite goodbye.

Gran came back to the table. "Careful with his words, that feller." She didn't sound like she disapproved of that.

"Why?"

"Said he hoped I didn't mind, but I had said I wanted to shift some cows, and he run into a feller who was talking about buying some in Whitemark. That abalone diver yer work for. And he said he was coming in to fetch you tomorrow, so he'd talk to me about it then. Depends on the price, but it'd take a weight off my mind. That kettle boiled yet?"

The saucer of beer was empty. Gran refilled it, which was a first.

The next day brought Jon. "Now, I was told you wanted to sell some cattle. I'm looking for some young stock for my block."

"Could be. It'd depend on the price," said his grandmother, as if she wasn't eager to sell. Tim couldn't help grinning to himself. By now he was more than sure Jon McKay wouldn't rip anyone off.

"Well, I'd say the average price from the last sale would be a good starting point," said Jon, fishing a magazine from the seat of his ute. "Says here that was..."

And he named the figure Tim had quoted to his grandmother.

Her mouth fell open. And then closed with an audible snap. "I don't take charity," she said angrily. "I'll sell at a fair price. Now, get..."

A huge branch came hurtling down off the pine tree, with an enormous crack and crash, and it sent pinecones flying like shrapnel all around them.

It took more than a falling half-ton branch, or an angry grandmother, to worry the diver. "Mrs. Ryan. That is the current price. You've got a phone. Let's call the auctioneer at Roberts and ask him. Or any farmer on the island. I don't know when you last sold cattle, but the price is up again, because so many people sold off in the last drought."

There was something about his steady, calm voice, or maybe the flying pinecones that cooled his grandmother off... a bit. "Yer'll be right with me checking?"

"Sure. But it is right here in the agricultural report..."

He was speaking to her back, as she'd walked inside. Tim was cringing. "Sorry, Jon," he said awkwardly.

The diver smiled. "No worries, son. Mike Symons said she could be a bit touchy about things."

"I told her what Mark's dad got, but she didn't believe me either," said Tim.

"Tim, come find the number for me," called his grandmother. "Roberts. I call them to order wire and dip and now I just can't think of it. Maybe my mind is going." She sounded slightly shaken.

Tim got the number—he only got as far as the first five digits, when she said the rest. He waited while she asked.

He had the satisfaction of watching her say, "Well now, thank you," in a very quiet voice, a stunned look on her face.

She put the phone down and marched outside. "I owe you an apology, Mr. McKay."

"No worries," said Jon again.

"It's... it's a lot more than I expected."

"Well now, it might go higher at the sale," said Jon easily. "We can check after and see if I owe you anything."

She shook her head. "I'm... well. I wasn't expecting more than half that. It's left me feeling like a beached mullet," she said with one of those fleeting smiles, "as my man used to say. I'm... I'm... embarrassed. You could have taken me to the cleaners, and I'd have been thanking yer. Yer did the right thing and I insulted..."

Jon laughed. "I'd end up like the beached mullet, Mrs. Ryan, if I'd ripped you off. Seriously, I'm not offended.

Glad it is good news to you. Now, I just want about fifteen or twenty head of young steers."

"Yer come have a look at them, pick the best. I owe yer that."

"I'll come along with the trailer when I bring Tim back. I'll have to do a couple of trips. It might be cheaper and easier to get the truckers to do it."

"I'll get them in by this afternoon," said Nan.

"No you won't," said Jon, with the cheerful confidence of a man who makes decisions of life and death, underwater, and wasn't that afraid of grandmothers. "I'm taking your labor away. Tomorrow's good. Will you take a check, or do you want cash? I'd have to go into town for that."

"From you, I'll take a check," said his grandmother.

"I think that's a compliment," said Jon. "Right. I'll sort it out when I see the cows. We'll make it twenty, if that's all right by you. Come on, Tim, we've got a live-fish tank to paint."

She nodded. "And those ones have got a pine branch to clear up. But they'll be well rewarded for that."

Driving down the track, Tim was awkwardly silent for the first bit. Then he sighed. "I'm sorry my gran was so...you know. She's just like that."

Jon grinned at him and looked back at the road. "Relax, Tim. Mike warned me, but I thought having it in the stock listing would be enough."

"She, um, well, her eyes aren't too good."

"Aha. Well, it must be a godsend to her having you there. And don't worry, Tim. The world could use a few more people like the old duck. You should be proud of her."

"I think she was being ripped off."

"I'm damned sure of it," said Jon, not sounding at all amused. "And I'm not overpaying either, just giving her a fair go. She deserves it."

Tim hadn't thought of himself as being useful, or his grandmother deserving anything, before. But it was kind of true, now that he did think of it.

Áed did enjoy the diver's Land Rover. It had an aluminum body, which was better than the cold-iron chariots. He liked the boat more; it had even less iron... but even with all the iron around, this place was better, at least for him, than the endless realms of Faerie. Here a lesser spirit got to doze a little in the sun, and to feel the wind, and taste the rain. Faerie might be endless, but it was also hard work for his kind, and boring. Tim didn't use him much. Áed had to guess his will, use his own judgment. He worked quite a lot with the old fenodree—a task he would have thought below himself, once. But it too had its rewards.

The master was a little angry now. The old *cailleach* had been cheated by that other one. If Fenn got to hear of it, he'd be sharpening his scythe again.

"I'm off into town in about twenty minutes," called Molly's mother from the kitchen. "Dad says we're to give your friend Tim's grandmother a call if we're going, ask if there is anything she needs."

"Well, can't Dad do it, then?" They made her do these awkward phone calls. She hated it.

"He's busy with yet another e-mail to the ombudsman about the hot water service and those...insurers. You really don't want to bug him right now." It had cost her parents a fortune to fix the faulty hot water system for the cottage they rented out, and the insurers weren't paying out. Her father started steaming when it even got mentioned.

"Can't you phone her?" asked Molly, in a last-ditch avoidance move.

"If you'd rather wash dishes, which is what I am doing, yes. Otherwise, my hands are wet, and she won't bite you."

Molly wasn't that sure, but made the call anyway. Maybe Tim would answer, or no one would. But she got his grandmother.

And the old woman sounded cheerful, and pleased to hear her on the phone. And... well, talkative. Not at all clipped like the previous times. "Ah. You're the girl with the big sheepdog. You're in school with my boy. Tell yer parents to come and have a cuppa tea with me sometime, when they've got a chance. I owe yer father a big cream cake. I haven't baked for a while, but I'm going to."

"Um. Yes. Mum just asked me to phone 'cause she's going into town, if there was anything you needed."

"Hmm. Not today, but if yer father is going in on Tuesday, well, I think I'm going to town. Actually... I think I'll splash out today. He's an honest man, I think."

"Who? My dad? Of course he is!" Molly was rather offended.

She got laughter down the line. "I'm sorry, dear. It's my day for saying stupid things. I'm just a bit relieved. I was talkin' about that diver feller, McKay. He's buying some of my young cows, thanks to your father, bless him. And at such a good price too." She named the figure.

"That's what one of the girls in my class said they were getting last sale. Everyone is trying to restock after the drought."

"We could use a bit more on our land, but we didn't really get hit by it because of that. Too few cows. I should hold onto them too, but we need some cash, and I'm so relieved to be getting it! Eh. I'm babbling. Sorry. Could you ask yer mother for two bars of plain chocolate, and some icing sugar? And a bottle of golden syrup... I'll do Tim a good sticky pudding for his tea. I'll go up to the gate with the money so she can pick it up on her way past."

"Isn't Tim there?" asked Molly. "Or I'm sure you can just pay Mum when she comes back."

"Tim's gone to work on Mr. McKay's boat. And I don't pay later."

"We'll come down. Don't come up," said Molly, thinking to herself that anything was better than the old woman driving and crashing because she couldn't see.

"That's too much trouble," said Mrs. Ryan.

"I have to walk Bunce, the dog. I'll bring him along on the lead and walk him back along the beach. Really, that would be fun for me," said Molly searching for excuses. "Otherwise I'll be sitting here alone." With a book, a computer, music and a project for school, but she didn't say that.

That got Molly a chuckle from the old lady. "You get used to it. I'd got used to the quiet before Tim came. Now, I miss the noise when he's not here. There's the radio, but it's not quite the same."

"It doesn't answer back, like he does."

That got another laugh. "Oh, too right, he does that. All right. That'd be good of yer. I'll see yous later."

"So? Did she bite you?" asked her mother, coming through, wiping her hands.

"No. She was quite nice. Actually, chatty. She says she owes Dad a big cream cake. She wants some stuff, wants to give you the money. I said I'd go down with you with Bunce and walk back."

"But I've just cleaned the car. She can pay me on the way back."

So Molly had to explain. Fortunately, Mum was pretty easy about that kind of stuff, and Bunce was of course delighted. "He'll be disappointed not to see Tim. The two of them behave like hooligans together," said Molly, patting him.

"I didn't know they got on," said her mother.

"Bunce? You'd swear he thinks he's Tim's guard dog. Honestly."

"Oh, really? I remember he was a bit protective of you at first," said Molly's mother.

"They behave like two lunatics together now. He even swam out to rescue Tim. They're besties now. Whenever I yell at Bunce, he runs to Tim."

"You didn't tell me about this rescue."

"Oh, Tim swam after a nautilus shell, and saw a seal and got a big fright. Buncy swam out to him and they swam in together. It wasn't a big deal, and Tim got a scare and learned a lesson. Don't tell his nan. She'd have a fit and ban him from the beach."

"It's really not safe swimming..."

"I know," said Molly, feeling guilty that she'd told her mother the story. "And I think he does too, now. He said he wouldn't do it again, and he really meant it."

At the farm house, the old woman was waiting with a list—written in a painfully neat hand on a page of an old exercise book, only she'd missed the ruled lines—and the money neatly folded. "Thank you. And maybe if your man is going in on Tuesday or Wednesday, I could get a lift down."

"He's got some guests to fetch on Monday morning. I'm going down to do some shopping to feed them and to get a new seal for the toilet cistern. That has to be done before they get here. I'll get him to call you."

"You wouldn't be buying vegetables, would yer?" asked Mrs. Ryan.

"Well, yes. Some. Our growing isn't as good as Mike says yours is."

She clicked her tongue. "We've got tomatoes coming

out of our ears, and more than we c'n use of just about everything else. I told that man of yours..."

"I know, he told me, but he's got his pride," said Molly's mother.

"It gets in the way, sometimes," said Tim's grandmother wryly. "Nearly tripped me up this morning, and it turned out I'd been made a fool of by someone else. I'm more in debt to your man for that bit of kindness than I can say, or I'd never have found out. I'll have a basket of tomatoes, beans, lettuce and spuds for yer. And if yer run out with these guests, well, yer don't have to drive all the way to town."

"You're a honey, Mrs. Ryan. People on the island have been so good to us."

It looked like it'd been a while since anyone had called the old lady "a honey." Molly's mother did it to everyone, of course. She even called Bunce a honey, sometimes. But after a few moments Tim's gran gave a skewed smile. "They can be if they like yer. How long do yer think you'll be? I don't want to pick the veggies too early."

"About two hours. I'll be back just before one, I should think. Whitemark is never quick. Too many people talk to me. Molly can give you a hand."

Molly rather resented being volunteered. "I've got to get back to my project, Mum."

"There's the afternoon, and tomorrow, love," said her mother, getting into the car and waving as she started to drive off.

"It's fine," said the old woman. "I've done for meself for nearly seventy years, girl. I don't need no help." And she promptly stumbled over a pinecone, proving that wasn't entirely true.

"Oh, I don't mind. I'd actually like to see your garden," said Molly hastily coming up with a politeness. "It was just Mum organizing my life again."

That got a snort. "I'll tell her how well it didn't work for me. So you're in class with my grandson, eh? Does he work hard? Have friends?"

"We share some classes. Yeah, I think he does. He's kind of quiet. He goes to the library a lot, but he seems to get on with the guys in class. Whenever, like, group stuff is going on, he's involved."

"Different from my time," said the old woman as they walked to the garden. "Black girls had to watch while the others played hopscotch." She pointed to Bunce. "You stay outside, or I know his kind, he'll help us dig."

That kind of got over the awkwardness of the previous statement, and Molly told the story of Bunce burying the potatoes her dad had dug up. They talked, picked beans— Molly noticed the old woman was doing it essentially by feel, and missing a few. But she seemed in a very mellow mood and wasn't that hard to talk to. She had some fascinating stories too, about the island fifty years back when it was far wilder and even more isolated.

Tim's gran straightened up. "I need a cup of tea," she said. "I'm dry with all this talking. And yer ears are bent double with it. Sorry. I had such a good surprise with them cows, and no one to tell. Best news since they told me Tim was comin'. And that was the best news I'd had for twenty years. I didn't tell that woman that, though."

"So...you want him here?" asked Molly. That hadn't been the impression Molly had gotten from Tim.

She nodded. "Oh my word, yes. This is Ryan land. It's empty without one. And...ah well, girl. Let's go and have a cuppa. There's a bone your hound could have."

It was weird, now that Molly realized how little Mrs. Ryan could see, how well she knew her own kitchen. She moved the kettle onto the heat on the woodstove. Got out mugs...looked faintly guilty. "You wouldn't be wanting proper tea cups, would you?"

"Um. No. We don't have any at home. I, like, never know what you have to do with the saucers when you need to use your hands."

"Heh. My husband's aunt, she was very posh, had them cake forks. I always thought it was just to embarrass me. But I bake a better sponge than she ever did."

The old woman went to the ancient refrigerator, and came out with a bottle of beer . . . and walked over to the corner and poured a little into a bowl on the floor. "Yer deserve it," she said, and put the beer bottle back in the fridge.

Molly wondered if it was milk . . . but that came out of a jug. So she asked. The old lady smiled. "The wee folk. I have one working on the farm. Tim has one following him about too. They'll drink milk, but this is a reward for them."

Molly was glad to drink her tea in silence then. Just when she had started to think Tim's nan was kind of normal.

It had been a good week, Tim thought, whistling to himself as he carried the cardboard box to the little curio shop. Jon was pleased with Gran's cows, Gran was pleased with Jon's check, which she'd turned into money, promptly, and paid the "thieving council" their rates. She'd even given Tim money to buy new jeans before putting the rest into her tin box. "Yer old ones feel all worn out," she'd said. It was true.

The day he'd taken six paper nautilus shells to the curio shop, he had not even moved the money into his secret neck pouch. Instead, he'd gone into the little shop that sold clothes, cutlery, newspapers, books and all sort of other things. It had been his lucky day—although he felt he'd let himself down, not keeping the money—because they had some really cool runners out on special, and in his size. So he'd splashed out and bought them.

Anyway, he'd been down to the beach again, and found more shells, and had brought them with him into town that Friday. He was so busy doing mental calculations about the value of the shells and where his money supply was right now that he wasn't paying a lot of attention, and the person coming the other way around the corner wasn't either, until they walked smash into each other.

The policeman's take-away cup of coffee went flying. So did Tim's box.

This time it was Tim's turn to start apologizing. "I'm sorry. I wasn't looking where I was going."

The copper looked thoughtfully at him, obviously placed him. "What's in the box this time?"

What did it have to do with him? thought Tim, cross, and yet irrationally nervous. "Shells." And the worst of it was he felt himself flushing, like it was box of drugs or something. And the copper must have noticed.

"Nothing protected or illegal, I hope?" said the policeman.

Were they? "Nautilus shells I found on the beach," he said, opening the box, resisting the temptation to run. Several had broken in the fall. That was just so . . . so infuriating.

"Looks like a bit of catastrophic damage there. So many! I've only seen a couple in the months I've been here, and they were broken," said the cop. "And how was the contents of your last box? I meant to call, but the old lady didn't seem welcoming."

That sounded . . . suspicious. Tim found himself even more nervous. "It was a lifejacket. It wasn't damaged," he said, shortly.

"Good. So how come you're still here on the island?"

And the pile of fertilizer bags that the guy at Roberts

was shifting with the forklift...came crashing off their pallet and splattered pieces of fertilizer everywhere.

The policeman left at a run, and Tim sidled into the shop. He'd rather have left completely. Gone as far away as possible, back to the farm. But even there...The only place he could be sure he wasn't going to somehow have the past turn up and spoil everything was going to take a lot more money from nautilus shells.

And to add insult, some were broken and the shopkeeper said he didn't want too many more, right now. He said he also collected them himself.

Áed knew by now that the master feared the consequences of Áed's actions, when he tumbled the bags by shredding the plastic wrapping. It seemed wise, though. The young master was in a terrible state of mind, both fear and anger, and some misery, when it happened. Much as he had been back in the iron-full city, where he had not belonged and not known it. Here, he belonged, but still did not know it.

Tim didn't really relax until he was on the farm again, shoes off to save them, toes on the hard sand. His feet were getting like old leather underneath; he could walk over stones or stubble without noticing now, and it felt good. Like his feet, at least, were out of prison. They couldn't prove anything, surely? And was it chance that pallet of fertilizer fell off the forklift? He had to admit to himself that it probably wasn't. If he could get paper nautilus shells from a seal-woman...the rest of what she said might be true too. It was quite hard to get his head around it all. So...could this lesser spirit rob a bank for him? Not on the island, of course. You couldn't do that kind of thing here! It might be tempting...but Tim really hadn't enjoyed being arrested, and considering how many things he hadn't done that he had been blamed for... And also... well, he got the feeling that while Hailey had thought shoplifting was cool and exciting, some other people he wanted to think well of him, didn't. Actually, he didn't himself, at least when he wasn't trying to impress her, he admitted to himself.

Later that afternoon, Molly and her dog came down along the beach and walked up to the garden, where he was digging over a bed. She waved, and Bunce bounced eagerly on the lead. "You look a bit more cheerful now. I thought you were mad with me about something. I brought you some anzacs. They're not your gran's cooking, but I made them."

"Oh, cool!"

"Yeah, they are now, but I burned my fingers on them. You better be nice about them even if they're terrible. I'm learning about tact. My dad's, like, getting up my mum's nose by raving on and on about your gran's cake."

Tim grinned. "Good thing he didn't get the sticky pudding I had last night, then."

"So, are you going to be able to come for a run with me and Bunce? I'm training for the cross-country."

Tim pulled a face. "Got stuff to do. Gran keeps finding..."

"Hello. It's young Molly and the odd sheepdog." Nan actually sounded pleased. "Come for tea? I'll make pikelets."

"Oh, no. I'm just going on a run. To get fit. It's...it's very kind, but I can't..."

"Do! I'll get pikelets that way," said Tim. "And anzacs. Gran, Molly made me some anzacs."

Tim saw his grandmother's face go from an almost-smile to a tightening of the lips, and tears start to run

down her cheeks as she turned away from them. They
both looked at each other—and Molly ran after her.

So did Tim, a few seconds later, not knowing quite
what to do, or what had gone wrong. At least it seemed
Molly did know, or had more of an idea than he did.
She had put her arm around his nan's shoulders. "I'm
sorry, I didn't mean to upset you."

His grandmother shook her head, but didn't say anything. She didn't push Molly away as she led her back
into the kitchen and sat her down. "Make your gran a
nice cup of tea, Tim," Molly said.

She sounded just like her mum, just then, thought Tim.
She'd probably call him "honey" any minute. He went to
the kettle, which was hot and ready on the woodstove,
and did as he was told, gave his gran the tea, putting
the handle of the mug to touch the back of her fingers,
as he'd gotten used to doing.

Nan took it, took a sip. Wiped her eyes on the back of
her sleeve, and then felt in her pockets and pulled out a
handkerchief. She was a great believer in handkerchiefs,
was his nan. Molly was still standing there, looking a
little awkward, one hand on his grandmother's shoulder.
"I'm sorry," she said again.

Tim saw his grandmother reach up and squeeze her
hand. "It's all right, child. Yer didn't do anything wrong.
It's just . . . I used to make tins of them. Post them to
my John in Vietnam. Even sent him salted muttonbirds
like that. I haven't had an anzac since . . . since he died.
I didn't want to remember that."

"I'm so sorry . . ." It looked like Molly might start blub-
bing herself any minute.

"Yer weren't to know." She took a deep breath. "Tim,
you'd better make yerself an' Molly a cuppa. Sorry, I
don't have any of that cordial . . . and then we'll have one

of those biscuits. And all of us in the kitchen with our boots on!"

Personally, Tim thought Molly had overcooked the anzacs a little, but his nan did seem to enjoy them and told Molly what a great cook she was. And then she told the two of them to go off and do something because she needed to clean the kitchen now. And she said that Molly was welcome to come down any time, even without anzacs.

CHAPTER 16

Molly told her mother about it... which reduced her mother to sniffles, too. "Imagine that... it must be forty years or more. I think she must have been terribly lonely."

"She's pretty strange, Mum. She puts down beer for the fairies." So Molly had to tell that story too. Over the next month or so, she found her parents had obviously decided to adopt Tim's grandmother and just hadn't told Tim about it yet. Like they needed any more expenses. Or more vegetables. Still, Molly had carte blanche to go down there, anyway. It was company, and made being on the island more than just something her parents wanted to do. Tim and his grandmother, they did stuff. Went spearing flounder at night. Went fishing, netting, and even trying to teach Bunce to herd sheep. So far that was not a success. At least he didn't want to kill them, but to play with them was another matter, and the sheep didn't get it.

Tim had tried to hold her hand a couple of times.

She'd shoved him away with a laugh. She wasn't too sure how to handle that, or if she really wanted to, or, well, anyway...He was a bit younger than she was, and the girls at school said...

Still, she was kind of glad to be able to go over, right now. Things were just a bit tense at home. There weren't that many out-of-holiday-time bookings for the B&B or even the self-catering cottage, and not only were the insurers still arguing about paying for the new hot-water service and the repairs, but money her mother had been expecting from an inheritance had been held up, and was possibly never going to be paid out, because a distant cousin—a lawyer and therefore able to cause maximum trouble at minimum expense, her mother said, was causing all sorts of strife. It wasn't a lot of money, but it would have helped right then, and they'd expected it. Counted on it.

Running around over on the Ryan place, she could mostly forget that sort of thing. Not worry too much about all the grown-up stuff.

Just when life seemed to be settling into some kind of normal, Tim's mother called from Melbourne. She sounded...harassed. Upset. "Tim. I've got a Mr. Scranson here. He's an insurance assessor. He wants to...to talk to you. To ask about that fire."

Tim's heart sank down into his new trainers. "Mum, I didn't do anything. I was there with two men, all the time."

"Just talk to him, Tim. He's...he keeps coming around here. He's come in to work. I...I don't want to have talk there. Things are going so well now that..."

She didn't finish. But Tim knew it was "now that you're not here to cause trouble anymore."

He hadn't meant to. Well, he sort of had. He'd wanted to have something go wrong. Sometimes. But he hadn't done anything. And if he'd known that he could cause it...he'd, he'd...have not done some of it. And not been where they could blame him.

A man's voice came down the telephone. "Timothy Ryan? I just want to confirm a few details about the possible arson incident at Merlba Stores, on the day of the twenty-third."

Tim's mind was sort of numb with anger. "I didn't start any fires." He said sullenly. "Leave me alone. I don't want to talk to you."

"I just need to confirm a few details. Now when security officers Belsen and Marx left you in the office..."

"I was never left anywhere! They were there all the time. They're lying!"

"They say..."

"They're lying! Now leave me alone!" He slammed the phone down, stormed outside, wanting to burst into tears, hit something, just, just...leave it all behind. Jogging down the track to the beach, he did feel a bit better. Let them try and make it all his fault. He could hide...Couldn't they just leave him alone? He could run away, live on fish...but he liked...people. Some of them, anyway. He didn't want to leave the kids at school, and Molly and Jon and...yeah. Well, the only person who knew he was in trouble was his nan. And she seemed to know what could have caused it. She'd hide him, Tim was pretty sure. But then she'd be in trouble. And though he'd resented being there, been angry that she made him work, that there was no TV, no Internet...he didn't want his nan to have any more trouble. It wasn't fair. Just look at what had been done to her with the cows. And he knew she was worried about them finding out she couldn't see too well, making her leave the farm. It wasn't right. She did fine. Better than Jon at gardening. Better than anyone at cooking, really.

The only answer was for him to leave, quietly and cleanly, before any more came out of this. He sat down at the side of the track and took out his pouch from around his neck, and counted the money. It had been coming in. Jon paid a bit over minimum wage, and there was the nautilus money. And he'd helped plant garlic for one of the teachers at the school, cleaned out the gutters for Mrs. Hallam, and she'd given him ten dollars... He hadn't added it up for a while, not since he'd worked out how much the trip to Ireland would cost. He piled the notes, carefully, bringing each pile to a hundred dollars. He bit his lip. It was more than he'd thought, but still a long way short. Once, a thousand, three hundred and twenty-four dollars would have seemed a fortune. Now he'd just have to earn some more. Soon. Before this guy went to the police or something. He was troubled and angry, and the wild rushes of wind made the she-oak branches above him shiver and dance like spears.

He gathered up the money and walked down to the beach to look for nautilus shells. The seal-woman always saw to it that he found a few. Maybe the shop would take a few more. And he'd ask around if anyone else needed jobs done. But it sat on him like a lump of lead. He'd forget it sometimes, when he was out at sea watching that diver air-line, or catching a fish, or when Molly was there with Bunce, and they were trying to teach the wolfhound to herd sheep.

But it always came back, especially when he learned the man had phoned his nan too. Nan had phoned his mother and told her off about it. Tim hadn't heard what his grandmother had said to the insurance assessor guy, whatever that job meant, but he certainly heard his nan giving his mother fifteen kinds of hell for giving "that feller" the phone number, or telling him anything all. It made Tim feel much better for about a week.

And then it came back to him that the assessor had pestered his mum at work. What if, instead of calling the farm, he phoned the school?

Just when you thought it couldn't be worse, it was.

Cnoc Meadha it would have to be. They didn't have telephones, or let in coppers, or whatever this "assessor" was. He wanted to make trouble, that Tim knew.

Áed knew the master was uncomfortable and worried about something that he did not fully understand. He knew too that the selkie had, at least for now, cried truce. Like all of the greater Fae, you could trust her just so far with that. She'd keep her word . . . to the letter, but not to the intent.

Still, he had less to fear from her now, and when the master was out on the land, and the land and the old spirits there were around this distant ancestor, well, the lesser spirit felt he was quite safe.

It had lulled him into a false security on this glorious May day. May still had its magic even here when it was the breath of winter, and not the start of the warm heady days of summer.

Today you could be forgiven for thinking winter far off. The air was almost warm, just a touch of chill in the breeze. The master had taken the ute down to the long forty paddock with some fencing wire. The girl and the great Cu joined him there.

And the snake, awake in the warmth, driven by body-knowing that cold was coming, hunted. A little slow with the coming of winter, and irritable. Áed found out from the magic marks, later, that Maeve had set it to watching, and it did, between hunting. That meant it was on the path by the fence line.

✧ ✧ ✧

Bunce, one moment trotting along the path in front of them, yelped and backed up, crashing into Tim's legs. He then flailed in a circle, as Tim, to his horror, saw the raised cold-eyed copperhead, its mouth still open, on the path.

"Snake!" he screamed, pulling Bunce away by the fur. Too late.

The huge dog was whining, trying to bite at his foreleg.

"He's been bitten!" screamed Molly, falling to her knees, arms around the wolfhound's neck, ignoring the snake. "Buncy! Oh, help!"

Tim flung the heavy coil of wire at the snake, then dropped to his haunches next to Molly. The puncture wound oozed a drop of red blood. The big dog whined piteously. "Oh, Buncy! Don't die!" said Molly clinging to her dog. "What do we do, Tim?"

For an answer, Tim picked the dog up. Bunce was nearly bigger than he was, but lighter. "To the ute, my gran..."

"The vet. I'll call Dad!" Fumbling, nearly dropping her mobile, Molly called as Tim walked toward the ute thirty meters away. He'd have run, but walking was hard enough. Normally, Bunce would not have put up with being carried, but now...Tim thought he must be dying.

Molly came flying up. "We'll meet Dad at the road; he's coming up as fast as he can," she panted. She helped Tim to get Bunce onto the tray and jumped up next to her dog, pulling his head into her lap. "Drive, Tim! Drive fast!"

Tim did. He was used to driving on the farm now. Not fast, usually, and he didn't want to crash or have them fall off, but he gave it his best. They skidded to a halt at the gate onto the public road. Molly's father was racing toward them in a cloud of dust. Tim opened the gate, and ran back as Molly was trying to lift her dog down. He took the big panting wolfhound in his arms—he had had enough practice with sheep—and carried him across to where Mr. Symons was opening the back door. It was easier just to get in with the dog on his lap than to try and put him in. Molly had run to get in the other rear door, taking the dog's big head onto her lap. "Dad! Get us to the vet! Quickly!" she said, her voice tight with panic.

"Quick as possible, Molly," said her father, jumping into the driving seat and pulling away. "What kind of snake was it?"

"Copperhead, Sir," said Tim. "I saw it, but too late."

"Oh, Daddy, will Bunce be all right?" she asked, her voice trembling.

"I don't know, sweetheart. We'll do our best. Mum's phoned the vet."

Molly didn't say anything. She just sniffed and buried her face in the dog's fur.

Tim didn't really know what to say. Didn't really know why he was here, except, well, it had been easier getting in with Bunce. He reached tentatively for Molly's hand clutching the wiry hair, intending to do no more than give it an encouraging squeeze. She felt it there, turned her hand and took it. Held it tight. Gave him a brief, watery smile before burying her face in the dog's fur again.

The vet was waiting as they skidded to a halt outside his doors. Tim got out, still holding the panting, whimpering dog. Molly's dad came to his rescue. "My word. You're a strong lad!" he exclaimed, taking Bunce.

"Take him into the surgery, first door to the left," said the vet. "Was it definitely a snake bite?"

"Yes," said Tim. "On his foreleg. A big copperhead." He gestured with his arms.

"Good thing he's a big dog. Shock usually kills the smaller ones."

"Will he be all right?" asked Molly. "Please say he'll be all right?"

"Well," said the vet, "I can give him antivenin, but look, it is only fair to tell you, it's very expensive. For

people, it's free, but it's going to cost about fifteen hundred
dollars to treat the dog, and there is no guarantee..."

Tim saw Molly's dad go whiter than a sheet. Take his
daughter's shoulder. "I'm sorry, Molly...we just...don't
have the money right now."

"But, Dad...I'll earn it. I'll work. I'll earn it back."

"Darling, we just don't have it. The credit card is maxed
out, the bank is giving us a hard time. We simply don't
have it. We...we'll just have to make it quick."

With a sob, Molly thrust away from him and dived
down next to Bunce, burying her face in his fur.

Tim heard a voice, quite unlike his own, but coming
out of his mouth, say gruffly, "Give Bunce the antivenin.
I'll pay for it." He pulled the neck pouch out and spilled
its contents onto the countertop. "That's a thousand four
hundred and forty dollars. And...a couple old coins, I
don't know if they're worth anything now. I'm working
for Jon McKay—the diver—tomorrow and you can have
the rest on Monday. Just help him. Now. Please!"

They all stared at him, even the vet. "You can't do
that, Tim," said Molly's father.

"I just did. Now will you get on with it, please, Mr.
Vet? He needs help right now. Do it! Do it now!" Tim
commanded.

The vet smiled at him. "Got my orders," he said to Molly's
father as he took a razor, knelt, and started shaving a patch
of the fur away. "We'll have it into him soon, son."

Molly still held onto Bunce, but the look she gave Tim
was worth every cent, twice over.

"Look, Tim," said Molly's father. "We can't take your
money. You...your grandmother needs it, and..."

"I'll earn more," said Tim, trying to be as light about
all that saving as possible. "And Bunce and I are friends,
see. If he didn't get that injection, he'd die."

"And anyway," said Molly in a hard little voice, "he's

my dog, Dad. I'll pay Tim back, every cent. It'll...it'll just take me a little time."

"You don't have to do that," Tim said awkwardly. "I... I don't need it."

"But I will!" she colored as she smiled at him, tear-tracks still on her cheeks, not hiding the braces on her teeth for once. "Thank you. Thank you so very much."

"I did it for me mate," said Tim, awkwardly, leaning down and patting the hairy hound. He actually got a tail thump for that. "And let's hope he'll be all right."

The next few minutes were an anxious period, time passing slowly. Tim wanted to hold Molly's hand, she looked so stressed out, but he couldn't with her dad and the vet there. So he just stood there, feeling awkward. After a time, the vet said, in a tone of some relief, "Well, I think we've won this time. He'll have to stay in for at least a couple of days, just to keep an eye on him, but I think he only got one fang of venom."

"Can I stay with him?" begged Molly. "I won't be in the way. I'll just sit with him."

The vet shook his head. "You can come in tomorrow. I'll phone if there are any other developments, but he's a big, young, strong dog. He'll be fine. You can go home."

Her father put his hand on her shoulder. She shook it off. "Tim needs to get back," he said. "Mum texted and said she hadn't been able to get hold of his grandmother. She's driven over there to try and find her."

"Oh. Yes. I'm sorry, Tim," said Molly, pointedly avoiding even looking at her father.

"No worries, Molly," said Tim, feeling quite adult.

She hugged Bunce again, and actually got a face-wash. "Oh, he is feeling better," she said, smiling tremulously, wiping her face on her sleeve. "Let's go, then."

When they got to the wagon, she said, "You sit in front, Tim."

"I'm fine in the back, really."

"You'll get all over dog hair."

"It's a bit late for that," said Tim, laughing.

She didn't quite laugh back, but he got half a smile. "Please, sit in the front, Tim."

So he did. He hadn't spent months on the bus with Molly not to know that "please" meant "You will do it!" He was a bit nervy about her dad, now. And he was suddenly realizing his getaway money pouch was empty. The way things always went wrong at the worst time, he'd need it tomorrow.

They drove in silence for a little while. And then Molly's dad said, "If you don't mind my asking, Tim—and we will pay you back—how come you had so much money with you?"

Tim had had time to prepare for this one. "I work for Jon McKay, and do quite a lot of other jobs for people. I planted garlic a week or two ago. And I collect paper nautilus shells and sell them. And there's not a lot to spend it on. I was keeping it in case I, um, needed it. Like, I'll earn more. Don't worry about it."

"I borrowed it, Dad," said Molly. "Not you. And I've thought about it. I'm leaving school. I'll get a job. I didn't know things were quite that bad. You should have told me."

"Molly, it is just cash flow. Really. And a few hiccups. We're slightly behind on the mortgage, but things will look up in the holidays. And your education is important to us, dear."

"Hey, I didn't do this so you would quit school!" said Tim. "You don't have to pay me back anyway. I did it for Bunce, not you. He can pay me back!" Trying to make her laugh, he said hastily, "I...I'll make him let me gel his moustache into big curls. And give him a pink mohawk. And you can't leave me on the bus with all those little kids."

It worked—to some extent, anyway. He did get a brief snort of her laughter, and a grateful look from her father. He said, "It's just really that damned insurer. They're doing their best not to pay out. The company that made the hot-water units went bust, so they can't get the money out of them. They've tried claiming it was either my fault, or the builders, or the council. There is no length they won't go to, to avoid paying up, even though it's quite a small amount to them, but they're very happy to take our premiums. Look, Molly, if things are really slow and don't sort out, we have other options. I'll take a contracting job somewhere for a few months. We just got caught short at a bad time. But your education is not something to be messed with. And Tim agrees with me, don't you, Tim?"

"Uh. Yeah."

"Huh," said Molly. "You're bullying him, Dad."

"I don't think he's the sort of guy anyone bullies easily," said Molly's father. "Or who needs my approval or anyone else's. Anyway, we'll talk about it with your mother when we get home."

Bullying... Tim thought about St. Dominic's. He'd taken a pounding there from just about everyone, both with their fists and their tongues. He'd kind of wanted to be noticed, to be cool. And the cool kids let him know where he stood, like, small and not cool. Here on Flinders he hadn't, but there were far fewer kids and he'd just been trying to be invisible. He was probably a bit stronger now, too. Well, yeah, he was stronger. He couldn't have picked up a sheep when he'd gotten here, last year, let alone have carried Bunce.

He was glad to find that Molly's mother had smoothed things over with Nan, too, and that he didn't have to explain there. It was odd with the empty neck pouch, partly frightening and partly relieving. He couldn't go...

but they could still take him away. It was an odd real-
ization that he didn't actually want to go. Yeah, some
things might be cool, and being a prince...but he had
something really exciting in the morning. Jon McKay had
lined him up to do a motorboat handler's course with the
local dive instructor, who also did the boat handling. "I
know you can do it, Tim, but I've got to comply with the
law. And Rob is planning to take leave for a month and
go to Bali with his partner during the holidays. You'll
like Mike, he's a top bloke, and I'm paying for it." Tim
didn't care what his teacher was like. It said Jon McKay
thought he was doing a good job.

Molly had told Gran how wonderful he'd been, too,
but had not said a word about the money. He was glad
about that too.

Mike Symons had a great deal to think about on that
trip home. He didn't find his wife entirely on his side,
either. He found she'd reached her own conclusions and
taken her own steps. Molly was subdued and yawning
her head off by the time they got home. "Poor honey,"
said her mother. "There's leftover lasagna. Warm it up in
the micro, eat, wash and get to bed. We can go in early
tomorrow to see Bunce."

Molly had been flat enough to just nod and smile and
do it. That worried her father. It wasn't like her. He was
feeling a failure enough as it was, without more trouble.
But there were chores to do, and by the time the wood
was in, the veg watered, and plants covered, his daughter
was abed. "Let's have a glass of wine, and you can tell me
about it," said his wife. "Before you tie yourself in any
more knots, I've taken that temporary teaching assistant
job at the school. It's school readiness, so it shouldn't
be too hard on Molly. And I spoke to your sister Helen.

Told her about the inheritance money from Granddad, and the mess with the will, and the trouble we've had with the insurers. I know you didn't want us to talk to her, but this is going to cost a fortune."

"Well, you need not have bothered," said Mike. "I wish you'd talked to me first, at least."

"You mean the dog is dying? Why didn't you tell me, Mike? She's going to be torn apart..."

"I mean, I said we didn't have the money and young Tim Ryan pulls it out of a pouch around his neck, then and there."

"What?"

"The kid had more than a thousand four hundred dollars with him. He says he earned it working for Jon McKay. I'm going to give him a call. I need to know more about this."

He picked up the phone and dialed. "Hi, it's Mike Symons. Look, I have a question to ask about young Tim Ryan."

"Best boatman I've ever had," said the voice down the phone. "He reads the water like a book. I can recommend him."

"Oh. So, he does a fair bit of work for you?"

"Yes, quite a bit, why?"

So Mike explained. It was embarrassing, but, well this was important. "And then he produces all this money... and I just wanted to know..."

There was a laugh. A slightly sharper tone. "Barking up the wrong tree, mate. I think the kid is straight as a die. He found the pouch on the old boat I bought when we were cleaning it up. Brought it to me, offered me the money. I told him to keep it. I pay him twenty bucks an hour, and he works a lot harder than my usual deckie for it. I haven't seen him spending it on designer clothes. I thought he was spending it on computers or the girlfriend. But he's probably just been keeping it. Good kid, but he's had a hard time, I reckon."

"Thanks. Thanks a lot. I was worried because of my daughter. I hate to think it, but there are drugs on the island, and I just wanted to make sure."

That got a snort. "Don't tell him I told you, but he admitted to me he tried dope once. He ended up in the E.R. Now if you were talking about your other neighbor, I'd say you had reason to worry. But I think your daughter has gotten involved with a very good kid. Think yourself lucky, mate."

"I'm beginning to think I must be. But I had to ask. I try and look after my kid, although I sometimes think I'm not much good at it. So, if you don't mind my asking, what's this rough time he's had? I'd like to help if we can."

"Search me," said Jon McKay. "I know he came here from Melbourne, miserable. But take him to sea, put tools in his hand, livestock to shift, or a boat to handle, and you'd swear he'd been doing it all his life. Look, he's Aboriginal, and maybe he took a hammering about that."

"He is?"

"His grandmother is, so he must be. They're good people."

"His grandmother is the salt of the earth. You know she started crying the other day when my daughter took some anzacs over to their place . . . she said she hadn't had them since she used to make them to send to her husband in Vietnam, what, forty years back. I gather he was killed there."

There was a silence down the line. Then Jon McKay said, "I'll need to have a chat with someone at the RSL. You can't just ask her, but I bet she's not getting a pension. I'll look into it. I've got a friend or two. But don't you worry about Tim. I'd trust my life to him. I do, when I'm underwater."

"Thank you. That's what it looked like to me. You've taken a weight off my mind."

"Well, you can be easy. Now, while I've got you on the line, someone said you designed websites? I need one, and I thought I'd do it myself, but I just don't ever get to it. And I'd rather hire a local if I can, because that way it's easier to get things changed and fixed. Can I come and have chat about it?"

"Sure. Whenever suits you. Or I could come see you."

"I'll drop in on Monday arvo."

His wife had poured him a glass of wine. Mike took a long sip of it. "Well?" she asked, raising her eyebrows.

"Jon McKay thinks the world of the boy, and pays him well, too. He reckons the money's honestly come by."

"I could have told you that," said his wife tartly. "I can't believe you were going to let Buncy die."

"I didn't see any way out just then. And it didn't happen. But now we have a problem with Molly thinking she's got to leave school to help out, to pay him back. I'll say this, Tim was quick to back me up on that. But I still can't quite see why a kid like that was wandering around with that much money and his grandmother was struggling to find five cents to scratch with."

"Maybe he didn't realize. She wouldn't tell him."

"I suppose so. But he'll have to be paid back. And I don't like my daughter being obligated..."

"Ah. That's what it is. Listen to me, Michael Symons. Trust your daughter. I'll talk to her, you stay out of it. But if she's going to get herself a boyfriend, I'd rather it was one who'd give everything he had for her dog than one who wasted his money on himself. And if Molly says she'll pay him back, then let her. Being broke and working will do her no harm. Molly's not going to squirm out of it. You know your daughter. We can help out, quietly."

"Yes... but."

"I don't think feeling she owes him money is going to make Molly jump into bed with him, Mike. If I know our daughter, it's more likely to work the other way around. She's not for sale. And anyway, if that's how she feels, that's how she feels. Butt out."

"Well, at least he seems a decent kid, even if I don't think it's that simple."

Áed had examined the dead snake under the coil of wire. He doubted his young master had meant to throw it to kill, but the wire was heavy and the land had lent him its strength when he threw it. That was their way. A man would defend, and would kill that which might attack.

The marks of Maeve's magics were on the creature. So he went to the salt water to confront her. He was afraid, but he, too, would defend his master.

She was not far offshore, as usual. And she knew why he had come. "It was an old working," she said. "We have a truce of kinds now. I bring him the human treasure he needs to go to Cnoc Meadha, to return the key."

Áed had a grasp—of sorts—on humans' idea of treasure in this age by now. He had no idea why he'd not been told to fetch it. "That is work for my kind, not you," he said tersely.

"Ah. But your master has found there is a cost to your help, little one. Magic among those who are both human and Fae has such a price. It rebounds on him when he uses it to his own advantage."

Áed was briefly stunned by this. No wonder his master feared the consequences of Áed's actions. The reward of a human soul was such, was it? No wonder it was a precious thing that Faerie feared. Magic being magic, it would not be ill...if his master used it for others. But how to explain that?

It would not be simple.

✧   ✧   ✧

Tim was finding it anything but simple. Actually, it seemed to have made things slightly awkward between him and Molly. He'd kind of, without thinking it out or planning it like that, assumed she'd, well, be grateful and not respond to his attempt to put his arm around her by brushing it off and saying "Stop it, Tim."

"But I thought..."

"Like, well, I owe you money, but that doesn't mean you can own me."

"I don't want to own you. I was just giving you a hug."

"Which you think you can because I owe you a thousand five hundred bucks."

"Yeah, well, Hailey gave me a kiss when I lent her twenty bucks..." She never gave it back to him, actually. But he got a few French kissing lessons. He hadn't had any pocket money the next time she asked him for a loan. And then she'd ignored him...

That, it seemed, was the very worst thing he could have said. He hadn't realized Molly even knew Hailey. She gave him an earful that included some words he'd never heard her say, let alone about anyone else. She was usually pretty nice. She finished up with: "And I wouldn't speak to you again, but I have to give you the money for Bunce. I didn't think you did it for...for that!"

"I didn't. And you don't have to give me anything or pay me back! I told you so. I did it...well, for *him*. And for you because you were so upset. And for me because I didn't want to see him die! And you don't ever have to speak to me again."

Tim was just as mad and confused then as he'd been back when his mother said he had to leave home and come here.

But obviously something he had said in all that worked a bit better. "I'm sorry," she said. "I really don't like her. But I do have to pay you back, Tim. Because...because I must. That was the best thing anyone ever did for me.

But I'm not going to . . . get involved, um, date you or anything. Not while I owe you so . . . so much. It'd be too much like you bought me."

"I didn't do it for that reason. I never even thought of it. Really. And I was only . . . well, I, l . . . like you. A lot." It wasn't the cleverest speech he'd ever tried. But it did have her blushing to the roots of her hair.

"I quite like you too," she said attempting to be light and sophisticated and not succeeding too well, but at least the bad moment had sort of passed. And then it got worse. "So, like, I've been meaning to ask, what are you saving the money for? Entertaining the beauty queen?" There was just a tiny edge in her voice, and Tim knew that it was a spike in at Hailey, who had been in a modeling competition and won.

"No. Just . . ." he sighed. "It's not important."

She looked directly at him. "Tim Ryan, you're hopeless at telling lies. You can trust me. And I promise I won't go off spare again."

Tim shrugged. "If you must know, I was saving up to get away from here."

She blinked. "Do you hate it so much?"

He shrugged. "I did. But I kind of got used to it. I've got . . . friends now. Even if one of them is never going to speak to me again. It's not that . . . I, I, just need to go."

"You know I wouldn't not speak to you. I was just mad."

"Yeah. I did know. You are, sometimes," he said, trying to smile and to change the direction of the conversation. It didn't work.

"So why do you have to go? And where?" she asked.

"Ireland; you know, like, overseas."

She blinked. "Is your dad there or something?"

He laughed bitterly. "No. He's in Oman. And you wouldn't believe me if I told you. Nobody ever does."

"I would. You're not a liar."

"Yeah, well, all of this is impossible, but it's also true. But it's so weird nobody could believe it."

She sat down. "Tell me about it. Dad drives me spare, but he says a trouble shared is a trouble quartered, and he's sort of right. And...and you did so much for me."

"I don't know where to start."

"Like why you hated being here. I...I like having you here. I'd like to fix it."

"It's more about why I got sent here. Look, promise you won't tell? But, well..."

It came out of him like a boiling-over pot. About things breaking, about the trouble with cannabis. About the tagging. About stealing the DVD and being caught... "And then the building caught fire. And like, well, they'd already called the school and Mum...and." He stopped.

"So...what happened then?" She prompted.

He shrugged. "Then I got sent over here to my crazy old nan."

"So... you didn't get sent to court or prison?"

"No. I mean, the cops tried to get a statement out of the security guards, and they...I dunno, they never found it on me. And the CCTV record didn't show anything at all...well, turned out they picked me up because I just looked guilty. They thought...and the copper said they shouldn't have, that they'd find the stolen stuff on me... but, like, I hadn't quite left the shop. Um, they shouldn't have done that either...but my fingerprints would have been on the DVD that showed up on the desk. Only they thought it must have got burned. Only...only I found it in my stuff when I was packing up. I threw it away."

"You made a mistake, did something you were feeling bad about anyway. What happened to Hailey in all this?"

"Oh, she sweet-talked them into letting her go. She said she barely knew who I was. She had, like, a bunch of stuff in her hat, too."

"She would," said Molly, "But Tim, so, it's over. You came here, and we like you."

He was silent.

"Tim. I really do like you. Lots of people do. And it's over. You've left it behind."

"I haven't. Half the shop burned out, and...and the insurance assessor is hassling my mum. And he's called here, and it'll all come out. That's the problem, see. I don't want everyone to know."

"Well, it's not your fault it burned down. And, and anyway, like, almost everyone does stupid stuff. I pinched some lollies, when I was little, about seven. Dad made me take them back. I thought I was going to die of shame, but I didn't. And here, no one but you and Dad know I did that."

"It was my fault. Sort of," said Tim, awkwardly.

"You set fire to the building?" she asked, incredulously.

"Of course not!" he said, hurt. And then, quietly, "But it did happen because I was there. These things do. I told you. I...I can't explain. But they always blame me. And...they're right, kind of. They'll keep chasing me. So...I have to go."

She shook her head. "But you can't just run off. You're a minor. They'll just find you and send you back. And all sorts of horrible stuff happens to kids...living rough. Please, don't do it, Tim. I'll be on your side."

"Not where I'm going. They can't reach me there. I just have to get to Ireland."

"Overseas won't stop them sending you back," she said. "They've got like treaties and stuff."

"Not with King Finvarra they haven't," said Tim.

She looked blank. "Who?"

"Yeah, well, I said I couldn't explain. It's easier to go than to explain."

"Try me."

He looked at her doubtfully. Pulled a face, sighed, but started talking anyway. "Well, like, you know you said my nan was crazy because she talks to the wee folk, puts beer down for them? Well, she's not crazy. And neither am I. I really have got an invisible friend. Only he's pretty stupid and he breaks stuff, and, and does things. Things I might want to do, but wouldn't."

"That's crazy. That's not real, Tim, it's..."

"Yeah? Watch," he said, angry partly with himself for telling her at all, and partly with the sheer unfairness of it all. "Tip over that glass," he said. "Go on. I'll reward you."

The glass on the scarred wooden table wobbled and then tipped, pouring out the water, then it fell over and rolled. And then... righted itself.

Molly watched it happen in horror, wondered if she should run... and then looked at Tim. He was crying, tears on his cheeks. "See! And bet you won't believe me, either, even if you have seen it. No one does."

Without meaning to, she reached out and grabbed his hand. "I believe you."

He sniffed, and pulled his hand away. Wiped his eyes, blew his nose. "Thanks. Nobody else would, though," he muttered gruffly, trying to pretend he hadn't been crying.

They sat in silence, and then Tim got up and wiped up the puddle of water. Just like a boy! He used the tissue he'd wiped his nose on, and shoved it back into his pocket. This wasn't the time to point that out, though.

"What can I do, Tim?" she asked.

He shrugged. "Do? Nothing. I'll get the money together again, get on a plane and go to Ireland, go to Finvarra's hill and use my key. I don't belong here."

"But you could do all sort of things with... with your invisible friend."

"I think I can see him sometimes. He's got little sharp black eyes and a long nose," said Tim, morosely. "But I can't really use him to do things. It always seems to go wrong, and they blame me even if I didn't mean anything to happen. That's why they'll blame the fire on me, eventually. Just like all those vases at Harvey Norman. And because I took the blame for that, they'll think I must have done it."

It was probably his face that made people blame him, thought Molly. He didn't seem to be able to hide his feelings.

When she got home she took out her copy of Fire and Hemlock, by Diana Wynne Jones. It was one of her favorite books, read many times. She reread the part about the Fairy court living in the real world...and the poem...Tam Lin.

She was going to have to hold on to Tim tightly, because she was sure that there would be a price for living in Faerie, just like in the book. They wouldn't tell Tim that, of course. She wasn't going to tell him that she was planning to hold onto him herself either, at least not until she had finished paying back that money. Then she was going to have to find a way of stopping him from spending it. She sighed. Looked at the nautilus shell. This was kind of what her dad had meant when he'd said that it was never simple.

CHAPTER 17

Molly had been trying to reduce the number of hours she spent babysitting. Now, she had to take as much as she could, but she still found time to go down to the Ryan place a few times a week, and of course there was school and the bus, when Mum didn't take the car in because she was working. She'd organized day stints at the local café during the holidays. It was something that had to be done. Tim had offered to ask Jon McKay if Molly could come out to sea with them too, if she had some spare time, just to see what they did. She wanted to do that, but she was a little nervous about it, too.

Still, Tim seemed okay for now about the new line drawn . . . sometimes she wondered if she was. The other girls all talked about their boyfriends. It wasn't easy, as a geeky, reads-too-much girl with braces on her teeth, who everyone thought had a crush on Tim Ryan . . . not that some of them didn't think he was quite cute, especially some of the younger ones. He didn't respond to their baits, though. Molly noticed he was a softy at heart and could be conned into helping out anyone who was struggling...or pretending to. Huh. Some people weren't beyond using that against him.

She supposed that was a good thing in a guy, too, although she'd have to watch him.

Then, just before the June holiday, things went pear-shaped. Hailey came home, and it was the end of that line of babysitting. Not, to be fair, that Hailey wanted to take her job. She was furious to have it expected of her. Molly and half of the island's population heard all about it, because the argument took place in the small supermarket in Whitemark, the day after the ferry had come in, which of course had brought all the farmers and other folk in to town. As a time and a place to have a screaming match, it could hardly have been more a effective way of telling everyone on the island.

Molly wasn't there, but got chapter and verse both from Melanie and Jane at school, and her mother's friend Miriam, along with all the speculation. "It's not school holidays in Vic." "She's pregnant," in hushed whispers. "She's been suspended." "She's been expelled."

Whatever. Hailey was back, and her stepmother was furious with her, and she was furious to be expected to clean and cook and look after the younger two. She wasn't a slave!

Even if she wasn't a slave, she was back out at their modern glass-and-tile house with its magnificent views, and blocking Molly's chief source of income—and phoning to see if she could cadge a lift into town.

"No, sorry. I don't think Mum or Dad will be going in for a few days," said Molly.

"Oh. I'm so bored. Sarah expects me to look after her stupid kids all the time," said the sulky voice down the phone.

Sarah was her stepmother. Molly supposed she ought

to feel some sympathy. She'd been a bit bored here, once. Like, a lifetime ago. "I could lend you a few books."

"Oh, I don't like reading. It's boring. Anyway there's lots of magazines here."

"Computer games... I've got a few, and Tim has some too."

"Tim? Oh, you mean Tim Ryan." It was said dismissively.

Molly's hackles rose. "He's a nice guy. He..."

"Oh, I know him. He was at St. Dominic's. Daddy told me to be nice to him because that dump of a farm is a real estate dream for selling off as holiday and lifestyle blocks. Daddy was going to buy it from Tim's father, but the deal fell through."

"Like, what's that got to do with Tim?"

"I dunno. Apparently the old bat living there had a fit when her son suggested it, and changed her will. Daddy said she'd drop dead one of these days and leave it to Tim. So I must be nice to him. But he was such a boring little loser. And then he got kicked out of the school for stealing."

Molly slammed the phone down, and sat there steaming for a good twenty minutes, thinking of all the things she should have said.

She retreated to her room and didn't answer the phone when it rang again. She tried to lose herself in a book instead.

She was quite unprepared for her mother to come into her room, dancing and leaping around like a mad thing. That just so wasn't Mum. "What's up?" she asked, warily.

"Have I ever said anything nasty about your Aunt Helen?" asked her mother.

"Er. Yes. You said she was obsessive, and..."

"Well, I should eat my words. You remember when Bunce got bitten by the snake?"

"Like I could forget."

"Well, I called her then. I thought... well, I thought we might need to borrow money, because the little bit I was expecting from my granddad's estate, I wasn't going to get because of Cousin Tobias-the-little-toad, and that insurance mess. And being Helen, she asked me to send her the will. So I did. Only I sent her Granny's will as well as Granddad's; they arrived together, and you remember we got the little davenport writing desk and those opal earrings from her..."

"Get on with it, Mum."

"Well, being Helen, she checked both wills and all the details. And it turns out that the vague wording Tobias was using to lawyer away at getting a bigger share for his family... is all in Granddad's will, but that he indisputably left his entire estate to Granny May, if he died before her."

"But they died in the same car crash."

"Well, no, it turns out. Your darling obsessive-about-details Aunt Helen checked. Granddad died immediately, but Granny May was just unconscious and only died in hospital the next day. So her will is the valid one. And Granny, being an accountant's daughter, set it out very carefully and correctly and beyond any dispute, to be divided equally between her named children, and, if a child predeceased her, their share to be divided equally between their children, or if they're childless, their share was to be divided equally between her other named children. The little toad shouldn't have tried to grab so much, because now his family are going to get very little. He's got seven kids, and he's one of four, but my mother got a whole share, and only had me. That was a lady from the lawyers' on the telephone, the executor of Granny May's will. It is going to be far more money than I thought! The overdraft is off our backs, we're a long way towards paying off the mortgage, and you, my

dear, have money for Uni. And also for settling your
debts, as I am your trustee, and can decide if you need
it. That on top of Dad getting the ombudsman on his
side with the insurers, it's been a good week!"

"Wow!" She got up and hugged her mother. "I'm so
glad for you, Mum. I know it has been worrying you so
much." She took her lip between her teeth. Then said . . .
"I think, if it is okay, I'm going to rather go on paying
Tim back slowly. I've . . . got reasons, Mum."

"Probate won't be granted for a while anyway. And I
don't think it a bad idea, Molly. It just means you don't
need to babysit quite so much, especially up there. I
don't like them."

Molly knew who she was talking about. "Oh, the kids
are okay. But that Hailey and her dad. He's, like, sort of
oily feeling. And you know what she said to me?" She
told her mother all about Hailey's call, leaving out the
part about stealing.

"I'd sort of heard there was a big bust-up with Tim's
parents and the old lady about selling. They'd apparently
arranged a retirement home for her."

Molly stared at her mum. She just couldn't imagine
Tim's gran in a retirement place. "Where do you hear
these things, Mum?"

"At the hairdresser, I think. And some at the CWA.
I'll bet she never knew Burke was behind it all."

Hailey was somewhat surprised to have the phone
slammed down on her. It was kind of funny really. That
plain bookworm with railway tracks on her teeth must
fancy little Tim. She herself had no real interest in Tim
at all. He'd been sort of useful at times, but he was, like,
so uncool. He didn't ever have much money, or an earring or tattoos or a car or anything important. He was

such a weed he couldn't even be emo. And he was young too. Like, barely her age. But it would be fun to make railway-tracks suffer a bit. Tim would come when she whistled, desperate to please her, like a little puppy dog.

So she called his mobile number. Only he wasn't answering her. Or calling back. She needed a spliff, and she knew where Daddy kept his stash. So she went and had a smoke, watched TV, and then decided to call Justin and got told about the plan to have a jam session on Friday . . . she forgot all about Tim and Miss railway-tracks. She wasn't really interested in music, but she really fancied singing in a band. Not the singing part, but the whole scene. She only remembered railway-tracks a few days later, when her stepmother announced that she was off to Launceston for a week. When Daddy asked her if she was taking Hailey, Samantha and Troy, she had said "no."

"But you can't just leave them here. I've got a load to go out on Friday."

"I'm going to be in and out of the dentist, Ricky. I've got four appointments. I can't look after them while I'm in the chair, and anyway, school only breaks up on Wednesday. That's three days before I get back. Hailey is here. She can keep an eye on them."

"But I want to go to Lonnie," protested Hailey. "This place is so dead, Sarah. Oh, come on, please."

"You are in such trouble you're not going anywhere," said that cow of a stepmother of hers. "You're lucky not to be in jail, Hailey. How could you have been so stupid?"

"Like, I don't know what you're making such a fuss about. It's not like it isn't the family business!"

Eventually Daddy shut the argument up. "Look, you can't go away, Hailey. But you can hire that girl from the place down the road to do some of the kid-herding. To give you a break."

"Uh." Good thing she hadn't actually got around to

whistling Tim in yet, but even so ... "She might not want to."

"Trust me, they need the money." He tapped his nose. "I'll pick that place up on a bank repossession soon. They're in trouble deep."

Now that Tim had been brought to mind again, Hailey thought of checking his Facebook page. It would be nice to have some leverage on railway-tracks. There were no entries at all since he'd left Melbourne. And then it occurred to her that his mobile number wasn't a Telstra one. They were the only ones that worked on the island. He must have a new phone. She'd have to call him on the landline and get it. She could always use him for bait for railways-tracks. She'd need someone to babysit for Friday.

So she called the landline. And got a very sleepy Tim. "Hailey? What's wrong?" he demanded, followed by a long "aaaaaaah" noise.

"Nothing. What's wrong with you?"

"Nothing. Why? What did you call me about?"

He actually sounded ... irritable. "You made a funny noise."

"Oh. Yawning. Sorry. I was asleep. You woke us up."

"But it's only like half past ten at night!"

"Yeah, well, I've been up since half five. We went and got a couple of flounder. And I was working on scraping the boat for Jon this afternoon. Hard yakka. So what can I do for you?" he asked, not sounding in the least eager.

"Oh, nothing really. I just called to get your new mobile number. And to give you a hard time for not telling me what it was. And to say you should come and see me. I could use some company in this dead place."

"Still the same old number. It just doesn't work. Look, Hailey, I'm just so busy with stuff. If I'm not working this weekend I'll walk over. But no promises. Life is kinda full."

He didn't really sound interested. Well, she'd change that soon enough. "Too busy with your new girlfriend for me?"

"New girlfriend?"

"Oh, I know all about Molly railway-tracks. Don't the braces cut your tongue?"

"Molly? She's not my girlfriend, but don't you dare call her names," he said crossly. "Anyway, listen, it's late, and I'm working again tomorrow. I'm falling asleep talking. I'll chat to you sometime when I'm awake. Maybe this weekend; the weather doesn't look so crash-hot on the long range forecast. Bye."

Tim actually had a bit of trouble going back to sleep after that call. Blasted Hailey. She never thought about anybody but herself. But what he really wanted to know more about was why Hailey thought Molly was his girl-friend. He wondered who she'd gotten that from.

Molly was more than a little surprised to have another call from Hailey, being sweetness-and-light, the next afternoon. "Like, I didn't mean to tread on any toes about Tim. I was just being bitchy because he isn't talking to me. He's crazy about you, you know."

Molly literally didn't know what to say about that. "Uh," was the best she could manage.

"Anyway. Look, I know you're looking for babysitting work."

"Um, not really..."

"And I've taken some of it away from you. So I felt bad and talked to Daddy. Sarah's going to be away for a week, and Daddy said I could call you and he'd pay for you to do a few hours. The kids like you. They always tell me about you."

"Um, I am going to be away for a day or two. My braces are coming off at last. I'm not sure of the exact date, because there was some hassle with the flights. And, like, I've got work in the café, and Tim said he'd arrange for me to join him on the boat."

"Oh, well, I'll give you a call. Bye."

And Molly was wondering just what Tim had said to whom, and was both cross and a little pleased, and a little ashamed that she'd not said "no." But it would be hard for her to find a real gap in her own schedule, so it was safe enough.

Hailey found being bored was a lot better than having Samantha and Troy expecting to be entertained and fed. And they got up so early!

When Justin called on Friday morning, she realized that she had not actually gotten around to organizing for Molly to come. So she phoned. The phone was answered by Molly's mother. "Sorry, she's not home. And I am sure she doesn't want to babysit."

She sat there biting her knuckles—she wouldn't bite her fingernails, because that would spoil them. Daddy was away in his little shed in the bush packing the stuff for the plane. And she really didn't have any other friends on the island. Well...there was Tim.

She called. And got Tim's grandmother, "Hello, Molly. So I heard yer going to be on the boat while Tim is working." She sounded...amused.

"Uh. This is Hailey Burke. I was looking for Tim."

"Oh. He left with Mr. McKay at seven. They'll be in the boat by now." The voice was much more terse.

Tim had said something about scraping down a boat. Hailey had no interest and no knowledge about what one did with boats. "Where are they?"

"I wouldn't know. They've been using Port Davies and West End lately. Tim didn't say. Now I got to get ready to go to town. Goodbye."

So she was still stuck with the kids when Justin showed up. She was tempted to leave them and just go. But then Daddy might get really angry. "The babysitter is working on a boat, scraping it or something. So I can't go," she said sullenly.

"Oh. Is that on at the ramp at Port Davies?" Justin's parents' house looked down on the bay. "I thought it was Mike. Mind you, it looked like a woman was painting it. Oh well, pity. My folks are away and we've got the place to ourselves. We're going to have a little...party."

"That's her. Or rather them. Look, let me take Samantha and Troy to them, they can't, like, not look after kids. And your place is just there. Even if Molly isn't there, Troy and Sam can play in the garden or something if they have to."

"Are you sure?" he asked, doubtful.

She kissed him. Just a bit of tongue to get him loosened up. And three minutes later they were on their way to Emita, and down to the ramp at Port Davies. And sure enough, there were some people working on a boat down at the water. The girl in the hoodie waved. It wasn't an "oh, I am glad to see you" wave, just a kind of greeting. And suddenly Hailey had doubts. She didn't really know how Molly would take to her, right now. "Just go down and see if Tim and Molly can look after you. We'll wait," she said to the kids.

The two ran off down the steep ramp, and stopped to have a look at someone's kayak, and then went on down to the boat. Then Troy waved at them, and started jumping from rock to rock. "Cool!" said Hailey. "Let's go party."

They stopped to smoke a spliff and then several hours and quite a few coolers later...

It was her mobile. Her father. "Where the hell are you?"

"Um, Emita."

"What have you done with the kids? I just got a message on the home phone from that old bird-watching duffer on Wireless Road saying he saw them out at sea in a kayak, and without lifejackets on."

"That Molly! How could she!" said Hailey, angrily. "She was supposed to be looking after them. I'll never forgive her!"

"The Symons kid? She's off-island, Hailey. She was on the same plane as my mate Morton, yesterday."

"But she was down at the boat ramp. With Tim. I'll go down now, Daddy!"

"You'd better! I'll be there in ten minutes."

There was no sign of anyone at the boat ramp. No sign of the boat they'd been working on, no sign of the kayak, and no sign of Samantha or Troy.

CHAPTER 18

"Good to be off the water," said Jon, looking at the sky as they turned into the long driveway down to the Symons' place. Jon had reached an agreement with them to leave the boat and the towing ute there, saving himself fuel and wear-and-tear.

"Yes. She's going to be a bad one," Tim said worriedly... not because he was worried about the sea. He had huge faith in Jon, and the RIB. "I hope the plane will be all right. Molly's coming in from Melbourne. She hates flying anyway."

"They'll be fine, Tim. They'll divert if there's a problem. And they're good pilots. They fly the route all the time."

There was no one home, Tim knew, as Nan had been going into town with Molly's parents. So they parked the boat and ute, gave the boat a quick wash-down, and loaded the two fish crates of abalone into the polystyrene boxes in the back of the SUV for Jon to take down to the airport, and drove out.

They were just turning into the gate to Nan's farm

when they nearly hit the cop's Land Cruiser coming the other way.

The vehicle skidded to a halt and the policeman leapt out. "Tim Ryan? We're looking for Troy and Samantha Burke. Do you know where they are?"

"I haven't seen them since school broke up for the holidays," said Tim, surprised.

"We were told that they'd been left with you and Molly Symons at the boat ramp at Port Davies this morning..."

Tim shook his head. "No..."

"We've been at sea, launched from West End just after seven this morning," said Jon McKay. "Haven't been within ten kilometers of Port Davies."

"And Molly is away. Off-island. She's only flying back today," added Tim.

"Hell. I'd better get the SES out. The kids have been missing since eleven. They were seen by a couple of fishermen at the ramp. The kids told them their sister was watching them. And then later the kids were spotted fooling around in a kayak."

"Better get onto it, right now," said Jon. "The weather's turning nasty."

"Stupid kid," said the policeman, reaching for his radio as he got back in his vehicle. "I left a note on the door asking you to contact me urgently, Tim Ryan. You'd better take it down before your grandmother sees it."

"They're only little," said Tim. "Not stupid."

"No, I mean the sister. She was supposed to be looking after them. Now, excuse me." He shut the door and began edging his police vehicle past them while talking on the radio.

"I think I'd best leave you here, Tim," said Jon McKay. "I'm on the SES call-list. It's probably nothing and the kids will show up, but I'd like to get these abs to my pilot before they call me."

"I could come and give you a hand," offered Tim.

"It's probably a false alarm. They usually are, but better safe than sorry. I think you'd better go and take that note down."

"Too right!" said Tim as the diver got back into his SUV. "See you, Jon."

Jon nodded and waved. "Probably more boat repair work tomorrow."

It was only while walking down the track that it occurred to Tim that Nan couldn't have read the note anyway. But there were chores to do, and he thought no more about it as he went through the comfortable routine of splitting firewood. He found it a very satisfying job now, actually, easily swinging the heavy block-splitter, seeing the chips fly.

Presently the phone rang. He went in to answer it. It was Molly on her mobile, and just hearing her voice made him smile. She must be safe and back. "Hi, Tim!" she said, sounding just as pleased to hear his voice. "Just calling to let you know your grandmother will be late home. Mum and Dad are off with an SES search, and your nan is going to get a lift back with the woman who works in Roberts. Everyone is out looking for Troy and Samantha. They were seen paddling around in a kayak by that bird-watching guy off Emita."

"Oh, wow! I hope they're okay! It was getting bumpy already when Jon and I came in. The swell is picking up. There's a real storm brewing."

"Yeah. I've got to go. I've got a lift home, too. I've got to go and shut the outside windows on the guest cottage. Mum thought it would be a great day for airing the place. Okay, bye, see you soon!"

Tim put the phone down and stood there for a moment. Then he walked to the door, stopping to take down an old oilskin from the nails just inside it, and headed for the beach at a brisk jog.

The sea was no longer the blue that it had been when they'd come in. Instead it was whitecapped and gray, and the waves were rushing up the sand in a tumult of foam.

He felt foolish standing there, calling "Maeve! Maeve!" just for the wind to whip the sound away.

But she heard him all the same. Either she had been very close or had gotten there magically, but the seal-woman suddenly surfaced amid the foam. She didn't look a bit like Lorde this time. "And now, Fae-changeling's descendant? Why do you call me? You choose a poor day for your kind to make the long swim to Ireland's shores."

"I'm looking for two kids in a kayak..."

"A blond girl-child and a boy in a fragile cockle-shell boat, bickering like sea-gulls."

"So...you've seen them! Where are they?" asked Tim.

"Why would I care to tell you?" asked the seal-woman.

"Because they're kids. They could drown out there!"

"They are not my children or my concern. Why should I care for humans? Why should you care for humans?" she said, disdainfully. "They are not your blood, nor is this your birthright-place."

The master stamped his foot, raised his fist. Not as if to hit, but as if to throw the ghost of a long, dark spear. Áed could see it, and probably the old fae could too. And the strength of the old ones, of the spirits of the land flowed through the boy...but he was a man then. Not one of the Aos Sí, in the land of endless childhood, but a man who will work and die...but truly have lived. "Hear me. So I have a drop of that fairy blood in me. So what? I've lots of other blood, and it doesn't make any difference to me, seal-woman. I belong *here*. This is *my* place and these are *my* people. Not off in some weird magical place. Just here. I want those children, I want them safe and alive. You want this key. Well, I'll make you a bargain. You can have it, if you can get them back to shore safe and alive. Otherwise you can forget it. Forever."

On the sacred mountain, lightnings danced. Not lightnings of the world of the flesh, but of the place that Áed too was a part of. Dancing in triumph welcoming the prodigal home.

Maeve knew that he was beyond her reach now, on land or sea. She shook her head. "I cannot do that. The boy child is already dead in the water. The girl is on the reef." She pointed to the breaking surf on the rocks a kilometer from the shore. "The tide and sea come for her. And she is cold and small, and well up on the rocks. I cannot reach her. She will not come to me, and I cannot go to her."

Tim looked at the seal-woman in horror. "Marriot Reef! What...where?"

"The islet with the sand-spit. On the rocks at the far end. You will need a good boat and good seamen. It is wild out there."

Tim took a deep breath. "I'll get the SES guys. If we get her off alive, it's a deal. Keep her there." He was running back to the house before he'd finished talking. These days it didn't take him that long. He was a little out of breath, but not blown by the time he got there. He still had the crumpled note from the copper in his pocket, which had a mobile number on it. He called it.

"Hello, it's Tim Ryan here, I..."

"Yes, I'm sorry, young man," said the copper. "Wrong tree I was barking up. We've got the search and rescue in full swing down here at Port Davies."

"I know. Look, I think I know where the little girl is."

"Where? Does she have a favorite spot? Tell me."

"She's on one of the islets on Marriot Reef. I think the boy has drowned."

There was a pause. Then the copper said, "Son, Marriot Reef is right across Marshall Bay, maybe ten kilometers away. Two little kids couldn't paddle that far. I don't know what you're seeing, but it isn't her."

"I can't see her. I . . . I just know she's there. The seal told me." As soon as he'd said it, Tim knew he'd said exactly the wrong thing. But it was too late.

"Look, I have a search to organize. I've got no time for this now. And don't go spreading rumors about drownings." He cut the call.

Tim stood there, steaming, for at least half a minute. Then he bit his lip and got a dial tone and called Jon McKay's mobile instead.

It rang.

And rang.

And rang out to the automatic message service.

He put it down and tried again. This time he left a message.

After the beep, Tim said, "Jon. This is Tim Ryan. The girl is on Marriot Reef. On the middle island with a sand-spit. You've got to get there quickly!"

It cut off, and he stood there. Chewed his lip, nervously, thinking. He realized Jon McKay would be at sea in one of the search boats. Then he tried again. "Jon . . . um, I'm going to take your boat. Sammy Burke can't wait. I . . . I hope that's all right."

Then he took down his red lifejacket from its hook, put on his boots, and headed out, at a brisk trot, taking the shortest route. It was only when he was near to the shoreline that it suddenly occurred to him that he could have taken the farm ute. It had no rego, and he was underage, but what would a couple of extra crimes be?

It had to be done.

It came down to him to do it.

And it felt, right now, as if he could run forever, faster than any ute, cross-country anyway. It felt right to run, feet thudding against the track through the ti-trees and tussocks. Then across the wet sand of the small bay, and up to Molly's place. As he ran across the sand he looked out to where Marriot Reef lay. He could see the white of the breaking surf against the black of the incoming storm.

It had to be done.

Mary Ryan had learned patience from the finest of teachers, the land and the sea. She hadn't always had it, but, well, there were worse things than a chair next to the fire and a mug of tea in the shop while you waited for a lift home. And she was feeling distinctly mellow right now. Not from alcohol . . . she kept away from it, seen too much go wrong because of it. Saying that had not made her popular, back in the days when a black man had to go around to the side door of the pub to get his grog, or brew it themselves, but she'd had a bad habit of saying what she believed. No, she'd been drinking stronger wine than the pub sold. Young Molly's parents had been emptying the butter-boat over her Tim. And then, in town, the headmistress, of all people, had come to introduce herself, and told her how good the boy was doing, and that he was a champion for helping the littler kids. It seemed it was true, too, because the woman who was finishing up before giving her a lift home had said she was "only too pleased to do something for Tim's grandmother. Such a nice boy. He's so good to my Mark."

Mary didn't like being dependent, but it was hard to not accept under those circumstances, and she had to get home, after all. The town was abuzz with the news of the search going on. Half a dozen people had come into the shop, talking about it.

But, sitting there, suddenly, she got the feeling that she was being called. And there—looking out from the wood-heater, or at least playing tricks with the fire-shadows as they could, was the long-nosed, dark-eyed wee-folk mani-kin that followed her Tim around, beckoning frantically.

It was an illusion, she knew, but she understood what he was doing only too well.

She stood up, and carefully made her way over to the counter. "I have to go home, now. Now! My grandson needs me." She couldn't see the people behind the coun-ter, of course, just their blurred shapes. But one of them said, "There, Tania. You better take her. I'll finish up for you." And they'd left together, Tania's guiding hand on Mary's elbow, which she really needed now.

Bunce had heard his second favorite person coming, of course. Molly had looked out of the window to see what her fur-face was barking at. You could tell it was a "happy-to-see-you" bark, but she hadn't heard the sound of a car. So she looked out, and there was Tim, loping up the beach-track like a wolf, carrying his life jacket. So she went out.

"Hi, Tim! What's up?" she asked.

He could have lied, it later occurred to her. Instead, he just said, "I'm borrowing Jon's boat. I know where little Sammy Burke is, and I need to go and fetch her."

Molly looked at the sea, at darkness of the storm com-ing. "Call the SES!"

"I tried. I told them. That stupid copper won't believe me," he said, opening the passenger door of Jon's ute. "Habit...I forget I'm going to have to drive." He slammed the door. "Fair do, I guess. I wouldn't believe me either. I shouldn't have said anything about the seal-woman. Now I've got to go and do it."

"You're going to be in a lot of trouble, Tim."

"Yeah. I know. But I have to do it." There was a kind of grim determination in his voice that there was no point in saying no to. If Tim Ryan had to swim, he'd do so. She couldn't exactly stop him from taking the diver's boat.

"Look..." she said. "I'll come with you. You can't get the boat off on your own."

He pulled a face. "I don't want you in this mess too, Molly." He climbed into the driver's seat. "I've got to do this. I can't know where she is, and that she needs help, and just do nothing."

"Budge up. I've at least got a P-plate license."

He hesitated for a moment, and then weakened, moved over. "As far as the boat ramp. Your dad'll kill me if I take you out to sea in this."

"You don't take me anywhere, Tim Ryan," she said, getting in and turning the key. "I'll go if I choose to. And I would trust you. Like, anywhere."

They drove in silence, other than one gear-grind, for some distance. Then Molly said warily, "There's something I've been meaning to say to you. About Hailey. Please don't be mad."

"Oh, I'm over her. Like, it was never anything...well, she's pretty, but..."

"She never was into you, Tim. Her father just told her to be nice to you, because you'll inherit the farm. And he wants to break it up and sell it as holiday places."

Tim was silent. Then he laughed. "That sort of makes sense, you know. I often wondered. She was always after the sports-jocks and the rich kids, and always, like, a couple of grades ahead of her. I thought it was because I came from the island, and her dad knew mine."

"Yeah. He tried to get your dad to get your gran to move into a retirement complex and sell the place."

"Nan started to say something once, and then clammed

up. I never knew why they...like, barely talk. I guess
I thought he was trying to make things easy for her."

"Maybe he was. Or maybe that's what he believed."

"Could be. My dad's not bad or anything. He's just
weak. He slithers out of everything my mother says,"
said Tim, sounding depressed.

One thing she couldn't say about Tim, right now, was
that he was squirming out. "It's a good thing, too. Your
gran couldn't live anywhere else...and if you hadn't
come to her, I would never have met you."

That did make him smile. "Yeah. And the same for me."

"So, where are the kids?" she asked, changing tack,
although she didn't really want to.

"Marriot Reef," he said. "Well, at least little Sammy
is on Treasure Island, and the tide is coming in with
the storm."

That was the island with a small sand beach, maybe a
hundred and fifty yards long, and a third as wide across,
at low tide. At high water most of it disappeared, meaning it had nice white sand, popular for low-tide picnics,
and it was out of range of the marsh flies on the main
shore. With the storm surge, and full tide, waves would
break over it.

"Oh. Exactly how do you know? I believe you; I just
want to know."

"The seal-woman," said Tim, matter-of-factly. "The
selkie Bunce came to rescue me from. She was sent to
fetch the key, like it's...it's my birthright, she told me."

"Um...is she telling the truth?"

"Yeah. I said she could have it if I got the kids back
alive, when I heard they were out in a kayak in this
weather. See, she wants that key back with Finvarra. And
this way she gets it as soon as I can give it to her. Otherwise she'd have to wait until I...I fly over to Ireland.
So I guess you don't need to hurry about paying me. I'll

probably end up in deep trouble about this. That's why I don't want you involved."

"But . . . you wanted to get out of here. To be safe."

"Yeah. But I guess I don't really want to go. I'll just have to try to stand my ground here. They can't punish me forever. Keep both hands on the wheel, Molly!"

"Sorry. I just . . . wanted to hug you. I'm glad you're going to stay here. I want you to be here. Not away in Faerie. I'm selfish, I guess."

"This is where I want to be too," said Tim Ryan. "Only I kinda didn't know it before. Slow down for the turn. The track is coming up just before the corner."

She concentrated on bringing the ute around the corner of the loop road to the West End slip before getting out to look. Her mind was still dealing with what Tim had said.

The wind flurry brought angry drops of rain hissing down the blue-gray wall of the surging swell. It roared up the ramp in a seething ravel of white water and rolling stones. The inky blackness across the water devoured the outer islands, and the horizon had vanished into the rain haze. Suddenly it was backlit by a tracery of jagged lightnings showing every black billow of the vast, stark roiling mountains of cloud above the whitecapped gray sea.

"It looks a bit ordinary out there," said Tim, zipping up the red life jacket. "I'm going to a get a little wet."

Molly said nothing. She just looked at the little RIB as Tim checked bungs and hooked up the fuel line. She took a deep breath, hauled out the life jacket from behind the seat of the ute, and buckled it up. She looked at the sea and pulled the buckles tighter.

His eyes widened as he looked up at her while he freed the bow-shackle, but he didn't try to argue. He just said, "Take your shoes off too, I think."

She did. He didn't need to explain that shoes and swimming didn't go together well.

"Can you back her down?" he asked.

She shook her head. "I don't know how to reverse with a trailer," she answered. "I've tried. My dad had to take over."

"I'm not too crash-hot at it myself, but we have to. Okay. Look. I'll back down around the curve and then if you just reverse straight down the rest, I can get the boat off." Tim edged the ute slowly down the rock toward the water. Molly watched from the back, pointing out the holes to him. A wave surged up and hit her feet, spraying up her legs and wetting her. Tim stopped. "Your turn," he said. "Don't go too far or we'll lose the ute into the sea too."

Hands damp and white-knuckled on the steering wheel, Molly eased her foot off the clutch. A wave crested up the ramp, and the sea plucked at the rear wheels of the ute, jerking and bouncing on the trailer. For an awful moment the rear end swayed. Cold sweat beaded her forehead as she thought that the sea would pull the ute, her, and the trailer into the deep. She'd never get out. She cracked the door open. Tim was yelling above the wind, "More! Quick!" She bit her lip and pushed back into the next wave. Both the trailer and then the ute bucked.

"Take her out, Molly!" shouted Tim, frantically pushing the boat's bow around to meet the next wave. She clashed and ground the ute into first gear in desperate haste... and stalled. Started again, as a wave came racing along pulling the trailer and ute sideways with casual brute force. The tires spun and bit and the ute bounced and humped, and Molly desperately straightened her wheels and put her foot down as hard as she dared. Something metal screeched on stone and the ute bounded higher, away from the hungry water.

Now she could look back, and to her horror, Tim was clinging onto the side of the boat, already out on the swells. She shouldn't have looked away, as the front wheel went over the edge of the ramp and the ute came down with a sickening bump. She scrambled out, rain stinging her face, screaming at the sea. He hauled up onto the boat, and... to her relief, was at the outboard. The boat's nose reared, there was a welter of foam at its tail, and he swung it back to the shore as she pelted down the slippery water-polished granite and towards the boat. A wave nearly pulled her feet from under her as Tim swung the boat around.

"Jump!" he yelled as the next wave mounted, and she did, grabbing the bowline and sliding over the pontoon as Tim hit the throttle. The boat hit the crest and whacked down, motor roaring as it churned in the foam, before it bit water and kicked them onwards, out into the open water, as she lay there, gasping. Water sluiced down the deck around her.

"Get a hold of something and get your weight up front," shouted Tim, urgently. "Hold the bowline and stand, legs apart, bend your knees."

Molly did what she'd been told. As she stood up, she saw, in the bow wave, scything through the water like a black oiled flexible torpedo, the black seal as it made slight of the power of the sea.

"Maeve! Is the little girl still there?" yelled Tim.

"Indeed," said the seal. "But the waves splash her and she cries."

Tim opened the throttle and the nose of the RIB rose under Molly and then flattened, as they rode, skimming and bouncing over the whitecaps. Looking back, briefly, Molly saw Tim, his face intent with concentration... against the backdrop of Roydon Island and the looming storm. He saw her looking, and smiled.

CHAPTER 19

The rain battered down on Alicia Symons's collar as she walked away from yet another empty holiday house. They were checking all of them. She sighed, looking out at the sea. The rain haze was sweeping across the bay and she could just see the boats coming in to Port Davies. Thank heavens it wasn't her child out there. She was worried enough about Mike going. She'd just gotten back to the car when a walker appeared. A stranger, with a small backpack, which in itself was unusual for the island, especially at this time of year. He smiled and raised a hand in greeting, looking tired. It was worth asking, even if he turned out to be one of the searchers. She wound down the window the window and said, "Hello. You haven't seen two little kids, have you? A girl of about six, blonde, ponytails, and a boy of about eight?"

He shook his head. "No, I haven't. I've been for a bit of a bush-walk. Took a lot longer than I expected to, and look at the weather now. It was lovely when I set out. You don't know where I could find a reasonable B&B around here? I don't fancy camping in this lot."

"Well, we own one. But it's at West End. And we're in the middle of a search and rescue operation. Look, walk back along this road, first right, about the second house along there is a sign—John's with the SES guys, but his wife is home, I think."

"Great, thanks," said the hiker. "I'll just go and get my gear from my kayak. Best of luck with the search. I'd offer to help, but I don't know this place. I've spent all day being lost."

Only one word registered. "Kayak? Where did you leave it?" she demanded.

He looked a little startled. "Right next to the slip. There was no sign saying you can't or anything."

Alicia flung open the other door. "Get in, please. I'll run you down there."

"Well, sure. What's wrong?" asked the hiker, strapping in as she turned the car.

"Tell me about the kayak. Did you leave the paddle with it?"

"Well, no. I tucked it in the bushes. But it's got a Minn-kota. One of those electric motors. Takes the pain out of paddling. I've got a solar charger, and she'll do fifteen kilometers on a charge," said the kayak owner, proudly.

Alicia almost forgot she was driving and closed her eyes. Then she said, "Oh, no!" and accelerated, putting her foot flat.

"What?" asked her startled passenger, "What's wrong? What's the rush?"

"I think those kids are in your boat. Look, the island police are there. Just let me concentrate on the road."

"What? You mean..."

They skidded to a halt at the ramp, just as one of the boats was being hauled out of the water by the police ute.

She jumped out of the car, recognizing her Mike among the life-jacketed men, and ran over to them. "I've got the kayak's owner. The kayak had one of those little electric outboards! It's got about a fifteen-kilometer range."

A moment of horrified silence spread across the group.

"They could be out as far as Prime Seal Island," said the SES captain. "We've just got a much wider search area."

"They're kids. They probably wouldn't head out to sea," said one of the men who had just come in with the boat. Alicia had hardly recognized him, the hood of his waterproof tight around his head and wearing a grim expression instead of his usual smile. It was the abalone diver. He was unzipping his jacket as he spoke. "We'll have to plan a new search. I'm just going to see who the hell has tried to ring me. Had three calls while I was out there." He looked at the number. "Hello. It was Tim Ryan."

"Ryan!" said the policeman, and Alicia saw him turn pale. "He called me to say the girl was on Marriot Reef. I...I didn't think it was possible."

"What?" demanded Mike.

"Hang on. He left a message," said Jon McKay. "Shut up so I can listen." There was instant silence. "Marriot Reef. Middle island, the one with a sand-spit."

"But...I mean, how could he know?" said the policeman.

"He's my boatman," said Jon, tersely. "That kid reads the sea like you read a book. It's in his genes. He'll find good abs at twenty meters down while he's on the surface, reads currents and waves like they were talking to him. I've been cursing all afternoon that I didn't take him up on coming along with us."

"I thought he was Melbourne...trouble," said the policeman slowly. "Up to something."

The look he got from Jon McKay was pure scorn. "I'm calling back, but in the meanwhile let's get this boat tied down well enough to tow down there. If we take the track just past the Wheatleys' place, we can probably manage a beach launch at the mouth of the creek there." He turned to the SES captain. "If that's okay."

That worthy smiled and nodded. "Yer beat me to the punch. I'll send the next boat in to West End. It'll be an easier launch, and better than trying to push across Marshall Bay in this. I wish we could have had got the chopper out, but it was already just too wild by the time we got the call out."

Men jumped about, tying the boat down. Jon shook his head. "No answer. I better check my message bank. There was another message."

A moment later he said, "The boy has taken my boat to go and get her."

There was a stunned silence.

"Come on," yelled the SES captain. "We might have a second search and rescue. Get going. I'll send the guys on quads down the beach from Castle Rock."

Alicia felt the sudden cold in her stomach, looked at her husband and pulled out her mobile.

Tim knew things were going to get worse before they got better, once they got out of the lee of Roydon and the Pascoes and got the full force of the swells and wind. The shallower waters of Marshall Bay would do two things— push the waves into peaking and then rob them of some force as they broke and expended their energy in foam. He knew that. Knew how best to deal with it. It was still incredibly hard, and took all his concentration, running just behind the break, then over at the right moment, to zig out and do it again. The sea was a churning mess of white, and the squalls of sheeting rain made it hard to see more than a few hundred meters ahead. He had to rely on his senses: his ears for the roar of the waves, his eyes to see what he could, and the feel of the water and wind biting to help with direction.

It would be better once they found the lee of Marriot Reef, but even that would be wild, he knew. And he had to find his way there...he could ask the seal-woman. But he didn't need to. He also didn't know if she could move as fast as the RIB did, anyway.

Molly felt the vibration of the phone in her inside pocket. There was no way she could get to it. She was amazed it still worked; the scything spray had soaked her and she'd thought that she was wet to the cold skin. She'd have been frightened out of her wits if it hadn't been for the glance back at Tim. He had one of those easy-to-read faces. And he wasn't miserable or afraid. He was just...intent. And he seemed to be smiling. He looked, simply, in control.

He caught her look, gave her a brief thumbs-up. "Five minutes," he yelled. "Nearly there!"

How could he tell? But his confidence lifted her spirits.

"Thank yer!" called Mary Ryan, as she hastily opened the door and scrambled with all the speed she could manage out of the woman's car. She was running through the rain for the house, not waiting for polite goodbyes. There wasn't a light on in the house. The stove was warm, had been lit, but hadn't been recently fed, by the temperature. She added wood out of habit as she demanded of the air: "Where is he?" Well, of the furry little feller of light and shadows that she could half see.

It pressed the ute keys into her hand.

She jog-trotted out of the house, trying not to shake.

It was hard to start the old brute in the cold, but she got it going. Her little-folk helper clung to the outside mirror, as he always did, pointing. Her heart sank still further, because that was the beach track he was pointing her down.

"She's out there, Mike," said Alicia Symons. "Not answering the mobile, and now it has stopped ringing."

"I'll kill him, if he isn't dead," said Mike Symons, driving too fast, but just keeping up with the police vehicle towing the boat in front of them, cursing that the trailer lights had obviously not been hooked up.

His wife was silent. Then she said, "If Molly is out there, and he brings her back alive, you'll listen to her first. Because I bet if she went along, Tim did his best to stop her."

"He should have done more, then."

"Like what, Mike Symons?" she asked. "You never managed to stop me skydiving."

"I just hope to God she's all right."

"I thought you were an atheist?"

"Not when my daughter is at sea in this."

"Yes. Look out, they're turning."

They bumped down the rutted, muddy trail to the beach behind the police vehicle. It was raining hard again, difficult to see, even with the wipers on fast.

"How can they hope to find anything in this? I just hope they give up and come home," said Alicia, fearfully.

Jon was in the front passenger seat of the police vehicle, with three of the other crew in the back, as they headed away from the ramp at Port Davies. The sergeant said, "Tell me about this kid. Seems I got it wrong. He said he was from Melbourne and all he wanted to do was to get back there."

"Maybe he did," said Jon. "But Ryan's ancestors were among the first sealers to settle here. The people who became the Straitsmen. You know, took Aboriginal wives, lived on the islands off the sea, lived off muttonbirds and a bit of farming. A lot of them came from little islands off Scotland or Ireland anyway. They were suited to the life, they knew the sea, and they survived and stayed on. The kind of people who couldn't cope with it either died or left. Seamanship is in their blood, Sergeant. That boy works as my boatman. He doesn't think about how to fish or read the sea. He just notices small details you and I don't. He doesn't even know, consciously, that he's doing it at all. I've asked him dozens of times what he's picking up. He shrugs, tells me what he can, but it's not all of it. He's uncanny with the sea. I've seen him dealing with sheep and cows too... he knows what to do without thinking much about the job."

"I had a boatman like that when I was running sheep on Chalky," said one of the men in the backseat. "He could find his way in to Whitemark, drunk as a skunk, in mist so thick you couldn't see your hand in front of your face."

"He'd need it out there this afternoon. Is there a GPS on your boat?" asked the policeman.

Jon sighed. "It's in my pocket. I took it off to log the dive spots. We keep a record. Still, he does know the area. I just wish like hell you'd listened, Sergeant. I wish like hell the boy wasn't out there, especially if Symons is right and his daughter is on the boat too. The RIB is as good a small boat for a bad sea as you can find, and Tim is competent, keeps his cool, I think, but he doesn't have experience in these conditions."

"Look, I'm sorry. He behaved like ... well, he had

something to hide. And his grandmother confirmed it by chasing me off. So I..."

"She chases everyone off," said one of the men in the backseat. "Has for years, Sergeant."

"Well, as it happens, Sergeant, she told me why she was so upset," said Jon, angry with the man himself. "The last time a policeman came to her door, he was escorting the officer who came to tell her that her husband was MIA in Vietnam. You think she's going to welcome you?"

"Oh, hell...I thought, well, I know there's cannabis being grown somewhere close to that part of the island. I thought it was there."

"Dicky Burke," said one of the men in the back. "You won't catch him, Sergeant. He's a wily fox, that one."

"I know. But they're relations...He collects mail for her, goes there. And we tracked some of the money from a deal. She spent it."

Jon snorted. "I can tell you how that happened, all right. And it's not a pretty story. Burke's been selling her cows for her, and gypping the old lady something terrible. I found that out when I agreed to buy some instead. You know what the bastard was giving her?" He told them, knowing that at least one of the fellows in the back was a farmer. "And to add insult to injury, I reckon laundering some of his money through the sale, giving her your tracked notes instead. I'll bet she's no dope grower. For starters, they're as poor as church-mice, and I reckon as honest as the day is long, by her standards, and I'll bet that doesn't cut it with her."

"I'm sorry. Still, that boy just has to see my uniform and he's in a panic. Don't tell me there's no history of trouble."

"You're probably right. I got into strife as a teenager, you probably did too. I was trying to prove myself a man and impress the chicks. Trouble is, for a kid like that in the city...he can't do it without getting into strife. Here he can. In Melbourne, he's just another kid who doesn't really fit. Here, he's a round peg in a round hole."

The radio crackled. "Bad news, Sergeant. The guys on the quad-bikes...they just found the little boy washed up on the beach, near Marshall Rock."

There was silence in the vehicle. Then Jon said: "Can't you drive a bit faster, mate?"

CHAPTER 20

Áed's powers were far too small to fight the might of the sea, but his master was doing that well. Still, he used what little strength he had to aid. A little magic: the rain he made fall ahead might wet... but it beat the swell down, and behind it, as it often is behind a rain-squall, the light was a little better and air a little clearer. The day was dying, and it was growing darker. That raised Áed's small power, but it didn't help the master.

But the selkie was out there, moving as fast as they were, and she had her watchers keeping the child on the rocks. Áed could taste the selkie spell-work.

"Rocks! Rocks ahead!" shrieked Molly.

"Marriot Reef!" Tim swung the tiller over slightly, and they raced along a wave and in behind the rocky Islet in its seethe of foam and breaking waves.

It did give some shelter, but even on the lee of the chain

of little islands there was no way they could safely land. "Treasure Island ahead," shouted Tim. "Can you see her?"

"No . . . Are those sharks?"

"Dolphin! And there's the seal-woman. And look! Look! Up against the rock!" He shouted, triumphant.

There was a huddled child—a wet blonde head and a scrap of red shirt. "Sammy!" screamed Molly along with Tim. The child didn't move. Then she lifted her little head and started waving frantically, plainly screaming too. But the wind whipped her cries away like a seagull's mew. A sheet of spray shot up behind her, drenching her.

"How close can we get, Tim?" asked Molly.

In answer he fiddled with something next to the outboard. "I've unlocked the motor, I'll run in as close as I dare. Grab the anchor rope." He had his knife out. "I'll cut the anchor off. We'll throw the rope to her."

Starting from the anchor end, Molly hauled the anchor chain until she got to where it connected to the rope. There was a shackle, but she knew Tim was right, her fingers were too cold and weak to undo that. She struggled back to him in the tiny pitching boat, nearly going overboard. "She's too little. She can't. Tie it onto me. I'll get her."

"I'll go," he said, slashing the rope free. It was a very sharp knife.

"I can't drive a boat," said Molly. "And I am not strong enough to pull you out of the water. And I can swim well."

He didn't waste time arguing. Just tied knots.

"Bowline. Tie one on her too. Let's go."

Tim edged the boat in, the breaking surf bouncing it around.

Molly could only hope he was right about them being dolphins. But sharks ate seals, didn't they?

"Go!" he shouted. "Now!"

Molly dived overboard.

She was a good swimmer. It couldn't be more than

ten meters to the waves sloshing almost over the rock. She was still totally unprepared for the cold, and for the sheer strength of it . . . she couldn't swim in this! She had a moment of terrible panic. And then she was carried upward, something muscular, warm, and immensely powerful thrusting her along, ripping her jeans as she shot up the rock with the wave. She scrambled clear. There wasn't much island left. The little girl flung herself into her arms.

"Bowline! How the hades do I tie that? Sammy, honey, let me tie this onto you. Quickly." She did her best, and then ran back to the rock edge. The sea looked huge and hungry. Tim and the boat seemed so far. "Take a deep breath, Sammy. Seal lady! Maeve! Help us!" she yelled as she backed off and ran at the sea, jumping as far clear of the rocks as possible.

Tim wasn't pulling the rope. Instead he'd tied it to the boat and used the engine to drag . . . and the seal lifted them, away from the rocks. Tim was hauling at the rope now, like a runaway steam-train, pulling them up the side of the boat. She shoved Sammy up, got a kick for her pains, but then Tim heaved her over the pontoon too, as she pulled and the seal shoved. Molly sprawled in the bottom of the boat, but she was on-board.

"Sorry!" said Tim, his arm strong and warm around her as he lifted her to her knees. "Had to get you away from the rocks, Maeve said. Crawl up in the bow and let's get out of here! We've still got to get in!"

And he turned to the water. "Maeve! Thank you!"

"I'll hold you to our bargain," said the seal-woman. "Sail. There are bigger waves coming."

Molly didn't try to stand. Instead, she clung on to the bow-rope with one hand and cuddled Sammy on her lap with the other. The child was even colder than she was. Fortunately, now they were running straight for the shore, riding on the back of a foaming wave, so it wasn't the pounding they'd taken quartering the sea. She couldn't see the shore. Ahead were the backs of more monstrous waves, peaking and breaking. The beach must be there, somewhere. But could they get in through the shore-break?

And then as the wave peaked and Tim dropped the throttle back slightly, she caught a brief glimpse of car lights on the beach.

Jon and the crew in the police vehicle arrived at the flooded creek mouth, with the sea breaking into it just as another elderly ute came bumping and swaying down the track over the dune on the other side. It stopped, barely at the edge of the water, and the door was flung open. A small, white-haired woman got out and strode into the water. "Who is that?" asked someone.

"Tim's grandmother," said Jon. "Someone must have told her. Let me do the talking, Sergeant. Coo-ee, Mrs. Ryan," he called out.

She nodded at them, briefly, but looked intently at the sea. "My boy is out there, Mr. McKay. I can't take a third heartbreak. It'll kill me."

"We're here to do our best, Mrs. Ryan. Be strong for him. He'll do it if anyone can."

She nodded. She didn't say anything, but Jon could see the tears coursing down her cheeks as she stared intently at the sea.

He looked at it himself, and it was not encouraging. He knew there was a shallower bank of coffee-rock and mud about seventy or eighty yards offshore, and the waves were peaking and breaking on it with a fury that would toss most boats. It was merely a strong, thundering foam running about a meter high and racing up the beach and into the creek-mouth beyond that.

"We'll never manage a beach launch in this! She'll be swamped before we can turn her," shouted one of the men. The sea was far worse here than it had been when they'd left the Port Davies ramp.

"We'll put the boat in the creek, turn her, and push out with the waves. You're going to get wet," shouted Jon McKay. "The trick is going to be getting through the big break out there."

"There's a boat! There's a boat out there! Oh, dear God, it must be them!" shouted a woman—Alicia Symons.

Jon turned to see his own RIB rising with the wave just short of the mudbank.

But it would be suicide coming in over that.

And plainly the red life-jacketed skipper knew that too, because he turned on the wave top and scooted for slightly deeper water again.

From the wave top Tim had seen and assessed the break on the mud bank. He'd seen it from the shore, before, but only at very low tide. There was a slightly deeper water channel here on the seaward side, so the half-breaking waves started to reform, and it was slightly less hectic than it had been further out. A bigger wave could still come through and flip them. He opened the safety drum. Dug with one hand, watching the sea, working by feel. Pulled out what he was looking for—a spare yoke—a basic life-preserver. "Tie that on her. We're probably not going to get in here." But what alternatives did he have? Trying to batter their way back into the wind and waves to West End? That could take hours, and there was no guarantee it would be possible to land there. The sea was getting rougher, the swells bigger.

And then he had an odd experience, rather like the seeing of Faerie, but sort of inside his head. Eight men, dressed like they came out of one his mum's favorite English romantic movies from long ago, but much scruffier than in any movie, in a long, narrow, wooden boat, rowing—in a storm, in this very place. In the bow, a few huddled women and children. And at the stern, holding an oar in the water like a rudder, was someone who made him feel he was looking in a mirror—but wearing fancy old-fashioned sailor clothes. "We'll never get in!" said one of the rowers fearfully.

"On the double wave," said the mirror-image, ice-cool. "On my call, on the double wave."

Tim looked at the sea, and turned outward again, looking for the wave. He understood now what he had to do. He unlocked the outboard again so the engine's keel would not dig in. Now to choose the wave...

They circled three more times, and then he saw it. A monster, already capping beyond them. He gave the RIB full throttle and cut across the smaller wave, and up the steepening face to get over the top, and then turned and chased it inward. "Brace yourself and her," he shouted. And then, for reasons he never quite understood until years later, yelled, "Two six, stroke!"

"What's he doing?" demanded Alicia, anxiously.

"Looking for a break in the waves or somewhere to get through," said Jon, staring. "But I can't see one." He wished he hadn't said that. But there wasn't a gap. Just big waves. He saw Tim lip a monster... and turn to follow it. *Why?* part of him screamed... it was worse than the rest.

And then he understood. The big wave was catching up on the wave behind, making for much deeper water, so instead of a dumping break it was curling over, and the boy was keeping the RIB just behind the breaking edge, where the water was fast, but still rushing forward, not tumbling and crashing. As it finally broke he'd tapped off the throttle and then, on the surging uprush of foam, opened it fully. Jon was with rest of them running into the water...

But Tim had judged it just right. The RIB skimmed up the wave onto the sand—going right past the first few men. Then Tim was over the side, yelling, "Help haul her in. Quick! Haven't got an anchor."

Mike Symons thought his heart would burst when he saw his daughter, wet hair plastered to her head, stand up in the bow of the boat, with the young girl in her arms. "She's really cold," she called, as strong hands lifted the RIB further up the beach, with her still in it. "Can someone take Sammy and get her somewhere warm?"

The cheering was loud even above the tumult of the waves and storm.

And Mike was only one of the men carrying her, and the child, to the police vehicle.

"Ambulance is on its way," the cop yelled. "Get the little girl in here, I'll want a first aider, space blanket, and the boat unhitched, fast, gentlemen!" Men leaped to do it. But that didn't include Mike or his wife. They were too busy hugging their wet child to do that.

"Sorry, Mum, Dad. I had to do it," she said.

"You're back safe and alive and you got the child, honey, and that's all that matters," said her mother. "And we'd better get you somewhere warm and dry and into some dry clothes. Your bags are still in the car."

She nodded. "Just got to make sure Tim is all right, Mum. Dad. You won't let them take him away or get him into too much trouble? If he hadn't gone out, little Sammy Burke would be dead, too, I think."

"Huh. I might give him a little trouble for taking you out there," said Mike, giving her a squeeze and a smile to show it wasn't... really meant. "But no one else is going to."

"He tried to get me to stay behind. But he needed me, and I knew that. So I went. He couldn't exactly stop me. He was... careful as he could be. He's a really good skipper."

"I don't think anyone is going to disagree with you about that! Or think that he's going to be in any trouble. Honey, if the sergeant had only listened to him... I just wish you'd called me."

"I should have. But I thought you'd say no, and I didn't think you'd believe. Good grief! Mum, that's Bunce. How did he get here?"

The wolfhound was leaping and licking in delight as she hugged him. "I really have no idea," said her mother, "but he's also pleased to see you."

Jon McKay came over and handed them a silver blanket. "Wrap it round her. We're all going back to the Ryan place, to get the boy and his nan settled, and to all get dry and warm. The young man needs a bit of support from me, I reckon. Are you going to join us? Or are you going to take our heroine home? Well done, girl. Tim has been telling us about how you swam over to get her. Brave as a lion. Uh, lioness."

"They do all the work," said Alicia. "What do you want to do, Molly? And what do you think, Mike?"

"How do you feel, girl?" asked Mike, turning to his daughter.

She smiled up at him. "Cold. Tired, a bit sore, hungry... and I would not let Tim... or his nan down for anything, Dad. He may still need me. Us. I want to go with them. Please?"

"So long as the wolfhound doesn't mind."

Áed felt there was some justice in letting loose the great Cu. It was a noble beast, even if it was not well suited to boats. It was a small magic, and he was feeling tired but generous. He would not be going to the hollow hills to serve, and that suited him well.

Tim had seen his grandmother as he had hauled the boat up and, leaving it to the others, he had run to her. Without thinking, he'd hugged her, and had seen the tears on her cheeks, even in the rain, as she put her hand up to touch his face. "Nan! Nan, it's all right," he said, holding her. She wasn't really a huggy person, but right then she was clinging to him, as tightly as any limpet did to the rock. He led her up, away from the water, looking across to see Molly and Sammy being carried over to the police vehicle. That was good. And so was the ground under his feet. "Is this Ryan land, Gran?" he asked her.

"Reckon they call it Crown land, down here," she said gruffly. "I thought I'd lost yer, boy. I thought my old heart would break."

He squeezed her shoulders. "Come on. Let's get back onto your land, then. They can sort things out, Nan. You need to get dry."

"It's your land, boy. That's all I was keepin' it for. It's not worth a damned thing to me without yer. And yer soaked, too."

"Bit of water won't do me any harm," he said, knowing it was her own words he was giving back to her. "Come on, Nan. Let's get back to our place, because I want to go home."

His grandmother kissed him on the cheek. She'd never done that before. "Home. It's so good to hear my grandson say that. Yer grandfather would be so proud, and they say joy don't kill, but I could murder a cuppa."

Jon came jogging up. "I said he'd be all right, Mrs. Ryan."

"Sorry about taking the boat, Jon," said Tim.

"It was the right thing to do, Tim. If you'd waited, well, she'd have drowned. And you did a good job in that sea."

"I thought it was getting worse, so I had to," he said, simply enormously grateful for the understanding and the trust. "But I want to get my nan home. She's wet."

"And he's a wet hen," said his nan acerbically, far more like her old self, but not letting go of him. "Now, why don't you tell all these people to come an' get dry and warm and have tea? That was you they was cheering for, Tim, and I want to hear why. All of it."

"He saved the little girl's life," said Jon McKay.

"That was Molly. She swam across to get her. Bravest thing I ever saw in my life, her jumping in there. Hey, Bunce!" The wolfhound danced and licked, and nearly knocked his teeth out.

"I guess, by the Huntaway, that she's here an' all right too?" asked his grandmother.

"She's here," said Tim, looking around. "I hope all right. I'd better check."

"You'll get your grandmother home," said Jon McKay, firmly. "She's with her folks and is fine. I'll check. Could you use someone to drive you?"

"No...I should be okay," said Tim, suddenly realizing how tired he actually was.

"Yes, we could," said his nan. "My boy needs to get warm and dry an' his tea in him. I don't never ask for help, but the old ute...well, I think she may have done her last drive. I pushed her a bit hard. Anyway...I have a grandson and we'll be all right, even if we have to walk."

"You can bet on it being sorted for you," said Jon. "Don't you worry about it. Come on, I'll get Brian to drive you. I'll come back for the boat in the morning."

"Um. There's your ute too. It's at West End," said Tim warily.

Jon laughed. "I didn't think you pulled the RIB there with your teeth, Tim. Stop worrying. Come with me."

So they did.

Tim didn't remember the evening too well. He was asked a lot of questions, which he couldn't answer too well, but it didn't seem to matter. There were a lot of people in a house that had always seemed so empty, and now it was noisy and cheerful, and then even more people came, bringing them tea, casseroles, an apple pie and even cake. It wasn't as good as his nan's, and he was tired enough to say so. That actually made people cheer, even if he was embarrassed by having said it aloud.

He was not too tired to put down a saucer of beer in the corner of the kitchen as soon as he got home, even before he went to get dry clothes and hang up his red life jacket. His grandmother touched the jacket as he hung it up. "Yer was wearing that, and off Roydon Island," she said, with quiet satisfaction. "Yer wouldn't believe, but I saw yer. I saw yer out there, the day yer came home from the city. I wasn't there, but I still saw it."

He hesitated a moment and saw the tiny ripples in the bowl in the corner. "I believe you, Nan...because I saw something like it when we were trying to come in. Like a big rowing boat with a bow at each end, with men in old-fashioned clothes, waiting for the double wave. That's how I knew what to do."

His grandmother took him by the arm and walked him into the main room of the house, the one with the slightly crooked wall. "See that mantelpiece over the fireplace. Yer grandfather said it came from the keel of the wreck of a whaleboat his ancestor first landed on the island in. During a storm. They didn't quite get to the shore and three men drowned."

Somehow Tim knew they'd all have made it, if, at the first grate of the keel and sideways judder, some of the men hadn't leapt from the boat to reach the shore. She'd rolled then, at the last, and trapped two, and an oar had struck one. But you couldn't explain that sort of thing. Besides, he had enough to explain to Molly's parents, who were just coming in with her.

Only it seemed he didn't have to explain much there, either. Molly rushed into talking first, grabbed his arm. "I had a bit of a talk with my dad on the way up. About you being scared of being sent away, or, you know..."

He was glad Nan was heading for the kitchen. He hoped no one else was listening. "I'll have to deal with it if it happens."

"Well, it's not going to. Over my dead body! But he said it was sometimes better to go and face your fears than to run. And he can be right sometimes. He said he is ready to help, if you want to talk to him. And he won't tell anyone. You can trust him, really."

Tim cast a nervous look at Molly's dad. "Uh, okay."

"But tomorrow, not tonight. No one is going to bug you tonight."

She was wrong about that, though, in an odd way. After they'd eaten, and people were talking, Tim got up and went through to the kitchen, taking the excuse of looking at the stove. But actually, he quietly opened the door and walked outside. The ground was wet, but the wind had died down, and the moon peered through the tattered cloud. It was dark out. Dark the way Melbourne never was. And there were more stars up there than he'd ever seen in Melbourne. The distant sound of the surf-roar on the beach drowned out the talking people inside. It was nice having them here. Good to feel that that they'd done the right thing. But...

"Too many people," said his grandmother from the doorway.

"Yeah." He'd never thought he'd say that. "I always thought Flinders Island small and Melbourne big. But that was the wrong way around, Nan. Over there you only have a tiny bit of it to yourself, and now that I am used to having something big to myself, I need a lot of space."

She nodded. "Come in, Tim, and I'll send 'em all home. The Symonses are wanting to go anyway."

So he did. He was already home. And he got a hug and kiss from Molly before she left. He suddenly realized that he hadn't noticed that the braces were gone from her teeth. He didn't care anyway. She was Molly, with them or without.

EPILOGUE

Of course life didn't just go back to normal—except where it did. The cow still needed milking early the next morning. Nan was still up before the sun, baking, by the smell of it. But his day of working on Jon's boat didn't happen. Instead Jon arrived with his ute, empty trailer, and two other four-by-fours. "We've come to fetch my boat, the other boat and Mrs. Ryan's ute. I need my boatman," he informed Nan. It felt pretty good, being called that.

So when the ABC reporter showed up, he was down on the beach, cranking a winch, sweating and laughing. He was never going to be much good at being interviewed, but it seemed everyone else said it for him. They'd been to Molly first, and she was better at talking on camera than he was. That was fine. She always had more to say than he did, anyway.

"I was just doing what had to be done" seemed a good answer to him, so long as they didn't ask how he knew it had to be done. He told them about her swimming to reach Sammy, though. He had fun doing that. But then that reminded him of Troy, and he was silent again.

Mary Ryan was sitting on her bed, her box open, and the letters out . . . she couldn't see more than the shape of the paper, and certainly not the words anymore. But she knew the letter by heart anyway. And now at last she could smile about it. "Eh, John, dearest," she said, "yer heart would burst with pride at our grandson. He's done you proud, my man."

Someone knocked at the door. She gathered the letters and said, "Comin'." They were old and needed to be put away carefully . . . she'd cracked a couple before she'd realized paper got old. And when you couldn't see well, it took time and care.

"Oh. I thought you said come in, Mrs. Ryan. Pardon me," said someone from the doorway.

It sounded like that damned copper! She stood up in a hurry, scattering the precious letters. "What do you want?" she snapped, defensively, ready to fight.

"I'm putting your grandson up for an award for his courage," said the copper. "I just needed his full name and date of birth. I tried to call, but the line must be down. So I came around to ask. He deserves recognition for what he did." He'd knelt down and was carefully picking up the scattered letters. That much she could see in the blurred outline. "He's a fine boy."

It was hard not to agree, or even to be angry with him. "Yes. My man would have been right proud of him."

"He'd have had every reason to be. I've never seen as good a piece of seamanship as him coming in yesterday. Where should I put these letters, Mrs. Ryan?" he asked. "Back in the box?"

She nodded. What else could she do? "You'll have a cup of tea, mister."

"I'd better report the phone for you," he said.

"I took it off the hook. People from them newspapers kept callin' to talk to him. He's out working. I should be too," she said, still a little tense.

"Well, if you can spare the time for a cup of tea, I'd be grateful. It's been a hard morning. Grim. I had to talk with Burke's wife. It's the worst part of the job. I hate it, but it has to be done. And thanks to your grandson, she has one child alive. A little longer and she wouldn't have either. The girl is still in the hospital. She got very cold, poor mite. Another half hour and the child would have been dead, the doctor reckons. Anyway, so, it's a relief to come here."

It had never occurred to her that it might be difficult to have delivered that sort of news. She'd only been on the other side of it. She nodded. "Cold'll kill yer, especially little folk or critters. I used to warm the orphan lambs up in me oven in the morning with the door open. Nearly forgot and put more wood in and closed the door and cooked one, one day. Only his yammerin' saved him."

They talked farming, and sheep, and about the sea. He'd also grown up on a farm, close to the coast, in Tassie. Talking like this, you'd have almost thought he wasn't a copper, and there wasn't an old .22 in her cupboard that shouldn't be there. It'd been her father's gun, and he'd never registered it, she was sure. Times had changed. A copper sitting having tea with a black woman . . . Then he went off to give the blokes a hand with the boat.

Mike Symons had gotten Tim to walk off a little way and chat while several of the men were fiddling with the old

Ford. He'd been braced for some fairly serious wrongdoing in Tim's past. Drugs. Car theft...that sort of thing. It had been all he could do not to burst out laughing when Tim told him about it, partly with relief, because unless he read it completely wrong, his daughter was very much in love with the boy. "Look. Honestly, forget about it. For them to charge you...well, you'd have had to take the DVD out of the shop and be caught. And as for that insurance scumbag—if he calls you again, you call me, and we'll talk to the sergeant or the ombudsman. He's overstepping the law. I'm amazed the school reacted like that."

"Well, there were a few other things. See, um, I tried some cannabis once, and got sick. And...and they told someone. But I swear I only did it that once, and after that I'll never go near it again! I ended up in the hospital. But my mum thinks I smoke it by the bucket. She's crazy. Even ordinary cigarette smoke makes me cough my lungs out."

Mike drew the boy out more, so he heard about Hailey. Heard and understood all too well how Tim...wanted to be accepted. Understood also how he wanted to leave it behind, and didn't want everyone to know what he'd done. "I'm not telling anyone, Tim. But seriously, after yesterday, I don't think you need to care. I hope it doesn't go to your head."

Tim Ryan looked up at Mike, and shook his head. "I didn't do it to be a hero. They're all wrong about that. I don't think I was, and I really didn't want to be heroic, just, there was no one else. I was really scared, to tell the truth. I wouldn't have done it if the cop had listened... Actually, I was really petrified I'd be in more trouble, too. I'd rather deal with the sea than that. I thought I would have to leave the island, or be sent away. I hated this place at first, but I've...I've kind of got used to being here now. The one who was heroic was your daughter. I just did what had to be done, stuff I could do."

Mike patted him on the shoulder. "You have no idea how worrying a heroine daughter is to a dad. I'm as proud as can be, of course, but...anyway. I think this island suits you, the way city life didn't, Tim. Everyone has the right place to be. You're lucky. It took me until I was forty to figure it out, that I wasn't happy where everyone said I should be, and I am happy here. And Tim...after the way you coped with that sea yesterday, I don't think you ever need to be afraid of what people think of you. Except maybe my daughter."

Tim blushed, and nodded, which Mike Symons, all things considered, decided was a good thing. "The sea's easy compared to women!" Then the boy looked toward the sea and said: "Excuse me...I've got to go and speak to someone."

There wasn't anyone there, but Mike did see a seal out in the surf.

"This thing ought not to be on the road," said the sergeant. "And she shouldn't be driving."

"I don't think it ever goes on the road. I doubt if it has been out of second gear in ten years. And it's proof of the curative properties of old fencing wire," said one of the volunteer mechanics. "And baling string. I've never seen a baling-string fan belt before."

"I don't think she drives it anyway. That's Tim, and it's all on the farm," said Jon McKay. "What's eating you, Sergeant?"

The man sighed. "I was looking for a reason to not be disgusted with myself. That old lady...I surprised her, startled her. She was sitting with her husband's letters on the bed. Scattered them all over the place when I got there. I picked them up for her...I'm a copper, and of course I was reading bits as I picked them up. And they've been read damn near to pieces. You're right, McKay. She's a battler and needs help. And she's half-blind. She shouldn't be out here struggling away like this. I don't know how it's been allowed to happen. We need to get something done. Social services or..."

Jon interrupted, explaining the pieces he'd put together himself. "Aboriginal girl, marrying into an old island family. Managed to make her family and theirs mad in the process, and then lost him in Vietnam. And didn't have any help, and wouldn't ask for it. All she had was her pride and this place. Take those away from her, Sergeant, or her away from here, and you might as well kill her. And don't try anything she sees as interfering, or charity. She won't take either," he said firmly. "Leave it alone, Sergeant. I've talked to RSL. She would have been getting help from them... if they'd known. The local crowd are as solid a crew as you'll get anywhere. And I reckon the Flinders Island Aboriginal Association folk will be out to look after her too, because one of the guys on my boat yesterday is part of the Association. They take care of their own, too. And the rest of us, we'll work on it. See to things quietly. Tim is her soft spot, and he's her eyes, too. He's a good island kid." He looked up at Mike Symons. "And he's got a good girlfriend. Where is he, Mike?"

"Talking to a seal. Seriously. And my girl will probably keep him on the straight and narrow, unlike that Hailey Burke he was mixed up with. What's happening there, Sergeant? How is the little girl doing?"

"She's due to be released from the hospital later. Nothing worse than hypothermia, and of course being terrified, and in shock about her brother. Her mother got in early this morning. Charter flight."

"And the older girl? And Burke? You going to take action there?"

The policeman bit his lip. Looked at his audience. "Well, this being the island, you'll all find out anyway. Burke's wife was so mad with him, she shopped him to us. We arrested him in his packing shed this morning, where he was trying to clear away what he'd been up to yesterday instead of keeping an eye on his daughter or the kids. He was sure that we wouldn't check on him yet, and he owes a lot of money to some nasty people in the trade on the mainland. As a result...I gather words like 'divorce' have been said. Apparently the wife never has liked the island, so I should think they'll be leaving. As for the older daughter...I don't think she'll ever be the same again."

It was some ten days later. Tim was glad Jon McKay could be so understanding, without asking hard questions. He'd taken them out without asking why or anything. Just taken Tim's "please can you give us a ride out there sometime soon, I've something I have to deal with" as enough. Prime Seal Island was someone's farmland, but the foreshore was crown land. And in that foreshore...

Áed led them, tossing sticks and pebbles to herd them along the trail toward the stench of the thing. Years it had been lying in the old hole, preserving the hole, as Fae lands are preserved.

Every now and again he paused to skip and dance a little in the sunlight and wind. To celebrate that he and the master would not leave here for the hollow lands.

The master stuck his hand down the hole. Hauled out an old silver teapot, a rotting leather bag, a candlestick with an engraved crest on it...and finally, a pendant. A long, silvery chain with a gem that glittered cold and bright, sharding the sunlight into fragments of rainbow.

The young master's lady gasped. He did not. "So this is what she wants," he said.

"It looks like it's worth a million dollars," said the young woman, awed by the stinking thing.

The master wasn't as impressed, it seemed. "Yeah. Maybe. I gave my promise. The seal-woman is waiting just offshore. I saw her as we came to the beach."

And he took it to the water and threw it ... as far and as hard as he could.

Maybe the master understood, somehow, that Faerie was a kind of hell, and not heaven.

Áed didn't know. He was just glad.

"Well, you've got nowhere to run away to anymore," Molly said, wrapping her arm around his shoulders, as the black seal with the glittering rainbow jewel around her neck dived into the deep blue of the ocean.

Tim shrugged, looking out at the sea and the distant mountain. "I guess so. But it doesn't matter because I'm not running anymore anyway. This," he pointed at the sea and the island beyond it, "is where I belong."